"McMILLAN DISPLAYS SHEER TALENT in a first novel that is touching *and* steadfastly unsentimental. *MAMA* is extremely funny throughout and at the same time honest about what a good woman will do to push her children higher than she can hope to go...."    — *Detroit Free Press*

"*MAMA* has Zora Neale Hurston's vernacular humor and John Irving's absurdity. McMillan is a master of black humor in both senses of the phrase...."    — *Village Voice*

"A tough, touching story about survival...with complex, believable characters who seem to sit across the kitchen table from you instead of sitting silently on the page.... *MAMA* offers not only rich characters but also prose that touches as it reveals a world seldom seen in literature."
— *Atlanta Journal & Constitution*

"*MAMA* is unapologetic about exposing the pain that blacks can inflict on themselves and one another, and concerned with emotional healing and recovery...."    — *Essence*

**Books by Terry McMillan**

Disappearing Acts
Mama

Published by WASHINGTON SQUARE PRESS

# MAMA

## TERRY McMILLAN

WASHINGTON SQUARE PRESS
PUBLISHED BY POCKET BOOKS
New York   London   Toronto   Sydney   Tokyo   Singapore

The poetry on page ix is from the poem "When I Have Reached the Point of Suffocation" in Gerald Stern's *Rejoicings,* published by Metro Book Co., Los Angeles.

I want to thank my editors at Houghton Mifflin: Janet Silver, whose insight and faith helped me to transform this book through many revisions, and Larry Kessenich, who said yes in the first place and gave me constant pep talks and reassurance. Thanks to them, I have developed something I didn't have before: patience.

I would also like to thank both the Yaddo and MacDowell artist colonies, where the first draft of *Mama* was written, and the PEN American Center, the Authors League, the Carnegie Fund, the Ludwig Vogelstein Foundation, and the New York Foundation for the Arts for their much appreciated financial support. I am also grateful to the many people who helped me get through the long revision process: Doris Austin, my family, the members of the New Renaissance Writers' Guild, the word processing department of PBW&T, Jackie Berke, Virginia Dunwell, Betty Hopkins and her entire family, and Leonard Welch.

Finally, I have to thank my son, Solomon, who, at two years old, discovered *he* could write, too.

## WSP

A Washington Square Press Publication of
POCKET BOOKS, a division of Simon & Schuster
1230 Avenue of the Americas, New York, N.Y. 10020

Published by arrangement with Houghton Mifflin Company
Library of Congress Catalog Card Number: 86-15367

ISBN: 0-671-74523-9

First Washington Square Press trade paperback printing December 1987

16  15  14  13  12  11  10  9  8

WASHINGTON SQUARE PRESS and WSP colophon are
registered trademarks of Simon & Schuster Inc.

Printed in the U.S.A.

*For my own Mama,*
MADELINE TILLMAN,
*whose love and support*
*made everything possible*

It takes years to learn how to look at the destruction
of beautiful things;

to learn how to leave the place
of oppression;

and how to make your own regeneration
out of nothing.

—GERALD STERN,
  "When I Have Reached the
  Point of Suffocation"

# *One*

MILDRED HID THE AX beneath the mattress of the cot in the dining room. She poured lye in a brown paper bag and pushed it behind the pots and pans under the kitchen sink. Then she checked all three butcher knives to make sure they were razor sharp. She knew where she could get her hands on a gun in fifteen minutes, but ever since she'd seen her brother shot for stealing a beer from the pool hall, she'd been afraid of guns. Besides, Mildred didn't want to kill Crook, she just wanted to hurt him.

She hated this raggedy house. Hated this deadbeat town. Hated never having enough of anything. Most of all, she hated Crook. And if it weren't for their five kids, she'd have left him a long time ago.

She sat down at the kitchen table, crossed her thick brown thighs, and rested her chin in her palms. An L&M burned slowly in the plastic ashtray next to her now cold cup of coffee. At twenty-seven, Mildred was as tired as an old workhorse and felt like she'd been through a war. Her face hurt. Her bottom lip was swollen and it would stay that way the rest of her life, so that she'd have to tuck the left corner in whenever she wore lipstick, which was almost always. It would serve as her trademark, a constant reminder that she had quick-firing lips.

Her left foot was swollen, too, from the tire Crook had backed

*I*

over it last night when she wouldn't move. She had gotten up at five o'clock this morning and soaked it in Epsom salts for a whole hour but that hadn't done much good. Now the combination of this pain and the crisscrossing of her thoughts irritated her like an unreachable itch, so she went ahead and took the yellow nerve pill Curly Mae had given her last week. Then she wrapped her foot in an Ace bandage, covered it with a fake-fur house shoe, and pulled another chair in front of her to prop it up. She took a sip of her coffee.

As Mildred waited for the pill to work, she stared out the kitchen window at the leafless trees and drew deeply on her cigarette, one strong puff after another. She twirled her fingers around her dyed red braids, which hung from the diaper she had tied on her head. She patted her good foot against the torn linoleum, something she always did when she was thinking.

The way she figured it, there'd been no sense trying to be too cute last night and get herself killed thoroughly. Crook had smacked her so hard outside the Red Shingle that she had forgotten her name for a minute or two.

He was the jealous type.

Everybody knew it, but Mildred had made the mistake of carrying on a friendly two-minute conversation with Percy Russell. Crook had always despised Percy because, as rumor had it, their oldest daughter, Freda, wasn't his, and could've easily been Percy's. Both men had skin the color of ripe bananas and soft wavy hair, which Freda had inherited. And both men had high chiseled cheeks, which, as time passed, emerged on Freda's face too.

Mildred ignored the rumors and knew that in a town as small as Point Haven people ran their mouths because they didn't have anything better to do. Crook never did come right out and accuse her of cheating because he'd been having an affair with Ernestine Jackson off and on for the past twelve years, before Mildred was even showing with Freda. And before they got settled good into their marriage. He wasn't whorish, except when he had more than eight ounces of liquor in him, which was just about every day.

And while Crook ran the streets, it was Percy who nailed plastic to the windows in the winter, bought Mildred maternity clothes, fixed the drip in the bathtub, and paid the plumber to fix the frozen pipes. It was Percy who had shoveled the heavy blocks of coal from the shack in the back yard and carried them to the house when Crook was too drunk to stand up, and then waited for the fire to pop and crackle in the stove. It was Percy who made sure Mildred was warm, who bought her cigarettes, aspirin and vitamins, lard and potatoes, and even paid her light and gas bills when Crook had done something else with the money, but pleaded amnesia.

The three of them had grown up together, though both men were six years older than Mildred. Percy had always had a crush on her, but he was so shy and stuttered so badly that she didn't have the patience to hear him out when he tried to express his true feelings for her. So Percy was forced to demonstrate his feelings rather than making them audible, which was a lot easier on both of them. And although Mildred always thought of him as kind and mannerly, his slowness and docility annoyed her so much that she never took his intentions seriously, except once.

Last night at the Shingle, Crook had barged in and broken up their conversation, grabbed Mildred by the arm, and pushed her outside through the silver doors. He'd ordered her to get in the car — a pink and gold '59 Mercury — and he jumped in and started gunning the motor. When she didn't budge, he backed the car up so fast that it stalled and ran over her left foot. Drunk and aggravated because his anger was being diverted, Crook leaped from the car and hauled off and slapped Mildred's face until she thought it was in her best interest to go ahead and get in.

She had pushed her platinum wig back in place, pulling on the elastic bands and pushing bobby pins against her skull to make sure it was on tight again. Mildred always wore this wig when she went out. It made her feel like she was going someplace, like she was an elegant, sophisticated woman being taken out on the town by the man of her dreams. She got into the back seat of the car and pushed herself as far as she could into the corner of the soft pink seat because she didn't want to be within smelling distance of Crook. He climbed behind the wheel without saying a word and slammed the door.

"Just take me home, Crook," she'd said, trying hard not to scream or cry, but tears were already streaking her cocoa-colored foundation so that her own lighter skin tone showed through. She rolled her eyes at Crook until the pupils stuck in the corner sockets hard, but Crook couldn't see her or else he'd have hauled off and smacked her again. All she could think of now was how she was going to get him when she got home.

It only took five minutes to drive home from the Shingle, straight down Twenty-fourth and a left on Manual to Twenty-fifth. Mildred's mind was clicking like a stopwatch, trying to remember exactly where she'd situated the cast-iron skillet among the other pots and pans. Was it underneath the boilers? Or in the oven with chicken grease still in it? Didn't matter. She'd find it. She pressed her forehead against the cold wet glass and stared at the clapboard houses, most of which belonged to people she knew, some even family. Crook was barely staying in his lane. Mildred knew he was drunk on Orange Rock, but she didn't dare say anything to him. She'd been on the verge of being tipsy herself, but the lingering sting of Crook's hand on her face had slowly begun to break down her high. Anyway, there were no oncoming cars. Not at this time of night. Not in this hick town.

"I'm taking you home all right, don't worry about that," Crook said, trying to keep his eyes focused on the wiggling white line cutting through the two-lane street. "You think you're grown, don't you? Think you're just so damn grown." He wasn't expecting an answer and Mildred didn't give him one.

"You know you're gon' get your ass tore up, don't you? Gon' get enough of flirting with that simple-ass Percy and all the rest of 'em. You my wife, you understand me? My woman, and I don't want nobody talking to you like you ain't got no man. Especially in front of my face 'cause the next thang you know, I'll be hearing all kinds of mess up and down the streets. You understand me, girl? You listening to me?" He looked at Mildred through the rearview mirror, his eyes dilated so big that it looked like someone had just taken his picture with a flash cube. Mildred simply stared back at him, her tears all dried up now, and kept fumbling with her wig. Her fingers smelled like Evening in Paris, probably because she had sprayed it everywhere — between her legs, under her arms, on the balls of her feet, and beneath the fake skull of her wig. She didn't utter a word, just tried to ignore the pain in her foot and hissed and sucked saliva through her teeth.

Crook pulled into the cement driveway, and the right headlight barely missed the bark on the big oak tree as he cut the wheel and brought the car to an abrupt halt.

Mildred opened the door before they'd come to a complete stop, jumped out, slammed the door, and screamed, "Kiss my black ass!" She limped up the side steps toward the porch, turned, and yelled, "I hate you! I hate you! I hate you!" like a cheerleader.

All the lights were out in the house, but Mildred knew the kids weren't really asleep. She knew that as soon as they'd heard the car pull up the driveway, Freda had sprinted to the TV and flicked it off and ordered the rest of the kids to "hit it." Money, Bootsey, Angel, and Doll would have scattered like mice to their two bedrooms, closed their doors, and dived into bed to hide under the covers and wait to hear the boxing match they knew was sure to come. It was something they always dreaded when their parents came home from the bar. They'd squeeze their eyes tight pretending to be asleep, just in case Mildred or Crook decided to check on them, but they rarely did on nights like this, when Crook forgot he had kids and Mildred was too preoccupied with her own defense.

Mildred flicked on the dining room light and walked toward the bathroom. Her foot was killing her. When she looked in the mirror she saw that the blood from her lip had smudged all over the white mink collar of her blue suede coat. The blood had made the mink come to slick points, like the fur of a wet dog. Mildred felt herself getting mad all over again. She had cleaned a lot of white folks' houses to buy this coat, had kept it on layaway at Winkleman's for almost a year, and she knew that blood never came out, never.

When Mildred looked down, she saw more blood was soaking through the seams of the pockets and staining the white stitching around the buttonholes. The scent of her Evening in Paris permeated the bathroom and started to stink. She wanted to throw up. Instead, she went into the kitchen, grabbed the dishrack, and threw it high into the air so that it crashed and hit the edge of the sink. Everything breakable broke and smashed in the basin. Plates, glasses, cups and saucers, cereal bowls. Some things fell to the floor and shattered into jagged chips. Mildred gritted her teeth, balled up her right fist, and pounded it on the pile of broken dishes. Her fist bled but she was too mad to notice.

She was just about to look for the skillet when she heard Crook stagger in the side door. Her rage welled up from a hollow cave in her stomach. "Oooooooo! You just irks me so. I'm surprised I ain't had a nervous breakdown by now. Always making a mountain out of a frigging molehill. Thinking thangs is happening when ain't nothing happening. You can't see for looking, you know that? I keep saying to myself, Mildred, leave this pitiful excuse for a man. I keep saying, Mildred, you know in your heart he ain't no good. Rotten, sorry. But how I'ma leave him with five growing kids to clothe and feed?" Her teeth felt like chalk and she scraped them together so hard that they slipped and she bit her tongue.

"Lord, have mercy on my soul," Mildred pleaded. "If somebody could show me the light, clear a path and give me an extra ounce of strength, I'd be out of here so damn fast make your head swim." Mildred was not a religious person, but she made sure her kids went to Shiloh Baptist every Sunday morning, though the only time she ever bothered to go herself was on Easter, Mother's Day, and Christmas. She shook her head back and forth, letting her eyes roll like loose marbles.

"Just keep on running your mouth, girl," Crook said, trying unsuccessfully to kick off his shoes.

Mildred's anger was flowing like hot lava. Pearls of sweat slid down her temples. Her jawbone was tightening as though she were biting down on rock candy.

"If I was trying to flirt with somebody for real, do you think I'd be stupid enough to do it right in front of your frigging face?" She put her hands on her hips and took soldier steps toward Crook. She didn't know where she was getting this courage from and surely it couldn't have been from God because he'd never given her any clue that being a fool would get her anywhere safe. "But you know what? Yeah, I'd love to screw Percy since you and everybody else swear I've been screwing him for years anyway. Who else was I supposed to be flirting with behind your back? Oh yeah, Porky and Joe Porter and Swift! I'd love to fuck all of 'em!"

"Mildred, you better shut your mouth up, girl. You know you're gon' get it. You know I ain't two minutes away from your behind." Crook had managed to get his shoes off, scattering wet red and gold leaves that had stuck to his soles. He slipped and fell backward against the china cabinet and plaster-of-Paris knickknacks tumbled all over the floor. He danced over the glass grapes, wishing wells, and miniature cats as though he were walking on hot sand at the beach.

Mildred didn't care at this point. She knew that whether she kept her mouth shut or open, she was going to get it anyway. His fist would snap against her head, or the back of his hard hand would swipe her face, or he'd hurl her against a wall until her brains rattled. It was always something, so long as it hurt.

Crook stumbled toward the living room and into the bedroom. He found his thick brown leather belt, the one Mildred occasionally used to chastise the kids for their wrongdoings, then he walked back out to the dining room. He pulled his shoulders back high, trying to act sober, and beckoned Mildred with his index finger. "Since you so damn smart, let's see if your ass is as tough as your mouth is, girl. Now get in here. You ain't had a good spanking in a while."

Mildred's courage vanished.

"Crook, please, don't. I'm sorry. I didn't mean what I said, none of it. I was just running my drunk mouth." Mildred was trying to move backward, away from him, but when she found herself in a corner and couldn't move another inch, she knew she was trapped. There was no one she could call to for help. She didn't want to scare the kids any more than they already were, and Mildred knew they were probably leaning against their bedroom doors, shivering like baby birds in a nest. All she could do was hope that he wouldn't take this any further than the belt to the point where he might just kill her this time. A drunk is always sorry later. "Crook, please don't hit me," she begged. "I promise I won't say another word. Please." Mildred was not the type to beg. Had never begged anybody for anything and now it didn't sound or feel right.

"Get on in here, girl. Your tears don't excite me," he said, snatching her by the wrists. "You think you're so cute, don't you?" Crook's face was contorted and had taken on a monstrous quality. It looked like every ounce of liquor and Indian blood in his body had migrated to the veins in his face. He yanked off her wig and threw it to the floor. Then he made her drop her coat next to it, then her cream knit dress, and then her girdle. When all she had on was her brassiere and panties, he shoved her into the bedroom where she crawled to a corner of the bed. Crook kicked the door shut and the kids cracked theirs. Then they heard their mama screaming and their daddy hollering and the whap of the belt as he struck her.

"Didn't I tell you you was getting too grown?" *Whap.* "Don't you know your place yet, girl?" *Whap.*

"Yes, yes, Crook." *Whap.*

"Don't you know nothing about respect?" *Whap.* "Girl, you gon' learn. I'm a man, not no toy." *Whap.* "You understand me?" *Whap.* "Make me look like no fool." *Whap.*

He threw the belt on the floor and collapsed next to Mildred on the bed. The terror in her voice faded to whimpers and sniffles. To the kids she sounded like Prince, their German shepherd, when he had gotten hit by a car last year on Twenty-fourth Street.

Mildred curled up into a tight knot and tried to find a spot that would shelter her from Crook. She hoped he would fall asleep, but he reached over and turned on the TV. Mildred crept out the end of the bed and put on a slip.

"Where you going?" he asked.

"To the bathroom," she said. She closed the door behind her and headed straight for the kitchen, tiptoed around the broken glass, and opened the oven. She yanked the black skillet out and slung the grease into the sink. Crook heard her and came into the dining room to see what she was doing. Before he knew what was happening, Mildred raised the heavy pan into the air and charged into him, hitting him on the forehead with a loud *throng.* Blood ran down over his eye and he grabbed her and pushed her back into the bedroom. The kids heard them bumping into the wall for what seemed like forever and then they heard nothing at all.

Freda hushed the girls and made them huddle under a flimsy flannel blanket on the bottom bunk bed. "Shut up, before they hear us and we'll be next," she whispered loudly. She tried to comfort the two youngest, Angel and Doll, by wrapping them inside her skinny arms, but it was no use. They couldn't stop crying. Since Freda was the oldest, she felt it was her place to act like an adult, but soon she started to cry too. None of them understood any of this, but when they heard the mattress squeaking, they knew what was happening.

Money ran from his room into Freda's. They all sat on the cold metal edge of the bed where the mattress didn't touch, sniffling, listening. They waited patiently, hoping that after five or ten minutes all they would hear would be Crook's snoring. They prayed that they could all finally go to sleep. But just when they had settled into the rhythm of silence — the humming of the refrigerator, the cars passing on Twenty-fourth Street, Prince yawning on the back porch — their parents' moans and groans would erupt again and poison the peace.

When Money couldn't stand it any more, he tiptoed back to his room. He flipped over his mattress, because the fighting always made him lose control of his bladder. He would say his prayers extra hard and swear that when he got older and got married he would never beat his wife, he wouldn't care what she did. He would leave first.

The girls slid into their respective bunks and lay there, not moving to scratch or even twitch. They tried to inch into their separate dreams but the sound of creaking grew louder and louder, then faster and faster.

"Why they try to kill each other, then do the nasty?" Bootsey asked Freda.

"Mama don't like doing it," Freda explained. "She only doing it so Daddy won't hit her no more."

"Sound like she like it to me. It's taking forever," said Bootsey. Angel and Doll didn't know what they were talking about.

"Just go to sleep," Freda said. And pretty soon the noises stopped and their eyelids drooped and they fell asleep.

The kids were already on the sun porch watching Saturday morning cartoons when Mildred emerged from the bedroom. She had a diaper tied around her head and a new layer of pancake makeup on to camouflage the swelling. The kids didn't say anything about the purple patch of skin beneath her eye or her swollen lip. They just stared at her like she was a stranger they were trying to identify.

"What y'all looking at?" she said. "Y'all some of the nosiest kids I've ever seen in my life. Look at this house!" she snapped, trying to divert their attention. "It's a mess. Your daddy was drunk last night. Now I want y'all to brush your teeth and wash those dingy faces 'cause I ain't raising no heathens around here. Freda, make these kids some oatmeal. And I want this house spotless before you sit back down to watch a "Bugs Bunny" or a "Roadrunner," and don't ask me no questions about them dishes. Just pick 'em up and throw that mess away. Cheap dishes anyway. Weren't worth a pot to piss in. Next time I'm buying plastic."

The kids were used to Mildred giving them orders, didn't know any other way of being told what to do, thought everybody's mama talked like theirs. And although they huffed and puffed under their breath and stomped their feet in defiance and made faces at her when her back was turned, they were careful not to get caught. "And I want y'all to get out of this house today. Go on outside somewhere and play. My nerves ain't this" — she snapped her fingers — "long today. And Freda, before you do anything, fix your mama a cup of coffee, girl. Two sugars instead of one, and lots of Pet milk."

Freda had already put water on for the coffee because she knew Mildred was mad. She had picked up the broken dishes, too. She didn't like seeing her mama all patched up like this. As a matter of fact, Freda hoped that by her thirteenth birthday her daddy would be dead or divorced. She had started to hate him, couldn't understand why Mildred didn't just leave him. Then they all could go on welfare like everybody else seemed to be doing in Point Haven. She didn't dare suggest this to her mama. Freda knew Mildred hated advice, so she did what her mama wasn't used to doing: kept her mouth shut.

When Crook finally got up, he smiled at the kids like nothing had happened. And like always on a Saturday morning after a rough night at the Shingle, he had somewhere important he had to go. When Mildred heard the Mercury's engine purring, she felt relieved because she knew she wouldn't have to see him again until late that night when he would most likely be drunk and asking where his dinner was, or tomorrow, when he'd be so hung over that he would walk straight to the bedroom and pass out.

Mildred counted her change and managed to muster up a few dollars. She decided to send the kids to the movies. Told them to sit through the feature twice, which was fine with them.

When they had finally skipped out the door and the house was as clean as an army barracks, Mildred had limped to the back porch and scrounged up the ax.

Her coffee was cold now, so she added some hot water to it and walked slowly into the living room. The house shoe helped cushion her foot against the hard floor, but it still hurt. She collapsed on the orange couch. Good, she thought. No Crook, no kids, and no dog. Mildred looked around the room, scanning its beige walls and the shiny floors she had waxed on her knees yesterday. The windows sparkled because she had cleaned the insides with vinegar and water. She had paid old ugly Deadman five dollars to clean the outsides. The house smelled and looked clean, just the way she liked it.

Her eyes claimed everything she saw. This is *my* house, she thought. I've worked too damn hard for you to be hurting me all these years. And me, like a damn fool, taking it. Like I'm your property. Like you own me or something. I pay all the bills around here, even this house note. I'm the one who scrubbed white folks' floors in St. Clemens and Huronville and way up there on Strawberry Lane to buy it.

Mildred sank back deeper into the couch and propped her good foot on top of the cocktail table. She tucked her lip in and took the diaper off her head. Then she ran her fingers over her thick braids. She began unbraiding them, though she had no intention of doing anything to her hair once it hung loose.

She looked out the window at the weeping willow trees. She remembered when she planted them. And who had had the garden limed? she thought. Paved the driveway and planted all those flowers, frozen under the dirt right now? Me. Who'd cooked hamburgers at Big Boy's and slung coconut cream pies to uppity white folks I couldn't stand to look in the eye 'cause they was sitting at the counter and I was standing behind it? Smothered in grease and smoke and couldn't even catch my breath long enough to go to the bathroom. And who was the one got corns and bunions from carrying plates of ribs and fried chicken back and forth at the Shingle when I was five months pregnant, while you hung off the back of a city garbage truck half drunk, waving at people like you were the president or the head of some parade?

She put her foot back on the floor and lit another cigarette.

Never even made up a decent excuse about what you did with your money. I know about Ernestine. I ain't no fool. Just been waiting for the right time. Me and the kids sitting in here with the lights and gas cut off and you give me two dollars. Say, "Here, buy some pork-n-beans and vanilla wafers for the kids, and if it's some change left get yourself a beer." A beer. Just what I needed, sitting in a cold-ass house in the dark.

Mildred's eyes scanned the faces of her five kids, framed in gold and black around the room.

And you got the nerve to brag about how pretty, how healthy and how smart your kids are. Don't they have your color. Your high cheekbones. Your smile. These ain't your damn kids. They mine. Maybe they got your blood, but they mine.

Mildred had had Freda when she was seventeen, and the other kids had fallen out every nine or ten months after that, with the exception of one year between Freda and Money. Crook had told her he didn't want any more kids until he got on his feet. Freda was almost three months old when Mildred realized she was pregnant again. She was too scared to tell Crook, so she asked her sister-in-law what she should do. Curly Mae told her to take three five-milligram quinine tablets. When that didn't work, she told her to drink some citrate of magnesia and take a dry mustard bath. A week later she went to the bathroom feeling like she was going to have a bowel movement and had a miscarriage.

Motherhood meant everything to Mildred. When she was first carrying Freda, she didn't believe her stomach would actually grow, but when she felt it stretch like the skin of a drum and it swelled up like a small brown moon, she'd never been so happy. She felt there was more than just a cord connecting her to this boy or girl that was moving inside her belly. There was some special juice and only she could supply it. And sometimes when she turned over at night she could feel the baby turn inside her too, and she knew this was magic.

The morning Freda came, Crook was in a motel room on the North End with Ernestine. Curly Mae drove her to the hospital. From that point on, Mildred watched her first baby grow like a long sunrise. She was so proud of Freda that she let her body blow up and flatten for the next fifty-five months. It made her feel like she had actually done something meaningful with her life, having these babies did. And when she pulled the brush back and up through their thick clods of nappy hair, she smiled because it was her own hair she was brushing. These kids were her future. They made her feel important and gave her a feeling of place, of movement, a sense of having come from somewhere. Having babies was routine to a lot of women, but for Mildred it was unique every time; she didn't have a single regret about having had five kids — except one, and that was who had fathered them.

Mildred lay down when she felt the heaviness of the pill beginning to work. Bells were ringing in her ears, and it made her think of Christmas, which was only two months away. For the past nine Christmases Mildred had had to hustle to buy Chatty Cathy dolls, Roll-a-Strollers, ice skates, racing car sets, sleds, and bicycles. Crook had helped her sneak them through the side door at midnight. She didn't know how she would manage this year.

She shook her head. Should've never let you come back after you got out the sanitarium, she thought. Should've let you have old sorry, ancient Ernestine, 'cause y'all deserved each other. But I felt bad for you 'cause I thought tuberculosis was gon' kill you. Guess alcohol must be the cure for what you got. You promised me, promised me, that when you got back on your feet you would take care of me and the kids like a husband is supposed to do. Told me I wouldn't have to worry no more about everything or work so damn hard. Well, *look* at me. My nerves is about to pop. Red veins in my eyes like freeways. My head always throbbing and my skin look like it been embalmed. I'm twenty-seven years old, and I'm sick and tired of this shit. And I don't care if I gotta turn tricks or work ten jobs — you getting out of here this time for good.

Mildred tried to grit her teeth, but the pill wouldn't let her. She wanted to scream, but the pill wouldn't let her. She felt like crying too, but the pill wouldn't let her. All it would let her do was sleep.

# Two

"KILL HIM," slurred Curly Mae, as she fell back in the recliner on Mildred's sunporch. The sun was piercing through the Venetian blinds, leaving yellow stripes across Curly's light brown legs. "As the World Turns" was on television, but neither of them was paying much attention to it. Liquor always made Curly talk crazy.

"And if he put his hands on you again, the sucker deserve it. I don't care if he is my brother, what give him the right to disfigure you?" She gulped down the rest of her drink and carefully set the plastic glass on the floor. It tipped over. "A skunk is a skunk," Curly said. She lifted her arm up as if it weighed a hundred pounds and plopped it in her lap.

Mildred was snapping string beans a few feet away from her. They were landing all over the floor instead of in the bowl. She was drunk too.

"I don't want to kill him, Curly, damn. I just don't want him jumping on me when he get back. It's been two days and I ain't heard nothing from him. I know where he is."

"He down there with that heffa, ain't he?"

"Yeah, I guess so. More power to him," said Mildred.

"Yeah, well, let me put it to you this way. You need something to protect yourself with. A gun'll scare a niggah."

"They scare me, too. You know that, girl."

"Now you tell me, what make more sense? To be waiting in here scared with these kids, or be holding something to get his ass on out of here? Remember the last time you called the police? How long it take 'em to get here? Forty-five minutes, and you know it take ten minutes from uptown. You could'a been dead. As long as one niggah is trying to kill another, white folks could care less."

"You right, chile, you right."

Mildred pushed the plastic bowl aside with her foot and went to get the rest of the Old Crow. When she came back, Curly was struggling to get out of the chair.

"Milly," she said, "I'll tell you what. I let you hold my gun till you get him out of here. Can you lend me twenty dollars?"

"Twenty dollars? That's my gas bill money. Till when, Curly?"

"Till Saturday morning or Sunday afternoon at the latest."

"Okay. But who's gon' show me how to use the gun?"

"I would, but I got so much to do over in that house today, and Lord knows some of this liquor gotta wear off first."

There was a knock at the door. It was Deadman. He often helped Mildred around the house. Of all Lucretia Bennett's dumb and ugly sons, Deadman was the ugliest and dumbest. He was in his early twenties and had the reading level of a fifth grader. But he was reliable and he was as nice as nice could be, so whenever he stopped by Mildred felt obligated to keep him busy, even if she didn't have anything for him to do. Trying to find things that needed to be fixed wasn't hard, because Crook had never fixed much of anything. After Deadman did whatever Mildred had asked him to, the next problem was getting him to go home.

Mildred opened the door.

"Hey, good-lookin'," she said. Deadman smiled, showing off his tiny yellow teeth. His head was shaped like a big almond from one angle and a small watermelon from another. Deadman knew he was ugly, and for that he was sort of cute. He kind of grew on Mildred and the kids. He had a contagious sense of humor. He'd have her and the kids on the floor in stitches when he'd tell them all the goings on in the neighborhood. He knew who was screwing who, who'd just been put out, who'd gotten her behind kicked, whose lights and gas were turned off, and whose car had been repossessed. He was more like a reporter than a gossiper, because he wasn't malicious. He also knew how to hustle and always had a few dollars in his pockets. Lots of times he lent Mildred money when she was short.

"I was going out to the butcher's and wanted to know if you needed something. Mama say they got a sale on neck bones and pork chops today."

"Why, thank you, Deadman, but I just lent Curly my last. We got enough meat around here to last us for a while, though. Tell me something, you know how to shoot a gun?"

"Yeah, everybody know how to shoot a gun. Pull the damn trigger." He started laughing, and his eyes darted past Mildred. He was looking for Freda. He had a silent crush on her, but he'd never let Mildred know it or else she would've probably changed her mind about him. He always bought Freda potato chips, fruit punch, chewing gum — small things he could give her without seeming obvious. As a matter of fact, that's what brought him over to their house so often. He would rake leaves when there were only a few on the ground. He'd clean out the stoker when it didn't need it; clean Mildred's storm windows; paint the bricks around the base of the house and along the driveway, and do anything else he could find.

"Can you show me how?" Mildred asked.

"Yeah, you got it here?"

"I'll send it over by one of the kids," Curly said, brushing past him. "I'll stick it in my old blue purse."

Mildred slipped her the twenty and Curly inched down the steps and pranced across the street to her house. A few minutes later, her oldest son returned with the purse. After Deadman showed Mildred how to use it, she hid it between her box spring and mattress.

Mildred knew how to pretend, and that's exactly what she'd been doing since Crook had come home from the hospital. Pretended she didn't know he was still messing around with Ernestine. Pretended not to know that Ernestine's oldest daughter looked just like Crook. She didn't know what he saw in that evil, bug-eyed drunk. Ernestine had never liked Mildred either, from the time they were kids. Mildred was not only better-looking, to put it mildly, but was much smarter and never had trouble attracting boys. Mildred always thought that just because she was poor didn't mean she had to look it.

Ernestine never smiled at anyone because her two front teeth had been knocked out by some man years ago. People said it was Crook who did it, but no one really knew. One thing Mildred did know was that even though Ernestine had had Crook's baby, he had married her, not Ernestine. At the time, she felt like the best woman had won. Hell, any woman can have a baby, Mildred thought, but can't every woman get the man.

When Crook still hadn't come home by evening, Mildred decided she couldn't wait another minute. She put her clothes on, left the kids watching "Million Dollar Movie," and walked down to Ernestine's house. She saw the Mercury parked in the alley. Mildred was furious, not because he had run to Ernestine, but because he wasn't man enough to face her. She contemplated picking up the brick she saw lying next to the car and breaking all the windows. Then she remembered that she was the one who had bought this car. She thought she might throw it through Ernestine's window but finally decided against that, too. Instead, she walked back home in the snow and packed everything Crook owned in cardboard boxes and trash bags. Then she called a cab and rode back to Ernestine's house and plopped them into a huge snowbank.

A week went by and Mildred still hadn't heard anything from Crook. It was snowing again on Sunday night, and she was watching a new group called The Beatles on "The Ed Sullivan Show." Funny-looking little white boys with suits that looked too small, with stingy little collars. There was a noise at the side door, and Mildred thought it was Prince, but she had put him on the back porch. She went to the door and there was Crook, sitting on the steps, snow soaking through the seat of his pants, his teeth hanging out of his mouth, looking like some orphan. She let him in, pushed him toward one of the kids' rooms and cracked open a window because he smelled like he'd been living in a flophouse. Crook passed out.

Mildred put on her snow boots and car coat, went to her bedroom, slid the gun from under the mattress, and put it in her purse. Then she eased the keys from Crook's pocket and drove down to the Red Shingle, where she knew she would find Ernestine.

There was nothing red about the Red Shingle, except for the trim painted around the white windows. And they weren't really windows either, because you couldn't see through them. They were squares cut into the brick wall. The parking lot could only hold twenty or thirty cars — big cars, which is what everybody drove in Point Haven. The bigger the car, the more stature you had, though a lot of the men who drove these cars lived in them, too. Kept their clothes in the trunk, their shaving equipment in the glove compartment, and a quilt in the back seat in case one of their lady friends wouldn't put them up for the night. Most black folks considered their cars evidence of their true worth. That and the gold capped over their teeth. And Lord, they flashed those. Some of them, mainly folks who had migrated from the South to work in the factories near Detroit, tried to out-tooth each other. They started out simple: a gold cap. Then they moved into gold and diamonds, then stars, and last, their initials.

Folks hung out at the Red Shingle because it was the only place blacks were welcome.

Drinking was the single most reliable source of entertainment for a lot of people in Point Haven. Alcohol was a genuine elixir, granting instant relief from the mundane existence that each and every one of them led. It was as though the town had some hold over them, always hinting that one day it would magically provide everything they would ever need, could ever need, and satisfy all their desires. No one was the least bit curious about anything that went on outside Point Haven. Here it was 1964, and most folks had never heard of Malcolm X and only a few had some idea who Martin Luther King was. They lived as if they were sleepwalking or waiting around for something else to happen.

Most of the black men couldn't find jobs, and as a result, they had so much spare time on their hands that when they were stone cold broke, bored with themselves, or pissed off about

everything because life turned out to be such a disappointment, their dissatisfaction would burst open and their rage would
explode. This was what usually passed for masculinity, and it
was often their wives or girlfriends or whores who felt the fall-
out.

Since the Shingle was in the middle of South Park and everybody lived within walking distance, the majority of these men
hung out here. And people came from as far as New Winton
and St. Clemens, thirty miles away, to hear an occasional live
band.

The Shingle was right across the street from Miss Moore's
whorehouse, three doors down from Stinky's Liquor Store. Dove
Road, at the mouth of Stinky's driveway, was considered a busy
street because it was the artery that led to the intersection at
Twenty-fourth. It was also the first side street in the black
neighborhood to be paved and get streetlights.

The only time the Red Shingle ever saw a white face swing
through its silver doors was when a Canadian came looking for
brown thighs and breasts. This had been going on for so long
that no one paid much attention to them when they showed
up, except for the few women who sat at the bar and called
themselves prostitutes. Most of them were just welfare moth-
ers trying to pick up some extra change, or wives whose husbands were out of work or had left them.

Fletcher Armstrong owned the Shingle. He was one of the
only black men fortunate enough to have some money in his
family. His father, who lived fifty-four miles away in Detroit,
was in the numbers business. It was supposed to be a well-kept
secret, but everybody knew it and always had. Fletcher lived
out on Ross Road in a house he had had built. It was a split —
three levels — like the white folks' houses up on Strawberry
Lane. Sometimes on their way out to the country, black folks
from South Park would drive by Fletcher's house just to ooh
and aah. Some were quite jealous, and the most considerate
thing they could find to say was nasty. "Niggahs thank they
something when they get a little money, don't they? Gotta throw
it all up in your face. Look at them pink shingles. Wouldn't
you say they was too damn loud to be on your house? Can't
take the country out of a niggah, can you?" But some people

were quite proud. "It sure is nice to see colored people moving up in the world, ain't it? Ten years ago, weren't no colored people even living out here. Now look. And look at them pink shingles — they beautiful, ain't they?"

Fletcher had green eyes and peach skin. He didn't associate with the regular black people of Point Haven because he thought he was better than they were. The closest he came was when he opened up the Shingle every afternoon and started heating up the grease in the kitchen for fried chicken and french fries and turned on the grill for the barbecued ribs he was famous for.

In one tight corner of the bar there was a platform barely big enough for a singer and piano player, but on many a night an entire four-piece combo managed to squeeze in and play forty-five-minute sets of jazz, blues, and rhythm-and-blues until the Shingle closed its doors at two o'clock in the morning, when most of the people were fatally drunk and still didn't want to go home. People like Ernestine Jackson.

Sure enough, when Mildred walked in she was sitting at the bar, with her stingy hair plastered down to her head with grease, and lint balls coating the tips of old curls. Ernestine was talking just as loud as always. Mildred sat down next to her and lit an L&M.

"I just want to tell you that you can have the sorry son-of-a-bitch if you want him. He's at the house. I'm divorcing him as soon as the courthouse open up in the morning, or God ain't my witness." Mildred got up from the bar stool, and walked toward the bathroom. She could hear the soles of Ernestine's shoes shuffling on the tile behind her.

Mildred was in front of the mirror when Ernestine barged in. She tucked in her lip and applied more lipstick on top of an already fresh coat.

Ernestine kicked the door shut and put her hands on her hips.

"Look, cunt, you ain't *giving* him to me, 'cause he was about to leave you anyway."

"Is that so," Mildred said, watching Ernestine from the mirror.

"Crook never loved you in the first place, and you know it.

You tricked him into marrying you. You was supposed to be so goddamn respectable. Hah! Now look. He done come back to me and his daughter after all this time. Life is a bitch, ain't it, Mildred?"

Mildred wanted to reach inside her purse and blow Ernestine's brains out, but she knew this hussy didn't have any. Besides, she wasn't going to jail for shooting some scag who wanted her trifling husband. She simply looked at Ernestine like she was a bad joke, shook her head back and forth, laughed, and left the bathroom.

So after ten years of sneaking, waiting, and loving the man who had married her rival, Ernestine finally had her chance. And like a fool, Crook went with her. Mildred felt like she'd shed ten layers of dead skin. She knew she'd made the right decision because when she sat down to think about it, the only thing she'd ever appreciated about Crook all these years was the fact that he was a good lover when he was sober and had given her five beautiful and healthy kids. But like most handsome men, she thought, screwing and making babies was about the only thing they did with dedication and consistency, without much thought or consideration, and were so damn proud afterward, that you'd swear they'd won the Kentucky Derby or something.

# Three

*E*VEN AFTER THE FIRST YEAR had passed and Mildred's endurance had sunk below sea level, she didn't have a single regret about divorcing Crook. She'd been fired from Diamond Crystal Salt because she'd called in sick too many times in the few short months she'd worked there. It was boring work to Mildred anyway. All she did from seven to three in the afternoon was add a free-flowing agent to the fine-grained salt so it wouldn't cake up from the humidity. It didn't make any sense to her. She always had to put a few grains of rice in her salt shaker when it caked up anyway, so what was the point?

It was mostly the kids who'd gotten sick, not her. Bad colds. Mumps. Measles. Then Freda started her period in the middle of her science class and threw up all over the bathroom floor when she got home. Now, Mildred was back out in Huronville on her knees six days a week, cleaning the Hales', Grahams', and Callingtons' houses.

Mildred hated cleaning up behind white folks (behind anybody, really), but it was steady work and most of the time they left her alone in the house and she was able to work at her own pace. Nobody was standing over her shoulder the way they had when she worked at Big Boy's and the Shingle, breathing out commands or hinting at what she should do next. Here she did everything the way she felt like doing it. Quickly.

23

One morning, after six months of listening to Freda beg her, Mildred let Freda come with her to see the rich folks' houses on the condition that Freda would help her clean, do something besides get in her way.

When they pulled up in the Mercury, Freda acted like she was getting out of a limousine. She walked proudly through the oak doors.

"Ooooooo, Mama, can you believe this?" Freda asked, as she glided through one room after another.

"Just don't touch nothing, girl, this shit ain't fake. Everything in here is real, and it's expensive. We barely had enough gas to get out here so you know we can't pay for nothing if you break it."

Freda promised her she wouldn't touch anything, but as soon as Mildred went about her business, Freda's fingers slid over the bronze and brass and alabaster. She was awestruck. When she heard the vacuum cleaner in the other room, she flopped down in the middle of the white couch and spread her arms across the back. Her bright black eyes scanned the airy room. She tried to guess how high the ceiling was. Fifteen or twenty feet? A chandelier with at least five thousand tiny lights glistened in the sun streaming through the tall windows. A fireplace big enough for her to walk in stood in the center of the room. Freda wondered how many times it had been lit, and if they roasted marshmallows or weenies there in the wintertime. What a way to live, she thought. She closed her eyes, let her head fall back on the couch, and imagined six of her best girlfriends lying by the fireplace in flannel nightgowns, eating popcorn and dreaming out loud about their prospective boyfriends. They were having a great time in Freda's house, and how they envied her. They loved her slumber parties because there was always plenty of everything to eat and her house was always spotless.

"Freda, what you doing in there, girl? You too quiet, and I know when you quiet you up to something. I told you not to touch nothing, didn't I?"

"I didn't touch nothing, Mama. I'm coming." Freda walked toward the yellow and white kitchen, where Mildred was running hot water into a tin pail.

"I'm hungry, Mama. Can I have something to eat?"

"Look in the icebox, girl." When Freda opened the door, her eyes zigzagged across each shelf. She had never seen so much food in a refrigerator. There were pickles and olives, a big leafy head of lettuce, stacks and stacks of lunch meat, and three different kinds of bread. There was fresh fruit — oranges and apples and grapes. Everything was neatly housed in plastic containers. But there was something so orderly about this refrigerator, Freda didn't feel comfortable about touching anything. Something was missing: it lacked a wholesome smell. She'd noticed it was missing in the rest of the house, too. That smell that meant somebody really lived here, tracked up the floors, burnt something on the stove every now and then. There was no smell of heat coming from the radiators, or any signs that rubber boots and wet mittens ever dried over them. Her own house smelled rich from fried chicken and collard greens and corn bread, from Pine-Sol and washing powder and Windex and Aero Wax and the little coned incense Mildred burned after she'd finished giving the house a good cleaning.

Freda decided she wasn't hungry and closed the refrigerator. Mildred hollered from the living room for her to go upstairs and start cleaning the bathroom. Freda slowly made her way up the winding staircase to the blue tiled bathroom in the hallway. The towels were folded neatly across the silver racks and looked like they had never been used. The blue bathtub was shining like a satin bedspread. Nothing in here needed cleaning. Freda pulled down her slacks to use the toilet, then remembered her mama had told her never to use a toilet when she didn't know the owners. So she put her hands on the seat and let her small behind support itself in midair. When she'd finished, she washed her hands, dried them on her slacks, and ran back downstairs.

"I'm done, Mama."

"Good. You may think we playing house, but I'm counting dollars and cents. All I gotta do now is wax this floor and we through. Look in that pantry over there and get the duster and swish it across the furniture in the front room and dining room, even if don't nothing look dusty."

While Freda was dusting, the real reason they were there finally hit her. Cleaning. She wondered just how long her mama would have to do this kind of work. Until something better came along? Like a new husband for her and a new daddy for them? One who could afford them all. When Freda finished, she stood in the doorway watching Mildred work on her hands and knees. She saw the sweat oozing down Mildred's temples, which made her red headrag look like it was soaked in fresh blood. Freda didn't like seeing her mama like this. Didn't care how much money she was getting for it. And on the way home, Freda tried to figure out the best way to tell her mama that one day if she had anything to do with it, she would see to it that Mildred wouldn't have to work so hard to get so little.

"Mama, guess what," she said, as they drove down the winding road along the river. It was a clear fall afternoon, the kind that children are anxious to go out and play in, and come home sniffling and hungry, their fingers too stiff to unbutton their own coats.

"What?" replied Mildred, only half paying attention.

"I'ma be rich when I grow up and I'ma buy us a better and bigger house than the Hales' and you ain't gon' have to scrub no floors for no white folks."

"That's what I need to hear, chile. I sure wish you was grown now. But you got plenty of time to be worrying about millions of thangs. Take your mama's word for it. And you don't have to worry about me. I *know* I ain't gon' be on my knees for the rest of my life. I got way too much sense for that. This is what I gotta do right now so I don't have to ask nobody for nothing. Ain't no sense in me whining like some chessy cat. This ain't killing me. Women've done worse thangs to earn a living, and this may not be the bottom for me."

Mildred pulled up to a stoplight and reached for her purse to get a cigarette. The light changed so she handed the purse to Freda.

"Light me a cigarette, would you?"

Freda found the pack of Tareytons (Mildred'd quit L&Ms right after she and Crook had broken up because they reminded her of him), and lit it. Freda thought of inhaling that first puff, but decided against it. She handed it to Mildred.

"One thang I do know," Mildred continued, "and you can

mark my words. Y'all ain't never gon' have to worry about eating, that's for damn sure. It may not be steak and onions and mashed potatoes and gravy, but you won't go hungry. And y'all ain't gon' never be caught looking like no damn orphans, either. If I can't give you what you need, you ain't gon' get it, and I don't care if I have to beg, borrow, or steal, every last one of y'all is going to college. I mean it. All y'all got good sense, and I'ma make sure you stretch it to the fullest."

Mildred took two quick puffs on the cigarette and tossed it out the window. Freda listened intently. She loved it when her mama went off on a tangent like this.

"And baby, let me tell you something so you can get this straight. That big fancy house ain't the only thang in life worth striving for. Decency. A good husband. Some healthy babies. Peace of mind. Them is the thangs you try to get out of life. Everything else'll fall in place. It always do. You hear me?"

"Yeah, I hear you, Mama," she said.

"What'd you say?"

"I mean yes. But I'm still gon' be rich anyway, 'cause from what I see being poor don't get you nowhere and just about everybody we know except white people is poor. Why is that, Mama?"

" 'Cause niggahs is stupid, that's why. They thank they can get something for nothing and that that God they keep praying to every Sunday is gon' rush down from the sky and save 'em. But look at 'em. What it takes is real hard work. Ain't nobody gon' give you nothing in this world unless you work for it. I don't care what they tell you in church. One thang is true, and this is the tricky part. White folks own every damn thang 'cause they was here first and took it all. They don't like to see niggahs getting ahead and when they feel like it, they can stop you and make it just that much harder. But with all you learn in them books at school, least you can do is learn how to get around some shit like that. Anybody can see through something that's crystal clear. Just keep your eyes open and don't believe everythang — naw, don't believe half the shit people tell you 'cause don't nobody know everythang. Not even your mama. Believe me, I ain't gon' steer you too far off in the wrong direction. Mark my words. If y'all just learn to thank for yourself, don't take nobody's bullshit, I won't have to worry about you. I don't care if they white, purple, or green. Always remember that you just as good as the next person. How many times I told y'all that? All you gotta do is believe it."

Mildred pressed her foot down on the accelerator and the car jutted forward in spurts. They began to see smaller houses ahead. Freda didn't like Point Haven and dreamed of leaving after she graduated. She had no idea where she would go, but she knew that there had to be a better place to live than here. Mildred had never given any thought to living anywhere else.

Most people who didn't live within a seventy-five-mile radius had never even heard of Point Haven. It was in the thumb of Michigan, and from a hundred feet above, the town would look like a blanket of gray and black stripes spread out beside Lake Huron. Most of the streets were pressed black dirt with rocks still stuck beneath it. There were so many trees and fields that no one appreciated them, except in hot sticky summers. There were blueberry, blackberry, elderberry, and strawberry patches in back yards and miles of woods.

And there was plenty of water, which meant good fishing, something the black folks cherished most about the town. They could never catch enough pickerel, catfish, perch, or sheepshead to satisfy their insatiable appetites for fillets dipped in egg batter and yellow cornmeal, dropped in hot grease, and smothered with Louisiana hot sauce.

A lot of people had drowned from undertows in the St. Clair River, where they often fished. Folks swore the currents came from Canada, which they could see when standing at the shore. Even when the sanctified preacher put on his white robe and walked through waves and over stones to baptize people, he wouldn't go out too far. Once he dropped his Bible in the water after dipping Melinda Pinkerton backward into salvation and a wave clipped his sleeve, sweeping his Bible away. He didn't try to go after it, either.

There were three residential sections in Point Haven. Half of the black population lived in South Park by the railroad tracks or near the small factories on the outskirts of town. In South Park there were five churches, one bank, two grocery stores, one Laundromat, one bar, and four liquor stores. Coming from Detroit, you reached South Park first, and the first impression people got was that this place looked like a ghost town. It was. Full of black ghosts who crept quietly up and down the mostly unpaved streets, with no place to go besides the Shingle. If you were under twenty-one, there was roller-skating twice a week, uptown at the McKinley Auditorium, but this was only in the summer. Uptown consisted of only three main streets, which housed stores that sold all the same items, only at different prices. There was no building in the entire town more than four stories, except the YMCA and the telephone company. They were six stories. There was one movie house, three drive-ins, three beaches, a softball field, and, in the fall, football games at the high school. In the winter there was outdoor ice skating but everybody's main source of entertainment was TV.

Word was that all the rickety houses along Twenty-fourth Street were going to be torn down to make room for an industrial park. Supposedly it was already in the planning stages, but the colored people didn't believe this for a minute. They had lived here too long, some for as many as three generations. Surely the city wasn't going to tear down the houses that most of them had scrimped and scraped to buy. Where would they go, anyway? There was also supposed to be a plan to build a housing project smack dab in the middle of South Park, but this too they thought was all talk. After all, nothing had been built in this town since the library and state office building uptown, and that was where white people lived.

Mid Town was where the so-called in-between black folks lived. These people weren't altogether poor because most of them had never received a welfare check, or if they had, they'd been working steadily enough to consider themselves middle class. Many of them were now buying instead of renting, and there were some white folks scattered in their neighborhood, but everybody called them white trash.

As you continued north on Twenty-fourth Street, past Mid Town, you began to see aluminum siding and the houses were set back farther from the street. The front yards became longer and wider and this was a sure sign you were entering the all-white neighborhoods. There was no name for this area. Directly behind it was the highway, which veered off to the left and led to Strawberry Lane, where middle-class white folks who thought they were upper class lived. The only black folks you ever saw up there were the ones who cleaned house, raked leaves, or picked up trash. Black people called this redneck country. These white folks didn't actually hate colored people, they just didn't like being too close to them. People like the Leonards, who ran the NAACP chapter, the Colemans, whose family was full of schoolteachers, or the Halls, who both had Ph.D's in psychology, couldn't buy a house in this neighborhood without fearing for their lives.

Even farther north was the North End. It was only ten minutes from Sarnia, Ontario. Here was a mixture of everybody: poor, not-so-poor, middle- and upper-middle-class black and white folks, all of whom considered themselves better than everybody else in town.

Half the reading and writing population of the Point — black and white — worked in factories. One, Prest-o-Lite, was in South Park. They manufactured spark plugs, shocks, and points for diesel trucks, and some car parts that were shipped to major car manufacturers near Detroit, like Ford, General Motors, and Chrysler. The women usually did day work, like Mildred, and the men worked for the Department of Sanitation, like Crook had. Or they were on welfare. Those on welfare looked for opportunities in all employable cracks and crevices but once they found jobs, many of them realized that their welfare checks were steadier and went a lot further. So a lot of them stopped looking altogether and spent their afternoons watching soap operas and gossiping.

# Four

**R**IGHT AFTER THANKSGIVING, it was snowing so bad that warnings were up. No one was supposed to leave the house, let alone try to get out of the driveway. Snow was piling up past Mildred's fifth step and there was no way she could go to work in this weather. She was supposed to get paid today and she only had one dollar and sixty-three cents to her name. Her left eye was twitching and jumping. Didn't that mean you were supposed to come into some money — or was it your left palm? Anyway, Mildred knew nobody was coming by to drop off a bundle of dollar bills unless it was God. And so far, she didn't think he was such a reliable source.

The kids were in the basement playing, and she could hear their screaming and rumbling through the vents that led upstairs. Mildred wasn't thinking about the noise, for once. She was trying to concentrate on dinner. Lately, she had so much on her mind, so much to consider at once, that one decision, or the wrong decision, could change all the others. So sometimes she made none at all.

When she opened the cupboards, an ache slid down her forehead into her nasal passage and throbbed on the roof of each nostril. It continued like an arrow into her skull, and skated up and down her neck until it had no place else to go. Mildred gave her head a good shake. Bags of black-eyed peas, pinto beans, butter beans, lima beans, navy beans, and a big bag of rice stared her in the face. She opened another cabinet and there sat half a jar of peanut butter, a can of sweet peas and carrots, one can of creamed corn, and two cans of pork-n-beans. There was nothing in the refrigerator except a few crinkly apples she'd gotten from the apple man two weeks ago, a stick of margarine, four eggs, a quart of milk, a box of lard, a can of Pet milk, and a two-inch piece of salt pork.

She put on a pot of pinto beans. Mildred knew the kids were tired of them, and so was she, but at least they would last a few days. Something good was going to happen, she thought. She didn't know what, but she always knew that when things got this bad they had to get better, just had to. She chopped up a yellow onion and sat it on the table, then took the lonely piece of salt pork from the refrigerator. She threw them both into the pot, sneezed, then wiped her tearing eyes. The only time Mildred cried on her own accord was when she peeled onions.

She wiped her eyes with a dishtowel and stood locked in place, as if hypnotized, watching the rainbow of spices, brown beans, and onions float to the top of the water. Something smelled funny. Like smoke and fumes. When Mildred looked toward the living room, she saw smoke coming out of the vents, leaving a sooty film on the beige walls. She dropped the spoon on the table and ran downstairs. She didn't see any of the kids.

"What the hell is going on down here? Y'all better not be near that furnace." Before she could get all the words out of her mouth, five charcoal-covered children walked sluggishly from the furnace room. Mildred stomped her foot and stormed past them. The handle on the stoker was dangling.

"Who did this?" she demanded, her hands on her hips.

They all stood like prisoners and hunched their shoulders up then down.

"I'ma ask you one more time before I tear up each and every one of your black behinds. Now who did it?"

"Not us, Mama," said Angel, holding Doll's hand. One of them always answered for both, as if they were Siamese twins, and they always agreed with each other. At six and seven years old, and only ten months apart, neither of them had opinions that weren't interchangeable.

Money just stood there, knowing full well he was guilty.

"Mama, we was just playing," he said. "I didn't mean to touch it, but Bootsey and Doll were chasing me and I bumped into it. I can fix it. Remember last time, Mama, when it broke, and I fixed it?"

"All right. I want all of you to go into that bathroom over there. Get that soot off of you. Then I want you to march back up those steps, sit down on that sun porch, turn on that TV or get a book, and don't say two words to me or else I'ma be two minutes away from your asses. You understand me?"

The girls ran into the bathroom. Money was used to this kind of thing: his sisters undressing and slamming the door in his face. He tried to fix the furnace while they were bathing, but it was really broken this time. When he heard them run upstairs, he made sure the bathroom door was locked and then he took his own shower. He loved his sisters, but sometimes he could strangle them for being girls. He had always hoped that the next one would be a boy, but no luck. While he took his shower, Money wished he could tell somebody how much he missed his daddy.

By six o'clock, the beans were thick and simmered but the house had grown colder and colder. Mildred knew then that the furnace was in fact broken. She called to find out when the repairmen could come out to fix it but they told her not until the roads cleared up. When would that be?

By eight o'clock the house was so cold the kids could see their own breath. They didn't want to leave the sun porch because they were watching "Get Smart," one of their favorite shows, but Mildred made them huddle in front of the warm open oven while they ate their beans and rice and corn bread. She wasn't hungry and just sipped on her last beer.

Two days later when the furnace people finally came, they told her it would cost $175 to fix, and since it had taken her so long to pay last time, they said they couldn't even start the job without at least a $50 deposit. "Just have a seat, and don't go nowhere," she told them. Mildred closed her bedroom door and called Buster, her daddy. She knew she was his favorite, and if she could just get around Miss Acquilla, she wouldn't have a problem. Mildred's mama, Sadie, had died in 1958 at forty-eight from a heart attack. Out of all Mildred's sisters and brothers, she took her mama's death the hardest. For the longest time, Mildred thought God had betrayed her by snatching Sadie away from her the way he did. Two years later Buster had married Miss Acquilla. He had told Mildred he was lonely in that big old house with no woman. And during those two years before Miss Acquilla had moved in, Mildred had made Crook watch the kids while she took her daddy home-cooked meals, washed his work clothes, and cleaned up his raggedy house.

Mildred and Miss Acquilla couldn't stand each other. Miss Acquilla didn't like the way Mildred could get anything she wanted from Buster, and Mildred didn't like Miss Acquilla because she was a selfish bitch, and reminded her of Ernestine: big, black, and evil. Ever since Mildred could remember, Miss Acquilla seemed to have had a head full of gray hair. She dipped snuff, too. But the main reason Mildred didn't like her was because she had married her daddy and ran him like a race horse.

Buster didn't tell Miss Acquilla he was lending Mildred more money. He knew he'd never hear the end of it. He took his white handkerchief from the old trunk at the foot of his bed, counted out three twenties and a ten, hopped in his Buick, and drove directly to Mildred's. She had asked for seventy because the kids had caught colds and couldn't go to school. She had to buy at least two bottles of cough syrup, a jar of Vicks, and extra toilet paper so they could blow their noses.

The kids stayed home from school the entire week, and Mildred didn't go to work. She was sick, too. Christmas was three weeks away and two of the families she cleaned for called to tell her they were letting her go. They were mailing her checks, along with a small Christmas bonus. There wasn't much she could do about it except walk down to the Social Services Department like everybody else and ask for help. This humiliated and embarrassed the hell out of her — Mildred hated the idea of begging, which is what she thought it boiled down to — and she also didn't like the nosy people in town knowing all her damn business. They talked enough as it was, which was one reason she didn't go to church, and she didn't want them to know just how bad off things really were in her house. She had always prided herself on being self-sufficient and self-reliant. But Christmas was right around the corner, so for once Mildred ignored her pride.

"Mama, here's my list," Freda said, handing Mildred a piece of notebook paper itemizing everything she wanted. The other kids handed Mildred pieces of paper with equally long lists.

"I want a Baby Sleepy," said Bootsey. "She pees and cries and then falls asleep. She comes with clothes too."

Money said, "All I want is a racing car set, a Mighty Moe, and, oh, I almost forgot, a pair of ice skates. My other ones are too small."

"We want skates too, Mama, with tassles on them," said Angel, "and a cooking set." Doll nodded in concurrence.

"Hold it! Just wait one damn minute here. Let me tell y'all something. First of all, now, you know your daddy ain't gave me a dime since he left. And you know I just got the first check and I still gotta pay off that furnace bill, and y'all be lucky if you get something to eat for the rest of the month, so all these elaborate lists y'all making can be cut right on down to three thangs. First I'ma get you what I know you need, then what I can afford. But ain't nobody in this house got no money to be going out spending hundreds of dollars on no damn toys that'll be torn up before the weather breaks good. You understand me?"

"Yes, Mama," they said, holding their heads down and returning to the sun porch.

"Chunky and BooBoo are getting bikes," Money whispered to the girls.

"Yeah, and Rita Morgan and those guys are getting new sleds and a toboggan and *real* skis," said Bootsey. "I don't want them cracking on me when we get back to school if I ain't got no new skis." Bootsey was the most competitive of the kids, and many times she and Freda would argue because Bootsey swore she was smarter. On one occasion, she decided she was stronger and asked for a fight. Freda slapped her so hard she made Bootsey's lip bleed. That was the end of that.

"I ain't never had my own bike," Freda said. "I want some

fabric 'cause I start homemaking class next semester. Boy, what I wouldn't give for a sewing machine. Then I could make all of our clothes!"

"I don't want no homemade clothes," Bootsey said. She was three years younger than Freda.

"Why not?" Freda asked.

" 'Cause they look too homemade." Bootsey stuck her tongue out at Freda.

When Christmas was two days away, Mildred hollered to Freda from her bedroom. "Can you come in here for a minute?"

Freda came to the doorway.

"Close the door, baby."

Freda closed it suspiciously and stood in front of it.

"Sit down," Mildred said, patting the mattress next to her. Freda sat down. Mildred had a worried look on her face. She'd counted her money ten times and every time it came out the same. She didn't have enough. There was no way she could stretch it to get the kids' things out of layaway. Somebody was going to have to do without — at least wait till she got her check after the first of the year. She knew the younger kids wouldn't understand. But Freda was almost twelve, and half grown. She could fry chicken better than Mildred, could put together a meal without even thinking about it, and had more common sense than some grown people Mildred knew.

"Freda, your mama gotta explain something to you and I want you to try to be a big girl and listen to what I'm saying, okay?" Now Freda was even more suspicious because Mildred never used this sweet tone of voice and had never asked Freda to close the door so they could talk.

"Okay, Mama, but you know I'm already a big girl."

"Yes, and Mama appreciate everythang you've done around here, from watching these kids for me like they was yours, and keeping this house in running order when I ain't here. You been doing a helluva job, baby, playing the mama, and you know I been working hard to make things better for all of us since your daddy been gone, don't you?"

Mildred was beating around the bush and she knew it, and so did Freda. But this was hard, and Mildred couldn't figure an easy way to do it.

"You be a teenager before you know it, won't you, baby?"

Freda nodded, trying to figure out what Mildred was getting at and wishing that whatever it was she'd hurry up about it and get to the point. The "Peanuts Christmas Special" was coming on TV in a few minutes and Freda didn't want to miss it.

"Well, baby, mama's money is real low and I got some decisions I gotta make and quick." Mildred gripped her hands together like she was praying. "If I don't pay this gas and light bill ain't nothing gon' shine on Christmas in this house, and we'll freeze to death if I don't buy no coal. Now you know the kids won't understand, and all I want is to see y'all, all of you, happy. I can only get a few toys for the little ones, you understand me?"

"Yes," Freda said, beginning to understand what Mildred was getting at. And although her chest was filling up with air and her training bra was rising and falling as if she had breasts, Freda was trying hard to be as strong as Mildred.

"All of y'all needs boots and new coats. I can't have y'all going to school or church looking like a bunch of vagabonds, can I?"

"No, Mama."

"Well, when I get all this stuff out the layaway, and buy a few toys, pay off these bills, we'll do good to get a chicken on Christmas, let alone a ham or turkey. Mama was just wondering if you could be a big girl and wait until after New Years, when everything'll be on sale. I can get the rest of the kids' thangs, too. I'll buy you that pink mohair sweater we saw in Arden's window. By February, I'll get you that sewing machine I heard you talking about. At least lay it away. Can you just let the other kids enjoy this Christmas? Can you do that for your mama?"

"Yes, Mama, I can wait," Freda said before she knew it.

Tears were welling up in Freda's eyes, and Mildred could feel something pulling at the center of her chest. She knew Freda didn't understand. She was still a child. Mildred's heart was signaling her to reach over and pull her oldest daughter inside her arms. But she couldn't. A plastic layer had grown over that part of Mildred's heart and it refused to let her act on impulse. She never showed too much affection because that made her feel weak. And she hated feeling weak because that made her vulnerable. Who would be there to pick up the pieces if she let herself break down? Mildred felt she had to be strong at all times and at all costs.

Freda wanted her mama to hug her, but she was afraid to make the first move. She didn't want Mildred to think she was being a baby about this whole thing. At that moment, Freda couldn't remember Mildred ever hugging her, or any of them. The two of them sat there stiffly, like starched shirts, but underneath, Mildred and Freda mourned for themselves.

Finally, Freda stood up and walked to the door. With her back to Mildred, she said, "It's okay, Mama. I can wait. I told you I was a big girl and I meant it." She closed the door softly behind her.

# Five

IN THE SPRING, the weeping willow trees Mildred had planted eight years ago were almost twelve feet tall. She had planted them in anticipation of Freda's sweet sixteen party. Mildred pulled the hose from around the house and put its nose at the base of their thin trunks. Her hands were caked with rich black dirt from where she'd been hoeing and weeding the small garden in the back yard. Each year she planted two rows of corn, a few string beans, some tomatoes and yellow squash, okra and cucumbers, and mustard and collard greens. Though none of them ever did too well, Mildred liked to smell the mixture of grass and spring air, and she liked the solitude of working her own soil. She had just finished cutting down the dandelions that had grown up through the grass. They left a fresh, tart smell around the yard. Mildred loved this yard. It was big enough for the kids to play hide-n-go-seek, and in the winter she'd let the hose run in the side yard and they ice-skated there.

She heard the screen door slam on Curly's front porch.

"Hey, sis'-n-law," yelled Curly. "What you know good?"

"Nothing, girl, just trying to get this garden in some kind of order. These weeds grow like ain't no tomorrow, I'm telling you."

"Got any coffee over there? I'm all out, and Lord knows I

39

could use a cup. The kids is at the playground and I got so much cleaning to do upstairs that I'm scared of what I might find once I start digging in them closets. A cup of coffee sure would be nice."

"Yeah, come on over, chile, I can let you have a couple of teaspoons until tomorrow, and you can have one with me. I don't have no sugar, though. You got any?"

"A drop, just a drop. These kids eat it like candy, but I'ma start hiding some just for my coffee."

Out of all of Mildred's so-called friends, the only one she truly liked and trusted was Curly. The others, like Geechie and Gingy and Sally Noble (folks always said both of her names as if they were one), were good over one or two cups of coffee, but they liked to drink, and when they did they got vulgar and loud and started talking about the first person who popped into their minds. If they got worked up real good, meaning they agreed with each other, they'd forget where they were and who they were with, and say, "Yeah, and that Mildred . . ." Then Mildred would cuss them out nicely, put them out of her house and tell them not to bring their poor tired asses back until they knew how to act like they had some sense, which, she said, would take about another twenty years.

Curly laughed as she sat down in Mildred's bright yellow kitchen. She had the kind of laugh that would automatically set you off to grinning right along with her, no matter what you had on your mind. Curly didn't have much to laugh about, though. Her big house looked much nicer on the outside than it did on the inside. It was full of dark, rickety furniture, which was why she kept her drapes drawn. And though Mildred loved her sister-in-law like a sister, she couldn't stand being in Curly's house for too long because it depressed her. "Why don't you open those drapes up, girl, and let some light in this place?" Mildred would ask her. And Curly would say, "For what? What's some light gon' do to these dingy walls but let all the hand marks and grease show?" Mildred saw her point.

"You heard from Crook?" Curly asked her.

"Naw, ain't heard from that sorry bastard since I had to beg him for twenty dollars for shoes for Money and Bootsey for

Easter. I ain't got nothing to say to him. He ain't working yet, is he?"

"Naw, him and Ernestine still down there living with her mama like savages. It's a shame, girl. I ain't never knew what he saw in that old hussy. She past trifling, ain't she, girl? Ugly as all hell, look like something the cat done dragged in, and I betcha, Mil, if the chile had some teeth in her mouth, don't you think she'd look just like a beaver?" She giggled and Mildred stomped her foot on the linoleum, almost spitting a mouthful of hot coffee in Curly's face.

"Well, I'll tell you, Curly, the way thangs is going around here, honey, I might have to pick up my kids and get the hell on out of here. I can't keep up these house notes. They kicking my behind. And the older these kids get the more they eat and the more they want."

"Who you telling, chile? Mine's is almost a football team. I swear, you lucky, you ain't got a houseful of big-head nappy and hardheaded boys. They stay in and out of trouble. Money don't seem to give you none."

"Not yet, at least, but you know he got his daddy's blood, no offense. How's Crook's health, anyway? Is he still dranking like it's going out of style?"

"Chile, that ain't the half of it. You should've seen him and Ernestine the other night at the Shingle. They had a band. Wasn't saying nothing, but girl, they acted like pure damn fools. Him and her just sloppy, I mean pissy drunk, and you know how loud she get."

"Yeah, I know how loud she get," Mildred said, lighting a cigarette.

"They could barely hold each other up. I acted like I didn't know 'em. Fletcher threw 'em both out. And I don't care if he marry that whore, she ain't never gon' be no kin to me, and won't never step one rusty foot in my door neither. She trifling, and besides, you'll always be my sister-in-law, sis."

"He know he shouldn't be doing so much dranking. That man is about as stupid as he looks. Got about as much brains as a field mouse, and he gon' end up back in that sanitarium if he keep this up."

"Well, he ain't been back to the doctor in God knows when, but that's all right. It'll catch up to him. You mark my words. If he live to see fifty it'll be a miracle and the will of God, and I'll tell you, Mil, God'a see fit to it that Crook obeys his laws. Abusing hisself like he do ain't nowhere in the Bible, is it?"

"Honey, I wouldn't know, been so damn long since I read it."

Since Mildred and Crook had broken up, she hadn't exactly resigned herself to being a widow, so to speak, but the men in Point Haven not only bored her to death but barely had a pot of their own to piss in, and if they did, helping out a woman with five kids was not their idea of having a good time, no matter how good she could make them feel in bed.

Mildred had stopped wearing that awful platinum wig, even though she knew she looked damn good in it. Now she wore her own hair, rusty red to suit her reddish skin tone. She let Curly trim it for her every now and then because it grew so fast and got too bushy and thick. A lot of colored women envied her shoulder-length hair. They thought if your hair was long and thick and halfway straight and didn't roll up into tight black pearls at the nape of your neck, you were full of white blood, which made you lucky. In 1966 most colored women in Point Haven wanted desperately to have long straight hair instead of their own knotty mounds. To get it like that, they wore wigs or rubbed Dixie Peach or Royal Crown hair grease into their scalps and laid the straightening comb over the gas burner and whipped it through their hair until it sizzled. Sometimes Mildred didn't feel like being bothered, sitting in that chair for almost an hour just for the straightening part, and maybe another hour to get it bumper-curled. Most of the time she would roll it up with brush rollers and let it go at that. Mildred usually didn't care what people thought.

Whenever she went to the bar, somebody's husband usually offered to buy her a drink. They always had that I've-been-waiting-for-you-to-get-rid-of-that-sorry-niggah look in their eyes. But Mildred would just accept their drink offer, make small talk — usually about the condition of their wives — then turn her back to them and continue running her mouth with her female friends.

Mildred didn't believe in messing around with anybody's husband, no matter what kind of financial proposition they made. The way she figured it, when and if she ever did get herself another husband, she damn sure didn't want a soul messing with hers. She truly believed in the motto that what goes around comes around. She'd seen it come true too many times. Janey Pearl got caught in the Starlight Motel under the Bluewater Bridge, laying up with Sissie Moncrief's old man, and Sissie tried to strangle Janey Pearl with her own garter belt and stockings. Shirley Walker's husband caught her in bed with his brother. Put both of them in the hospital with a .38.

This town was entirely too small to be sneaky and slick. Be different if this was a city like Detroit. Messing around was the surest way to get yourself killed by some jealous church-going woman, especially if she was a Baptist. Them Baptists could get the spirit all right, Mildred thought, right on your ass, and the very words they chastised their children for using would sizzle off their tongues like water hitting a hot skillet.

Mildred didn't have any trouble getting the attention of most men because she was still young — a few months shy of thirty — and well equipped. Her hips didn't exactly curve out now, but when she turned to the side her behind looked like someone had drawn it on, made it a little too perfect, and it was this luscious behind that drew many a man's eye. Even though she still stuffed her bra with a pair of the girls' anklets to give her breasts more cleavage, Mildred wasn't what you'd call promiscuous. She liked to look her best and had gotten tired of sitting around the house all those months getting sucked in by soap operas. It wasn't even so much romance she was looking for as it was to have some fun, maybe roll over and feel a man's body in her bed again. These days no one was there except maybe one or two of the kids, trying to keep warm.

One night a tall, caramel-skinned man strolled through the doors of the Red Shingle. He walked right past Mildred. She could hardly swallow her drink; couldn't believe something this handsome would set foot inside the Shingle without advance notice. In all the years she'd been in here and even when she worked here, she'd never seen anybody that caused her to do a double take.

This man had deep-set eyes and thick bushy eyebrows and a smile like you saw in toothpaste commercials. His hair was charcoal mixed with gray and he was as tall as a basketball player. He had a body like a boxer and instead of walking, he strutted like his ego was sitting on his shoulders. Mildred liked his style immediately. This man had class. She could barely speak when he walked up to her and introduced himself. His name was Sonny Tyler. She told him her name, then tucked in her lip and broke out her long-forgotten-that-she-still-had "Yes, I'm alone" smile. He sat down next to her at the bar and offered to buy her a drink but all she asked for was ginger ale.

Sonny told her he was stationed at Selfridge Air Force Base in St. Clemens, which was thirty-odd miles from Point Haven. One of his old running buddies was playing at the Shingle tonight and he had come to hear him since he hadn't seen him in almost a year. "Is that so," was all Mildred could say. She was trying to sound intelligent and figuring out the best way to carry on a conversation with this man, who was causing her panties to get wet.

They talked through two shows.

"I'm divorced and got five kids. The oldest is thirteen and the baby is seven," she told him.

"You sure know how to keep yourself up," he said, smiling. Mildred was shocked that he didn't go flying to the other end of the bar where there were quite a few women with less responsibility but also less sex appeal. They were all tapping their stirrers on the rim of their glasses to the beat of the music, and watching Mildred like hawks.

Sonny asked Mildred for her phone number, which made her feel seventeen again. She loved it. A few nights later he called her. He wanted to come over to her house; wanted to meet her kids. "Not yet," she said, but she met him at a motel in Canada. She told him she didn't let just any man in her bed, didn't care how good he looked or how good he smelled. "What's that you wearing anyway, Sonny? Lord, it smells good."

"Old Spice," he'd said, caressing her in all the right places. She knew it smelled familiar because Crook had always worn it, and so did Percy. It smelled different on Sonny. Tantalizing.

After a few weeks of making excuses to the kids as to why she'd been staying out so late or not coming home until daylight, Mildred decided to tell them. Hell, she was a grown woman with needs just like any other female. What was wrong with her feeling a little pleasure?

She made Sonny whisper when she let him in. "This is a nice house," he said softly.

"Shhh," she said, and guided him to her bedroom, where she hung his clothes over the door and left it cracked. She didn't want the kids to barge in unannounced and find her in bed with a man who wasn't their father. Sonny was a much better lover than either Crook or Percy had been. He was so warm and big that Mildred woke up whistling the next morning, anxious to fix him a hot breakfast. She wanted to make him as comfortable as possible because she wanted him to come back. And keep coming back. It had been so long since she'd been kissed, especially the way Sonny did. She'd almost forgotten what else lips were good for. And what he had rekindled between her legs was another story altogether.

Sonny put on everything except his shirt and walked out into the living room when he heard the kids laughing at cartoons. When Freda first saw his hairy chest, her eyes widened like she'd seen a ghost.

"Who are you?" she asked, turning up her nose at him.

"I'm Sonny," he said smiling, all friendly-like. "I'm a friend of your mother's."

"Since when? And how come you don't have all your clothes on? You coming or going? Did you spend the night over here? With my mama, in *her* bed?"

"Yes, your mother is a very nice lady, and I like her a lot. I hope to get to know you and the other kids better, too."

"Hmph. I hope you ain't staying long," she said, and huffed away.

Mildred walked back into the living room, not having heard this, and slid her arms around his waist like a high schooler satisfying a crush. She called the kids to introduce him. Each of them sat down on the couch, lined up like dominoes, and when Freda crossed her arms and grunted, the rest of them imitated her. They watched her for the next move, hardly even noticing Sonny.

"Sonny is a friend of your mama's, and he's nice. I like him, and I want y'all to treat him nice. He's in the air force and he's going to be visiting us quite regularly, so y'all might as well get used to him."

"Why we gotta get used to him? He ain't coming to see us." Freda said.

"You got a quarter?" asked Money, holding out his hand.

"Boy, stop begging, what I tell you about that. And Freda, you better watch the tone of your voice, you ain't grown. I'm still the mama in this house."

"How'd you get a name like Money?" Sonny asked.

Money hunched his shoulders. He didn't know.

It was Freda who had started calling him that. It seemed that Money always begged, and nobody knew where he got the habit from. He was barely old enough to tell you his address, but he'd beg coins from anyone who came to the house or wherever Freda had dragged him. "You got a dime?" he'd ask, and if they said no, he'd say, "You got a nickel?" And if they still said no, he'd press the point. "Well, you got *any* money?" Freda would smack his hand and tell him he shouldn't be begging and if Mildred ever found out he was doing it, she would beat the stew out of him. He ignored her threats. "Money! Money! Money! Those the only words you know, ain't it?" Freda would say. After that, to embarrass him she started calling him Money all the time. So did everybody else.

It was commonplace in black neighborhoods to have a nickname. By the time a child was sucking his bottle or thumb, people were already staring at him like a specimen, asking, "What you gon' call him?" Then they would give the child a name that showed no consideration for his own. Baby boys got names like Lucky, BooBoo, Sugar Pie, PeeWee, and Homeless. "Don't he look just like a little fat pumpkin?" And that's what he'd be called thereafter. Little girls' names were at least softer to the ear: Peaches, Babysister, Candy, Bo-Peep, and Cookie. There was a set of twins called Heckle and Jeckle.

Money kept his hand out when he saw Mildred take the plates back in the kitchen.

"Here, I've got a quarter, for all of you," Sonny said, reaching into his pockets. Their attitudes seemed to change then, but when Freda refused hers, the girls pulled their hands back too. Not Money. He slid his quarter into his pocket and told Sonny he could give all of the coins to him and he'd see to it that his sisters got theirs later on when he knew they'd change their minds. The girls looked at him like he was a traitor, but it didn't bother Money.

Sonny kept coming for a few months and Mildred was glowing, always humming some song. Then he found out he was getting sent to Okinawa. He told Mildred it was a strong possibility that he might not see her for at least a year. And if he was ordered to fight in Vietnam, he might not ever see her again. Before he'd met her, he'd asked to be transferred to Texas, which is where he'd be stationed if he made it back to the States. Mildred didn't whine or cry. She just thanked Sonny for the best four months she'd had since her divorce, especially since he'd gotten her juices back in circulation. It wasn't like she was madly in love with him. Hell, Mildred said to herself, wasn't no use crying over spilt milk.

Percy hadn't exactly given up on her, even though he'd married a shy woman who knew a good thing when she saw one. Percy was the kind of man who would try to enter a jalopy in a stock car race and wouldn't be able to figure out why he didn't qualify, and if by chance they did let him in, he'd be at a total loss to why he didn't win. The only thing he was good at figuring out was his long-overdue and stored-up passion for Mildred. Dreaming about her was enough for Percy. His wife suspected it, though she never said anything to him so long as he paid the bills.

Percy had told Mildred time and time again that if she ever needed anything, anything at all, to drop her pride and call him first. She decided to keep him on the back burner in case of a real emergency. After all, he *was* married, and she didn't want his wife knocking on her door in the middle of the night ready to blow her brains out. So Mildred left Percy just where he was:

on simmer. Besides, he was too nice, she thought, and not once had Mildred ever seen him lose his temper. She wondered if he had one.

Mildred applied for another job. This time at Prest-o-Lite, though they weren't hiring. Those welfare checks were barely making the house note, let alone everything else. She wanted to work, not sit around the house all day trying to drum up things to keep her busy. She was getting fidgety and the least little thing that didn't go right got on her nerves. She was sick of standing and waiting in line for the flour and cheese and margarine and Spam they gave her at the welfare office.

She sat at the kitchen table and started going through a stack of envelopes that she had already shuffled and reshuffled in order of importance over the past few weeks. It didn't make a difference. Most of them were going to have to go unpaid. Bills. The coal bill. The gas bill. The light bill. The water bill. The garbage man. The insurance man. The washer and dryer bill. The house note. Groceries. Lunch money. Special field trip money. Gym suit money. School books. Notebook paper. Tennis shoes. Sunday shoes. The dentist. Popsicles.

Everything was piling up and it was as if Mildred were caught in a snow storm and was constantly shoveling the sidewalk. It kept snowing over where she had just shoveled. In spite of the welfare checks and the occasional day work she managed to get on the side, Mildred was getting deeper and deeper in debt. Everything kept getting more expensive and her kids were growing entirely too fast.

It cost so much to keep up a three-bedroom house like this, and trying to raise five kids, she thought. Hell, twenty years is a long-ass time to be paying for anything. What will I do with all this room when the kids is grown? Which won't be long. Sit in here by myself and run from room to room? Maybe I'll have some grandbabies. But the thought of being a grandmother was unfathomable to her. She decided not to think so far ahead. Shit. Right now what she needed was some money. A decent job. Maybe even a sugar daddy, which Mildred was seriously considering about now.

"Mama, can I make some cocoa?" asked Bootsey, walking

into the kitchen. She was starting to look like a miniature Mildred. Everybody had been telling Bootsey this, but Bootsey didn't see it.

"I don't care what you make, girl," Mildred said.

"Here's the mail," Bootsey said, handing it to her.

Interruptions. Always interruptions. Mama this. Mama that. Mama Mama Mama Mama. Can I have this? Can I have that? Yes. No. Maybe. I need this. I need that. Not now. Mama, please? Why not? Because. Because why? Because I said so. Because because. Her kids were everywhere she turned and everywhere she looked. A hand. A mouth open. Asking asking asking. Do something. Anything. Gimme gimme gimme. And always the very things she didn't have, except her love, which they never once asked her for.

Mildred went through the envelopes quickly, tossing aside the ones she didn't want to look at, and then she came across a letter from her oldest brother, Leon. He lived in Phoenix. What would he be writing me for? she wondered.

She opened the letter and read it. She was surprised to discover that he was well informed about her financial situation and she wondered who had filled him in. It had to be one of her sisters, most likely old fat-ass Georgia or motor-mouth Lula. Mildred let the thought pass when she got to the part where he suggested she consider selling the house and moving out to Phoenix. He said there were better job opportunities out there for colored people, the weather was hot and dry all year long, which meant hardly any mosquitoes, the kids might meet some civilized children instead of those hoodlums running loose in Point Haven, and, above all else, Mildred might meet a stable and loveable serviceman with a pension and she might even consider getting her high school diploma.

She folded the letter and put it back in the envelope, letting her fingers crease it over and over again. She could hear the furnace clicking on. Heat, Mildred thought. Wouldn't need no furnace in Arizona. She walked over and flicked off the switch. She had never really thought of leaving Point Haven before. All her people were here. But she wasn't afraid of taking chances. Always knew something had to happen to make things better. Was this it? She looked down at her puffy hands and saw how years of bleach and ammonia and detergent had made her skin like spiderwebs.

Ain't nothing gon' ever change unless I make it change, she thought. And I need a change, that's for damn sure. Shit, I'm tired of playing catch-up. Working and scrimping and scraping, to get where? Nowhere. Not even past the starting line. She went to the sink and turned on the faucet though there were no dirty dishes in the basin. She poured almost two cups of Tide in the water and let the suds ooze through her fingers. She stood in front of the window and let her hands soak until they felt like liquid silk. Then she pushed the starched curtains aside to unblock the view. Her view. Of Herman and Beulah Dell's ugly brown house. The grass in the side yard was growing too fast. And before spring this house would have to be painted again. The Mercury was starting to fall apart too. Mildred dried her hands on the curtains and picked up the letter again. Then she found Leon's phone number in the junk drawer and picked up the telephone.

# ═══ *Six* ═══

ILDRED'S BROTHER had told her just what she would have to do before she could pack up and head for the desert. He instructed her on how to go about selling the house so she could make some money. At least a few thousand dollars. Her eyes lit up at the mere thought of having that much money in her possession. She had no idea how much she'd paid in interest and principal. Had never kept track. But since more white folks had started moving into the neighborhood, the house must have appreciated; the boundaries had started changing so that now the portion of Twenty-fifth Street where she lived was considered Mid Town instead of South Park.

It occurred to Mildred that this would be the first time she could make money off of white people. The agent didn't quite see it that way. First, the house would have to be appraised, then he would have to find a suitable buyer; said he didn't want just anybody moving into this house, especially since Mildred had kept it up so nicely. And there was no telling how long it might take to actually sell the house and consummate all the paperwork, which meant she didn't know how soon she would have a check in her hand. So when Faye Love told her there was an opening at Lapper Lakes Nursing Home, and since she was the supervisor and could hire anybody she wanted to on the spot, Mildred took the job.

Two months later, Mildred was so sick of smelling old people she didn't know what to do. Her patience had gotten clogged
up like hair in a drain. Curly Mae had told her she should get
herself a prescription for nerve pills, and Mildred did. Thought
they just might be the plunger. They seemed to do the trick.
Pushed about fifty pounds away from her skull, put each little
worry into its very own compartment, and gave her the keys
to unlock each one when she felt up to it. At first, she didn't
take more than she was supposed to — most of the time not as
many doses per day as she'd been prescribed. But after a few
days of taking them that way, she got so dizzy she slept for
almost thirteen hours. Mildred didn't like sleeping that long;
she liked knowing what her kids were doing and where they
were at all times. When she came home from work she would
pop one and sip on a beer, like she was doing now, standing in
the middle of the sun porch in her white uniform, which had a
stain on it from where old Mrs. Henry had thrown up on her.

She sipped the foam from the top of the glass and sat down
in the recliner. The kids were watching "Wagon Train."

"I got something to tell y'all and I want each and every one
of you to keep your mouths closed and listen to every word I
have to say, whether you like it or not, you understand?"

Her children turned around to face her.

"Now, y'all know that we've been through a few cold and
hungry days, but ain't none of you starved or froze to death,
have you? Well, sometimes you have to do thangs in this world
that you don't want to do in order to make thangs right when
they're wrong, easier when they're hard, you know what I
mean?"

They nodded their heads up and down, although they had no
idea what she was talking about. They figured if they stayed
with her, they would catch on.

"Ain't y'all tired of this old dull mangy town?" Mildred didn't
give them a chance to answer. "Wouldn't y'all like to make
some new friends and go to a nicer, prettier school? The main
reason I'm asking — telling — you this is because your Uncle
Leon, the one out there in Arizona, in Phoenix, wants us to
move out there with him and his kids. He say they got good
jobs out there for colored people, even women, and cheaper,

bigger, finer houses, and guess what? It don't even snow out there, and they ain't got those aggravating-ass mosquitoes. Y'all could learn to swim and play outside all year round without no coats and boots or gloves. Don't that sound nice?" She glared at them.

"But, Mama," Freda said, "I just tried out for cheerleading this year — the junior varsity team — and it might be my only chance! I'd be the first colored to ever make it!"

"What will we do with Prince?" Money whined. "He don't like hot weather. And what about my bike? How I'ma get it all the way to Arizona? Where is Arizona anyway? And what about Chunky, and BooBoo and Big Man and Little Man? Ain't gon' have no friends in Arizona."

"What I tell you about saying ain't, boy? You'd thank they didn't teach you how to speak English in school."

Bootsey, Angel, and Doll went along with their older sister and brother. "Yeah, we don't want to move to no Arizona. People die in deserts. How long does it take to get there? Probably weeks," Angel said. The other two huddled near her.

"What's wrong with *this* house?" asked Freda, crossing her arms and making a huffing sound. "We like this house. We don't want to go nowhere and I only got four more years till I graduate."

Mildred had figured as much, but it didn't matter, because her mind was made up. She clenched her fist and started gritting her teeth — this always scared the kids and made them see things her way.

"Look, I know what y'all *likes* to do too. Freda. Girl, you can cheerlead in Arizona. Don't you think they play basketball and football no place else besides Point Haven? They got better high schools than that little rinky-dink one on Twenty-fourth Street. And Money, you can always make new friends, boy, so stop acting like a sissy. And them little hoodlums you hang around with ain't worth a pot to piss in noway. Meet some civilized kids in Arizona. And Prince ain't never told you he didn't like hot weather, did he? Dogs go where their owners go. Look at it this way, most of the colored people in this town ain't never been no farther than Detroit, and it'll give your cousins and friends a good reason to go somewhere new for a change. They can come visit in the summer. Look, I'm trying to thank this thang out and I thank it's gon' be the best damn move I've made in thirteen years, and regardless of who don't like it, I'm the mama and daddy in this house, and we going, as soon as I can get myself situated."

Two weeks later Freda made the cheerleading squad at Chippewa Junior High School and Money ran away from home. Mildred had just come in from work.

"Where's Money?" she asked, kicking off her white hospital shoes in the middle of the dining room floor.

"He ain't, I mean, hasn't come home from school yet," Bootsey said. None of the other kids seemed to know where he was either, and since Money didn't participate in any after-school activities Mildred knew something was wrong. The kids were supposed to come straight home from school and had to do their chores and homework before they were allowed back outside. She said she'd wait a half hour, and as soon as he walked through that door she was going to snatch a knot in his behind.

Mildred was having a nicotine fit. She didn't want to send one of the girls to the store since it was getting dark, but she sent Freda anyway. "Get me two packs of Tareytons, would you? Ask Joe if I can have 'em till I get my check day after tomorrow. If he says yes, then get me three packs." What Mildred didn't know was that the reason her cigarettes had been disappearing so fast was because Freda had been smoking them at home and with her girlfriends after school when she went over to their house to watch "Dark Shadows."

Freda came back with the three packs about ten minutes later. Mildred told her not to take off her coat. She made the other girls put theirs on. "Go find that boy. Look everywhere. Check the Pattersons and the Howells, but don't come back in this house without him."

They were gone almost an hour, and when they returned they were all out of breath. They told Mildred they couldn't find him and no one had seen him.

"That's impossible. Y'all can't tell me that in a town this damn small ain't nobody seen a little nappy-headed colored boy." Mildred called over to Curly Mae's, who sent her boys to look for him. They went straight to the White Rose gas station, which had a pond behind it where they always caught polliwogs in the spring to scare girls.

Money was up to his knees in icy water when they spotted him. He was so cold his brown face was red and snot was running down his nose. Maybe he had thought of drowning himself, they thought, but the water was too cold and too shallow, and besides, he looked more scared than anything.

"Your mama is looking for you, boy, and you gon' get it when you get home. Come on out of there," one of the boys said.

"I ain't going no fucking where. I ain't moving to no damn Arizona. I hate Arizona and I hate my mama even more! I'm gon' drown myself if it kills me!"

But the boys just laughed and counted to three and ran into the pond and dragged him out. Then they tied a rope around his waist like a horse in a rodeo so he couldn't run. As they walked home, all Money could think of was the beating he was going to get.

But Mildred didn't beat him. When she saw him standing there wet and freezing, his teeth chattering and his eyes dilated as if he were in shock, she was too afraid he had caught pneumonia to even think of hitting him. She didn't even scold him or raise her voice one octave. Nor did she hug him, though she wanted to.

"Get out of those wet clothes, boy," she said. "And Freda, make your brother some hot Nestlé's Quik. Wouldn't you like some hot cocoa, boy?" Mildred couldn't stop looking into his cat eyes. Then it suddenly occurred to her that he might see in her own eyes her grief and confusion and just how responsible she felt, so she averted her glance. She didn't want Money to know that she was feeling like a collapsing bridge. Mildred also knew that if she hugged him she would be hugging a young Crook and maybe never let the boy go. She watched him gulp down his hot chocolate and sensed he was all right. Then she took another nerve pill and lay down.

That night, huddling on their bunk beds, which they were outgrowing, Mildred's children held a conference over popcorn and Kool-Aid. They decided they would simply boycott the whole idea of moving. Just refuse to go. She'd have to go by herself. After all, she couldn't *make* them go. "Shit, we ain't the one with the divorce problem or the money problem," Freda said.

"And we ain't trying to get away from nothing or nobody. Are we?" Money asked. All of them shook their heads no. The next decision to make was where everybody would live. This took some serious thinking. It soon became clear that Bootsey should stay with their Aunt Georgia since her daughter, Jeanie, was her age. Freda wanted to stay with the Wiggins family because they were clean, like her mama was, and always kept food in the refrigerator (a big consideration for her), and besides, she had a crush on Eric. Angel and Doll would have to stay together and could go with Ruthie Bates because her granddaughter, Cookie, left her dolls and toys in her spare bedroom until she came to visit in the summer from Chicago. Money would stay right next door with Curly Mae. That way, he said, he could keep an eye out on Freda's weeping willow trees. Make sure nobody else sat under them.

"Milly, you sure this is what you want to do, baby?" her daddy asked. Buster was standing at the wringer washer pushing clothes through the rollers. His big stomach was hanging over his pants, and his suspenders were making them hike up so his ankles showed off his white socks. His skin looked red and he was going bald. Miss Acquilla was sitting in the front room watching "The Price Is Right." She was dipping a piece of corn bread into a bowl of sweet milk. Her silver hair was parted down the middle into two thick braids.

"Buster," she called, "you almost finished in there? You know them beans need to be snapped if you want to eat 'em tonight."

Mildred rolled her eyes in Miss Acquilla's direction. She still couldn't stand the woman. She was too bossy and Mildred's daddy was too gullible. He did anything she told him to.

"I'm almost finished, sugarplum," he said.

"To tell you the truth, Daddy," Mildred said, "I don't know. It sound like it might be better for the kids. Who knows, I might be able to find a decent man out there. Leon say they all in the service. They suppose to have some good jobs on the base. Anything gotta be better than this."

Buster sighed. "You know your daddy would miss you and the kids. Don't too many of y'all come by and visit like you used to. You about the only one. Everybody else always too busy."

"Hell, with your asthma the way it is, you might want to consider coming out there too. They say it's dry heat, which is why a lot of people move out there. So they can breathe."

"Ain't nobody moving way out there," Miss Acquilla yelled from the other room.

"Wasn't nobody talking to you, Acquilla," Mildred said. Buster shook his head back and forth, as if pleading with Mildred to not say anything that would upset Miss Acquilla or get her started on one of her tangents. Mildred waved her hand at him as if to say "Forget her, I'm talking to you."

"I still got a few more years at the foundry before I can retire. The house is paid for, and by the grace of God, I'm still sitting here."

Mildred just shook her head, hugged her daddy, grunted a goodbye to Miss Acquilla, and stuck her hand through the hole in the screen door to open it, since the handle was only on the outside.

When the agent told Mildred he had found a buyer, he also told her it would be at least another month before the closing. Mildred immediately made it known to her neighbors and friends that they could walk through her house and take their pick of the junk she was going to leave behind, as long as she wasn't cooking or cleaning. For weeks afterward she made the kids take trips to the grocery store to get empty toilet paper and laundry detergent boxes so they could pack.

"I'm putting all this shit in storage until we can afford to leave. It's gon' take a lot more money than I'ma get from this house for us to move. Plus, I gotta give your daddy some of it. We gon' stay with Lula and Ike for a month or two, until I get some of these bills paid off and get enough money to haul all this mess out there. Maybe buy another car. Then we leaving."

When the kids heard this, there was a lot of heavy moaning. Lula Wilson was Mildred's baby sister and had six dumbbells for kids. They lived in a big old raggedy house on the other side of Twenty-fourth Street where the city had already torn down at least ten homes to make room for the industrial park. Lula had a simple husband whom everybody called Simple Ike, though he wasn't so simple he couldn't take care of his family. He also worked at the foundry, snapping steel parts together for diesel truck engines. Lula was even simpler than Ike was, which is why they got along so well. Everything was funny to them and they were always grinning. The kids, too. The entire family was a bunch of slobs, though.

When the kids saw that Mildred wasn't kidding, they circled around her.

"Mama, they got roaches," said Freda.

"And Junior caught two mice last week in the bathtub, and three upstairs in Linda and Cindy's room," said Bootsey.

"They ain't even got no dryer and they nasty! Where we gon' sleep, on the floor?" Money asked.

"Nasty ain't the word for it," added Freda. "Mama, you never even let them spend the night over here without leaving their bags outside to air out, and now you want us to go over there and live?" She crossed her arms and started crying. Everybody started crying.

"Mama, can't we stay somewhere else? What about Grandma Honey? Or Granddaddy Buster?" asked Bootsey, who was getting so that she had to put her two cents in whenever she could.

"They nasty too," interjected Freda.

"I don't like Grandma Acquilla," Angel said. "She's too mean, and all she do is spit snuff."

"If y'all open those little ignorant mouths and say another word about the subject, I'm gon' get your daddy's leather belt and beat your asses till they turn purple. Lula is the only one who got enough room and enough heat, and she's my sister and it's free and it ain't like it's gon' be forever. And since it's so damn nasty over there, maybe y'all will get a chance to help keep it a little cleaner. Do something for somebody else for once in your lives. Now leave me alone, please. I got a lot on

my mind. Freda, get me one of my nerve pills and a beer, would
you?"

For the next two months they endured life with the Wilsons,
and it was more like living in the Detroit zoo. There were eleven
kids running wild between two floors, all under the age of fifteen. And before they had been there a week, Mildred found
out that her children knew what they were talking about. Lula
was past simple, she was closer to stupid and beyond filthy.
And no matter how much Mildred's kids did around there to
clean up and pick up, Lula's would come right behind them
and tear up, mess up, or junk up what they'd just done.

Then Mildred found out that she wasn't getting as much
money as she thought from the house. She needed at least a
few thousand dollars in order to move herself and the kids, the
furniture, buy a decent car, and then find a place to live. She
didn't have any intention of staying more than a few weeks
with Leon. Shit, she still had to give Crook his part of the money.
For three whole days she calculated and recalculated her fig-
ures, which only made her head hurt. Maybe the time ain't
right, she thought. If it don't fit, don't force it.

And she changed her mind about moving to Arizona. Just
like that.

The kids couldn't have been happier.

"Mama, we don't have to stay here, do we?" asked Bootsey.

"Naw, not much longer. I'm thanking. Just give me a minute
to figure this shit out."

Mildred wanted her house back, but the agent had already
consummated the deal and sold it to a big black woman named
Carabelle, who dressed like a man, kept her hair in three skinny
braids, and ran a brothel full of tired whores. Mildred approached her in the dry cleaners about buying the house back,
but Carabelle, who smoked a pipe, simply blew smoke in her
face. No deal. Carabelle had plans for that house. Mildred knew
how to fight fire with flames and figured if she told the agent
what Carabelle's line of business was, the note would be recon-
sidered. But he just told her that what that woman did for a
living was her business, so long as she paid the bill.

"Now where we going, Mama?" Freda asked.

"Give me a minute. Just give me a hot minute," Mildred said. She patted her feet as she let her mind wander up and down the streets of South Park. Then she made a loud snap with her fingers and walked to the telephone. Baby Franks, an old friend of hers and Crook's, a World War II veteran who was fond of loose women, owned a house on Thirty-second Street, right at the railroad crossing. Mildred knew it was vacant because she always passed it on her way to see her daddy.

It was a big old house sitting in the middle of two acres of land, with a rolling front yard so long and so wide, most of the other inhabitants had used a riding lawn mower to cut the grass. There were pear trees, apple trees, a plum tree, and blackberry bushes in the woods that stood at the edge of the back yard. The rooms were huge, and everything else about it was quite decent. There was even a real fireplace in the living room. So what if there were only two bedrooms. Money would just have to sleep on the sun porch.

# Seven

$S$POOKY COOPER WAS NO GOOD and Mildred knew it. He was quiet. Slick was a better word, according to everybody in town. And he was so handsome that even he did a double take in the mirror when he combed his hair and mustache. Though he was supposed to be black, they said his daddy was white, and he resembled Clark Gable. He talked with a southern drawl, almost as if he were trying to prove his blackness. He was also married to a bony woman who looked like she was dying of cancer. Kaye Francis. Nobody ever did figure out how she snagged Spooky in the first place, and it was hard to ascertain if her three babies had anything to do with it.

When Mildred had worked at the Shingle, Spooky had often flirted with her but never actually came right out and approached her. He wasn't one of those husbands who had offered her more than a free drink after she and Crook were divorced. Oh, she'd watched him, but he had always made her feel too fluttery inside, so she had avoided his eyes all those years. And now, here he was knocking on her front door.

Spooky was puffing on a cigarette like a gangster and pulling his pants up like a pimp so his penis bulged and so Mildred could see that his socks were silk and his pointed-toe shoes were expensive. She opened the door and tried to remain cool, especially since it was one of those rare occasions when she was alone in the house. As the saying goes, you always want what you can't have. To Mildred, there was something so mysterious about Spooky it made him damn near taboo. And his seeming off-limits only made him more desirable.

Mildred knew she looked okay. Connie James had just pressed and curled her hair and she hadn't wiped off her peach lipstick yet. She sat her plate of collard greens and ham hocks on the dining room table and went to open the screen door.

"What brings you way over here, handsome?" Mildred heard herself asking.

"Oh, I was just driving in the neighborhood, and I said to myself, Baby Franks rented that house to Mildred, didn't he, and I just wondered if you were home. Can I come in?"

"Yeah, come on in. Have a seat. Ain't got nothing in here to drank but a beer. What you know good?"

The truth of the matter was Mildred already knew Kaye Francis had put him out — everybody knew it. She had finally gotten tired of all the women calling her house, claiming Spooky was the father of their brand new baby, or had given them gonorrhea, or owed them some money. A lot of people thought Spooky had married Kaye Francis because her people had money. She was the one who had bought him that white Riviera he was driving. Didn't make any difference to Mildred one way or the other. At this moment, all she knew was that he had been curious enough to stop by to see her, and for the first time in her life, Mildred felt whorish. She didn't want to talk about anything, just do it while the kids were gone and then put him out. Her panties were already getting slippery, and when Spooky put his cigarette out and finished his beer, Mildred felt a lingering weakness inside.

It had started to rain, and the sky was growing darker and darker. She walked to the sun porch to close the windows and a flash of lightning crackled and lit up the whole sky.

"You gon' get caught in this storm, you know," she said.

"I'm already caught in the storm," he said.

This would be the first time Mildred wouldn't stop to think about her kids. She was just glad they were gone. She and Spooky sat on the sun porch, listening to the thunder and the rain falling in the drain pipes.

"My daddy always saying a thunderstorm is the Lord doing his work and we should be quiet," she said, unable to think of anything else to say.

"I'm a quiet man," Spooky said.

She offered him some greens and corn bread, but he said he wasn't hungry. At least not for food. Mildred couldn't finish hers either. She turned off the television.

"Why don't we go into the living room," Mildred whispered.

Her heart hadn't pounded so hard since she fell in love with Crook. She had forgotten that feeling. Spooky Cooper sat beside her smiling into her eyes, and the gap in his tooth only added to his charisma and charm. He bent over and kissed her like a movie star, then led Mildred to her bedroom like he already knew where it was.

Spooky knew his power, and Mildred couldn't resist. His black eyes had hypnotized her, especially when he told her that he had always yearned for her, long before he ever married Kaye Francis, but she had married Crook. Spooky wasn't really lying, but his timing was brilliant. He knew how picky Mildred had always been when it came to men, and the only piece of a man she had had since she moved into this house was old smelly Rufus, who often stopped by to see the kids and lend her ten or twenty dollars, which he never made her pay back. Rufus had the hots for her too, and though he drank too much, a few times Mildred had let herself get loose enough to ignore his funk, his scratchy whiskers, and his unbrushed teeth. The kids liked Rufus because he was generous with his money and he was so silly. They would have never guessed in a million years, though, that their mama had actually slept with him. To Mildred, Rufus was like a spare tire when she had a flat.

Now, she had a real man in her bedroom. And one who smelled like Aqua Velva, not Old Spice, thank God. She was so nervous that you'd have thought she was going to bed with the president of the United States.

"Make yourself comfortable," she told him as she glided to the bathroom. Spooky had already taken off his clothes and was lying in her bed like a king. Mildred closed the bathroom door and took a quick douche, brushed her teeth and gargled, sprayed some Topaz between her legs and on the balls of her feet — like the good old days — and Q-Tipped her ears and na-vel. She didn't own a sexy nightgown, but it wouldn't have mattered. Spooky was so smooth and so cool that she wouldn't have had it on a minute before he would have skillfully slid the straps from her shoulders.

She turned out the bathroom light and tiptoed back to the bedroom. Before she knew it, Spooky was holding her in his arms and kissing her like she was breakable. He touched her skin in places she had forgotten could be ignited by a man. She'd never felt her body throbbing like this in all of her thirty years. She didn't even feel the house shake when the train rum-bled past her bedroom window.

And Spooky took his time with her. He licked her skin in slow motion, the way a kitten licks milk from a bowl. He swirled his tongue around in her ears at 33 rpm's, until Mildred felt like she would boil over. She had never, ever, experienced this kind of passion before. And when the room grew completely black and his warm pressure amplified inside her, she screamed out his name three octaves higher than her normal voice. Spooky calmly rolled over and lit a cigarette, knowing full well his mission had been accomplished.

During the weeks that followed, Mildred made him park his car four blocks away from the house. His wife had become a reality to her. Word had already hit the streets that Mildred Peacock had made Spooky Cooper fall in love with her. And it was true. Supposedly it was impossible because there had been so many women who would have given anything to be with him and Spooky hadn't given them the time of day. Mildred hadn't asked him for a thing in return and had not posed a single question to him about his wife. She knew how to make a man feel like one; everything Spooky had done to her, she had given back to him three times over. And the first time Mildred moved her head below his waist, she gave Spooky so much pleasure that he thought she knew what she was doing. Most of her girlfriends had always said they didn't go that way. The men said they would never eat at the Y. Just about all of them were lying, and would do damn near anything behind closed doors, so long as it guaranteed some kind of pleasure.

Spooky went so far as to walk in the rain to be with Mildred,

and this was something he had never done for any woman —
got his shoes wet. What the hell, Mildred thought, she was
fucking a dream and loving every minute of it. Spooky had been
the first man to drive her far enough to bring her to a full or-
gasm. And Mildred got greedy. She didn't just want more of
him, she wanted all of him.

But Spooky was still sneaky and no good, and when Mildred
sat the kids down to tell them that he was going to be spending
quite a bit of time there, they stared at her like she was crazy.

Freda, as usual, spoke for all of them. "Mama, that's Miss
Francis' husband! I know you wouldn't mess with no married
man. Please don't tell us you like him, Mama. Everybody know
he hang out at Carabelle's and Miss Moore's. He a ladies' man.
What you got that ain't none of them got?"

"Shut up, would you," Mildred snapped, not even bothering
to correct Freda's grammar. "I like the man and he likes me,
and I don't care whose husband he *used* to be, he makes me
feel damn good, better than your daddy ever did, and if you
knew how long it's been since your mama felt like this, all y'all
would be happy for me."

"Happy? Everybody at school know he take money from
women, and you ain't got none, so what he want with you?"
Money asked.

"If y'all don't shut up, I swear . . ." and Mildred couldn't say
another word. She ran some bathwater and soaked in the tub.
In her mind all she could see were Spooky's black eyes. And as
the bubbles burst over her brown skin, the only thing she could
feel was warm air leaving his lips and penetrating every pore of
her body. The hot water felt like Spooky's passion spreading
like an oil slick between her legs. And at that moment, as
Mildred let her shoulders slide farther into the water, she
couldn't remember her children, by name or by face, and in her
heart, she didn't even have any.

"Whose deal is it?" Mildred asked.

Zeke swirled the ice melting in his glass. "I guess it would
be kind of hard to figure out since we kicking y'all ass. Come
on, Geraldine, let's run a Boston on these mothas. Show 'em
how to play some real whist." Geraldine was his wife. Dead-

man was Mildred's partner and although he wasn't that bright, the boy knew how to play a hell of a hand; knew how and when and what to bid, and it seemed as though Deadman could read Mildred's mind or see right through her cards when she looked at him and started whistling. It was as if she were giving him some kind of secret signal that only Deadman understood. And when Mildred could get away with it, she would kick his foot under the table like she was doing now, before he had a chance to bid an uptown or a downtown, and sometimes he would switch his bid completely around.

The kitchen was full of smoke; the table was covered with overflowing ashtrays and bowls of potato chips and dip, and everybody had glasses next to their elbows. Ashes and crumbs were all over the floor, but Mildred didn't mind because they were having so much fun and nobody was keeping track of time. By eleven o'clock, they were all damn near drunk, but hell, it was Friday night, and Mildred had taken a nerve pill earlier, so she was feeling extra mellow.

The kids were still up, so she decided to put them to work. "Freda, put your mama's record on, would you? And Bootsey, come in here and empty these ashtrays. And bring us a bowl of ice while you're up. What you bid, sucker?" she said to Zeke, who was so high he could hardly put his hand in order. He never could hold his liquor, and Geraldine wasn't much better. She kept missing when she spit her snuff in the can she had placed next to her bunioned foot.

"I bid a three no," Zeke said, and Mildred just smiled at Deadman because her hand was pretty, so pretty that after she bid, she plopped down one card at a time so that it snapped and some of them flew off the table. They made every single book. Pulled a Boston on them, which would've aggravated the hell out of Zeke and Geraldine had they been sober.

Mildred laughed. "Now, tell your mama to bring her fat behind on over here if she want to play!" At that moment, Rufus knocked on the door and walked in with another fifth of Scotch. Nancy Wilson was singing "And you don't know and you don't know and you don't know, how glad I am" in the background and Mildred started popping her fingers, singing right along with her. "Turn it up, Freda, damn, I can't even hear the thang."

"Where's that white niggah at?" Rufus asked Mildred, breaking everybody's train of thought.

"Aw, shut up, sucker," Zeke said. "Don't come in here spoiling everythang."

"That really ain't none of your business, Rufus," Mildred said. "Now if you want to play, sit your behind on down, and if you wanna run your mouth about thangs that really shouldn't concern you, you can take it back on out that door. But leave that bottle where it's sitting."

Rufus just laughed. He hadn't slept with Mildred since she'd started seeing Spooky, and that was almost six months ago. He missed her luscious body and had continued to give her money anyway. Spooky never gave Mildred a dime.

Deadman got up and let Rufus take over his hand, and he eased into the living room where he was content watching Freda sewing on the machine Mildred had finally bought her, thanks to Rufus's generosity.

What Mildred didn't know was that Spooky had been parking his white Riviera in his own driveway on the nights he wasn't with her. Nobody bothered to tell Mildred, either. They assumed she already knew, and besides, nobody really wanted to get cussed out for meddling in the business of a woman who had such a distaste for it. All Mildred knew was that some nights Spooky just didn't come by, but when he did, he more than made up for it.

By two o'clock in the morning, everybody was too drunk to bid anything and Mildred put them out, including Deadman, who had been sleeping on Money's cot. The television was still on, even though the girls had finally gone to bed, and Money was spending the night with Chunky and Big Man. Only one more to go, Mildred thought, when she looked at Rufus.

"Do I gotta go too, Milly?" he asked, trying to act sober and busying himself by picking up glasses, throwing away bottles and dumping dirty ashtrays. Mildred looked at Rufus and frowned. He looked even more mangy than usual. "Yeah, you too. I ain't in the mood, Rufus." He took no for an answer like any beggar who didn't get a dime the first time but knew that sooner or later he would.

Spooky invited Mildred to Niagara Falls for a long weekend. Said he wanted to talk to her about something. Of course, the kids didn't like this idea one bit, their mama going away for an entire weekend, with a man, and Spooky at that. They thought he might try to throw her over a bridge since she still wasn't giving him any money. But Mildred didn't care what they thought and packed her suitcase faster than she could remember what she had put in it. This would be her first time leaving the kids this long.

By the time they reached Windsor, Spooky's desire for Mildred overpowered his urgency to get where he was going, and they pulled into a motel for a few hours. By the time they reached St. Catherines, the mixture of satisfaction and foreign air had become such a natural intoxication for Mildred that she wasn't able to contain her excitement. She sounded like a little girl, the way she oohed and aahed at the sights. Being someplace new gave a new keenness to everything. She was so exhilarated she thought she must not have heard right when Spooky told her the bad news — that he had gone back to his wife.

Freda was fourteen years old now, old enough to watch the kids and the house while Mildred was away, and Mildred had given her explicit instructions. No company, other than Deadman, who was supposed to stop by to fix a leak under the kitchen sink. Since Saturday was Crook's birthday, Mildred had left them twenty dollars, ten of which they were to use to buy his present. She had warned Freda to make sure they used every dime of it on him, and call to make sure he would be home. They had rarely gone by the shack he and Miss Ernestine had moved into; they didn't like her because she didn't like them. Ernestine never said two words to them when they did see her. And when they went by to visit, she and Crook were both usually drunk or asleep. Sometimes, when they saw their daddy on the street, the kids merely waved to him like they would anyone else. Money didn't even seem to miss him any more.

They bought Crook a tie and some cufflinks from the K-Mart that had just opened up next to the brand new McDonald's hamburger take-out. Totaled $4.93. They spent the rest of the money on submarine sandwiches and grape pop.

When they went by his house to drop off the presents, the door was open and flies were buzzing over plates of food that looked like they'd been sitting out for days. They opened the screen door when no one answered, then peeked in the bedroom. As they had expected, Crook was asleep, drunk, right next to Miss Ernestine. An empty bottle of liquor was on the dresser. The two of them were spread-eagled across the bed, half naked and drooling all over each other. Freda dropped the unwrapped gifts on the black-and-white TV set, made an about-face, and they all ran out of the house.

She decided to make fried chicken and pork-n-beans for dinner, and afterward told the kids they could have the privilege of going roller-skating at the McKinley Auditorium with six of the other ten dollars Mildred had left them to spend on entertainment. Freda loved the power she had playing mama. She didn't want to go skating because, just like Mildred, it was rare that she was alone and had time to herself. She wanted to finish making a wraparound skirt she was working on with no interruptions. A horn honked and the kids ran out to the car. Their Aunt Curly Mae told Freda she would have them home by ten.

Freda was sitting in the living room, sewing, listening to Della Reese, and puffing on a cigarette like she'd been smoking twenty years instead of just one. When she heard a knock at the kitchen door, she jumped up and smashed the butt out so fast that she burned her fingertips. But it was only Deadman. She hollered for him to come in.

"Hi, Freda," he said, slurring and smiling, showing off his bright pink gums. "I came to fix the pipe." Deadman sounded like he was drunk, though it was rare that Freda had ever seen him drink more than a glassful. Once in a while he followed in his brothers' footsteps and got drunk with them, but hardly ever in public.

"I know, I know." She waved him in. "You know where the sink is, Dead. Just don't come in here bothering me, 'cause I'm doing something." Freda unbent her cigarette, brushed it off, and lit it back up. Deadman wasn't nobody, she thought, as she inhaled and blew smoke out through her nose.

"Where the hell is everybody?" he yelled from the kitchen.

"Roller-skating. How come you didn't go tonight?" she asked.

"I didn't feel like skating," he said. Deadman usually hung out with the teenage crowd because grown-ups didn't take him seriously.

It was getting dark, so Freda turned on the light in the living room. Ten minutes later, Deadman came in and claimed he couldn't fix the pipe because he didn't have the right tools. But Freda didn't remember him carrying any when he came in. The next thing she knew he had flopped down on the couch near her chair. She sucked her teeth and made sure she kept her back turned to him. He still didn't take the hint. He pulled his pint bottle from his back pocket and took two long swigs. He could hardly sit up straight, but he managed to pull himself to a standing position. Then he crept up behind her and slid his arms around her neck.

"Are you crazy, Deadman?" she yelled. "Get your fuckin' hands offa me, niggah." Cussing came as easy for Freda as it did for Mildred, and if Deadman had been any drunker, he might have mistaken her for Mildred and left her alone. But he wasn't that drunk. "Ah, come on, Freda," he said, "let me have one little kiss. I'll give you five dollars. Just one little kiss."

"I don't want your money, Deadman, and you better get your fuckin' hands offa me before I scream." Freda tried to sound sure of herself but she knew that where this house was situated, no one would hear her no matter how loud she screamed. She got scared. It was only nine o'clock and the kids wouldn't be home for at least another hour. Sometimes Curly Mae took them to the Dairy Queen afterward. Lord, she hoped tonight wasn't one of those nights. She tried to squirm out of the chair but Deadman had tightened his grip around her neck, making it hard for Freda to breathe.

"You know I love you, Freda." he said. "I've always loved you. Since you was ten years old I loved you. I done waited all this time. All this time." Deadman didn't notice that Freda had carefully picked up a seam ripper with her right hand and when he tried to lift her from the chair by her neck, she jabbed it into his stomach. Then Deadman got angry.

"Just for that, I'm not gon' be nice. I *was* gon' be nice, but you act just like your old sassy-ass mama, don't you?" He grabbed the seam ripper, threw it on the floor, and slung Freda onto the couch. She was terrified, immobilized. Deadman pulled her slacks down past her trembling knees and told her that if she moved he would tell Mildred he saw her smoking and that he knew she'd been stealing from K-Mart, and then he would spread a rumor all over South Park that she had given him some without his even asking for it. Freda's frail body shook in spasms as he pulled his pants down and revealed his giant penis. She had never seen a grown man's penis before, only Money's, and that was when he was six years old. Freda was so frightened by what she knew he was going to do with it that she fainted.

A moment later, when she came to, Deadman was on top of her, fumbling with himself and pressing his body down hard against hers. Freda could feel his heart pounding and then saw his ugly face coming toward hers. Deadman's chapped lips scraped her mouth. This was a kiss. His breath smelled like garbage, but Freda couldn't move. He thrust himself inside her, but before he could fully penetrate her, Freda spit in his face. He pulled away, and then he came all over Mildred's orange couch. Then he zipped his pants up and left, satisfied.

Finally, Freda opened her eyes, but she couldn't move. She didn't want to move. She lay on the couch, staring at a button on one of the cushions. It was almost ten o'clock. She finally forced herself up and walked slowly to the bathroom, where she urgently washed between her legs, then tried to do knee bends to get rid of the stiffness. She hurt. She felt embarrassed and humiliated. Freda had always thought Deadman was a good friend of the family's. And just look at what he'd done to her. She took baby steps toward the living room, where she saw the wet spots on her mama's couch. She got a soapy dishcloth from the kitchen and tried to wash out the stains as best she could.

She was frightened when she heard the kids running up the steps, slamming the screen door behind them.

"Guess what, Freda, I learned how to skate backwards tonight," Bootsey said.

"Aw, she did not," Angel protested. "She just barely managed to turn around. I'm the one who can skate in this family, admit it, heffa."

"Oh, Freda, Money walked home with Big Man and Little Man," Bootsey told her. "We told him you was gon' be mad, but he said he was gon' walk anyway."

Freda tried to sound like she was upset about it. "I'll just tell Mama, when she gets home."

Doll went to turn on the television, and the rest of the girls followed her. Before they sat down on the couch, Bootsey saw it was wet.

"Oooooh, you spilled something on the couch, Freda! You know what Mama told us about eating and drinking in here. You gon' get it if it don't come out."

"It ain't nothing but some Kool-Aid and it'll come out. Besides, Mama ain't here. And when she ain't here, who's the mama around here?"

"You are, Miss Smarty, you are."

After Spooky had fucked Mildred's brains out and then told her he was going back to his wife, Mildred couldn't keep her food down for three days. She had lost, she thought. For the first time in her life, she had lost. She bathed her swollen eyes and made up her mind that this would be the last time she would open up her heart so eagerly and generously, only to end up feeling up like it was a fresh-cut wound that some man had poured salt into. No. Hell no. Her heart was made only to pump blood and keep her going. And that's exactly what it was going to do from now on.

"I'm marrying Rufus," she told the kids.

They just laughed, until they saw Mildred wasn't joking.

"Rufus, Mama? Come on, old stupid smelly ugly Rufus?" Freda asked.

"He may be stupid, and he may stink sometimes, but he ain't ugly and he treats me nice and keeps some money in his pocket at all times. He can help me pay these bills. It takes oil to heat up this house, and who you think been giving me y'all lunch money all these months? Who you think bought you that damn

sewing machine that you ain't been using lately, girl? Huh?
And Money, boy, where you thank that bike you ride all over
town come from? God? Not to mention all the steak and pork
chops and sausage y'all been eating around here. Ever since I
got laid off, y'all know we been having a rough time, but you
never once thought about where all this money was coming
from, did you. Them welfare checks and food stamps don't
stretch to buy no steaks. Besides, we need a man around this
damn house. Deadman never did fix that pipe, and where the
hell has he been anyway? I ain't seen him in damn near a
month."

A chill went through Freda when she heard his name and she
stiffened. Then, not wanting to look awkward, she shoved
Money, who shoved her back. She had tried to block out the
pain of that evening because she didn't know what else to do
with it. It had worked pretty well up to now.

"We got Money," said Doll, watching him tumble forward.
Doll was almost as tall as Money was. She was only nine, but
Mildred still called her baby. She was also cross-eyed, and wore
cat-eyed glasses. The kids always called her Jealous Eyes because her eyes looked like they were staring at each other. Doll
was kind of homely, when you looked straight at her. Her hair
was sandy brown and she had thick beige lips, unlike anybody
else in the family. Folks swore up and down she and Freda looked
alike, but Freda was darker and had nappier hair. Freda said she
had never been that ruined. They often made fun of Doll, made
her the brunt of a lot of jokes. But everybody always said that
when Doll grew up, filled out, and started fixing herself up, she
would probably turn out to be the finest of all four girls.

"Yeah, you got me, Mama," Money said, poking his small
chest out.

"Look. This ain't got nothing to do with love. I'm getting too
old to be thanking about marrying somebody for some damn
love. There's other thangs to consider. Y'all for one. It won't
kill me to marry Rufus. I've known the man for damn near
fifteen or twenty years. That's long enough to marry anybody.
Ain't like he no stranger. Plus, your mama could use some regular company. I'm tired of being by myself. Y'all is good company and everythang, but when you get older you may under-

stand what a man can do for a woman, and vice versa. And don't ask me no questions about it now 'cause I don't feel like explaining it."

They had never even bothered to ask her about what happened to Mr. Superfine Superslick Supercool Spooky. They were glad not to see his pale face around their house at night. And they didn't want to embarrass her. But now, here come Rufus, and they didn't know which one was worse.

Mildred married him downtown at the courthouse and when Rufus brought home three old suitcases full of dirty clothes, the scent of the whole house changed instantly. Freda threw everything he owned into the washing machine and dropped four capfuls of Mr. Clean in along with the detergent. He wasn't so funny to them any more, now that he was their stepfather. Even when he told a good joke they found it hard to laugh. Sometimes, though, they had to force themselves not to laugh at him, and just to be smart they would walk behind him with a can of Glade air freshener or Lysol disinfectant and spray it like a halo over his head. "Am I in your way?" Rufus would ask, and the kids would crack up, and say, "No, are we in your way?"

They never did call him Daddy, but Rufus didn't mind and Mildred didn't make them. It was true that Rufus always looked tattered and funky, no matter how many baths he took. And his face always sprouted a brownish growth of hair that stuck out like little porcupine quills, which he insisted on rubbing against their faces. Sometimes they would sock him in the stomach but he would only laugh, even though they were really trying to hurt him. The man just didn't know what the word deodorant meant and besides that his teeth were brown and looked too small for his wide mouth. His breath smelled like dry alcohol. And now they had to explain to their friends why their mama's last name was now Palmer instead of Peacock, and also why she married him in the first place.

Rufus tried to be a good stepdaddy, though, and bought them as much junk as he could. Now they had all the things they had dreamed would fill up the refrigerator one day. They had too many hot dogs and potato chips, too much popcorn, and plenty of soda pop and ice cream. They had five different kinds of lunch meat, American, Swiss, and cheddar cheese, and lettuce and tomatoes to make sandwiches. They had chocolate chip, sugar, peanut butter, and Oreo cookies to put in their bag lunches, but they never took them any more because Rufus gave them money to eat out. Mildred finally told Rufus he was spoiling them and she started making them take their lunch instead of buying it.

For three whole months now, they had lived in a house where nothing was threatened with getting cut off or taken away and Mildred felt relatively at ease. At least that was the front she was trying to maintain. The nerve pills helped. The kids still couldn't figure out how she could stand to get so close to Rufus, let alone kiss and cuddle up to him at night. And God, did they really do the nasty?

Like Crook, Rufus drank too much. At first he seemed to have it under control, but when Mildred started ignoring him under the covers at night — after the pills had long worn off — and giving him orders in the daytime like he was one of the kids, Rufus began hitting the bottle like he had grown accustomed to doing before Mildred had said "I do."

Rufus would go into a purple rage when he drank more than ten ounces of eighty proof. His brain cells became toxic and he choked on his own pitifulness, his own worthlessness and powerlessness, and began to spit it out at Mildred. She jumped back. Then he started looking slovenly all over again and began smelling like old rags and turpentine.

"You need to do something with yourself, Rufus," Mildred told him. "You make me sick just looking at you."

So Rufus went out and bought himself a brand new suit, a white shirt, and some cheap black shoes.

Mildred wasn't impressed. "I don't know who taught you how to dress, but that suit ain't hitting on nothing."

"You want me to take it back? I'll take it back, Milly," he said.

"Naw, why don't we go somewhere tonight? I'm sick of sitting in this house." The truth was, Rufus had asked her on lots of Friday and Saturday nights if she wanted to go down to the Shingle to have a drink, listen to some music. But Mildred had always said no. First of all, she was too embarrassed to be seen with him, but to be completely honest, she was scared she might run into Spooky.

And sure enough, who was sitting at the bar, sipping on a rum and Coke, when she and Rufus sat down at the other end of the bar. And he was not alone, of course. One of Mildred's so-called friends, Faye Love, was staring him in the face so he couldn't look at anyone else.

"It's hot in here," Mildred said, making sure her head stayed turned in the opposite direction.

"It ain't hot in here. That niggah down there is making you sweat. That's it, ain't it?"

"What niggah?"

Mildred turned her head in Spooky's direction. He was laughing with Faye Love and didn't seem to notice her.

"I want to go home," she said.

"Yeah, I think that's a good idea, a very good idea." Rufus finished his drink. Mildred had already hopped off the bar stool. Instead of heading for the door, she walked down the length of the bar and stopped in front of Spooky. Faye Love turned her head away.

"Hey, good-lookin', what you know good?" she said to Spooky.

"Nothing, Milly, not a thang."

Mildred turned away, pivoting like a ballerina, and slid her arm through Rufus's at the door.

For the next few months she tried to tolerate Rufus. Even though he went to Ford's every single day, he just couldn't pull himself together. She didn't love him and got sick and tired of making excuses for her feelings, of trying to convince herself that things would work themselves out. Rufus was making her miserable.

Finally one afternoon, while he was lying on the couch, she told him she was divorcing him.

Rufus didn't want a divorce and tried to explain why in a language Mildred was all too familiar with. He pulled a knife on her.

"I'll kill you first before I let you leave me. You know I've always loved you and now that you mine, I ain't letting you go for nobody. What I'ma do without you and the kids? Y'all my whole world." Rufus was crying and started kicking the wall over and over, harder and harder.

But Mildred did not feel sorry for him at all.

"Now who in the hell you think you gon' stab, mother-fucker? You better put that knife down. You just like the rest of 'em. Ain't worth a good fuck. I should'a known all along. But I ain't crazy. I know when I've made a mistake. Crook was a mistake, and you, you worse than one, you was an accident."

The girls were peeking through their bedroom door, where they'd been playing tic-tac-toe, and when Freda saw Rufus come at Mildred with the knife and grab her arm, Freda ran out of the room screaming.

"Let go of my mama, you son-of-a-bitch!" she screamed. Freda hollered at her sisters to run and call the police. Money was spending the night with Chunky and BooBoo.

Rufus looked at Freda, still holding Mildred's arm behind her back. "Move, girl, go on back in the room. This is between me and your mama."

And before knowing what had come over her, Freda was on him like lightning, and with the strength of any grown man, she pushed her mama out of the way, grabbed Rufus by his shirt, and flung him into their room, where his head hit the metal bar of the bunk bed. He fell backward on the mattress. Freda grabbed the knife from his hands and put it up to his throat.

"Now, who you gon' stab? Huh? I'll tell you something, and you better listen good, you hear me?" She stuck the point of the knife into his neck. "If you put your hands on my mama ever again in your life, I'll slit your fucking throat and cut your dick off and you won't ever be able to fuck with *nobody* else again. Do you hear me, motherfucker?" Freda was shaking and shivering like a puppy, but she soon began to regain her strength.

Mildred was in a state of shock and hadn't realized that Rufus had cut her. Her blouse was bloody. She walked to the doorway. "Leave him alone, Freda," she said. "I can handle it from here."

Rufus got up without saying a word and followed Mildred toward their room, which was right off the living room. The girls ran past them, back into their own room to comfort themselves with Freda.

"Here we go again," Angel said.

"You crazy, Freda, you know that," whispered Bootsey. "You fucking crazy. He drunk as a skunk and could'a cut you too."

Freda frowned. "I wish he would'a tried."

Suddenly they heard the sound of glass shattering and Rufus yelling. Mildred had grabbed a beer bottle from the end table, rammed it against the wall, and jabbed Rufus in his side, where the glass had formed a long, smooth, sickle-shaped cut. Blood was gushing out like a red waterfall. Freda ran to see what had happened, and Rufus crumpled over on the floor. She suddenly felt sorry for him. Police cars were pulling up, lighting up the long driveway, and the sirens and red flashing lights brought the other kids from their room again.

"You didn't have to try to kill him, Mama," Freda screamed. She ran to the bathroom to get a towel and Doll opened the door for the police. When Freda returned, a patrolman was asking Mildred what had happened. She told him nothing. Another policeman went back to his car to call an ambulance, while the other three, bored with the incident, left altogether.

Freda was hysterical. "Y'all both crazy! First you try to screw each other to death one day and then try to kill each other the next! First it was Daddy, now this stupid jerk. I'm gettin' out of this house if you keep this up. I mean it! I can't stand living like a bunch of savages!"

Mildred told her to shut up and go somewhere and sit down. Freda stomped out of the room.

"Get up, motherfucker," Mildred said to Rufus, and he did. The ambulance arrived and took him to the hospital, where he was given fifteen stitches. When the kids woke up in the morning, his shoes were outside Mildred's bedroom door.

# Eight

"CURLY, GIRL, I gotta do something," Mildred said into the phone. "And quick. Since me and Rufus broke up, I feel like I'm in a rerun. These damn bills done piled back up and I swear I can't get on nowhere decent. You know ain't nobody hiring, not even Ford's or Chrysler's or Prest-o-Lité. I'm back on the state again, did I tell you?"

"Naw, you didn't tell me," Curly said, cradling the telephone against her shoulder.

"Shit, these kids need winter coats and snow boots and Christmas'a be here before you know it. Now that Freda's in high school, every time I turn around she need money for this, money for that. That girl sews her behind off. Buys the most expensive fabric she can find. But let me stop boring you, chile, and get to the damn point. I need to get in touch with one of your friends."

"It ain't nothing to be ashamed of, Sis. I've been trying to tell you for years, when you get in trouble, you always need a friend. Somebody who can afford to do you a favor. The men around here can't even eat your pussy good, let alone help you pay for anythang."

Up until last year, Curly hadn't turned a trick for her husband, Clyde, in quite some time. Then he got burnt down at the foundry and they had to live off his disability. It was hardly

79

enough, so Clyde suggested that Curly do "something." She did. Drove their Buick across the Blue Water Bridge to the first nice bar she came to in Ontario and made lucrative propositions. All of Curly's "friends" were Canadian. And she had always been and still was good-looking, even after seven kids. It seemed like the more kids she had the dumber she got, because she wasn't charging her regulars the going rates any more. She used a declining scale and was damn near giving it away.

"How you do it, Curly? Tell me, what do I do?"

"You don't do much of nothing, really. Just take 'em up to some motel — I'd go to the Starlight 'cause it's out of the way. And wear something pretty. Then just take it off, shake your behind a few times, and don't give him more than a half hour, forty-five minutes at the most. Make sure he use some protection so you don't catch nothin' and make him drank something first. Then tell him about your kids. How hungry they is, and how they ain't got nothing to wear to school or church, and that your lights is cut off and you can't even see 'em," she said, giggling.

"Come on, Curly, I'm serious."

"I know, I know. Can't you take a joke, Milly? Just exaggerate every damn thang. Let him know that this could be a regular thang so long as he improve your financial situation. Promise him that you'll guarantee he'll feel good at least once a week. Don't give him your address or phone number, though. I made that mistake years ago, chile."

"How much do you charge?"

"How much you thank it's worth?"

"I don't know, I ain't never thought about it before."

"You'll find out after you finished, honey, believe me, you'll know how much it's worth to you."

Mildred took him to the Starlight, the same place, she remembered, where Sissie had tried to strangle Janey Pearl when Sissie caught her with her husband. Crook had spent many nights up there with Ernestine, too. As a matter of fact, the only time anybody from town went to the Starlight was when they were creeping.

It was snowing so hard that at first Mildred was going to change her mind. She was nervous and scared and didn't know whether she could go through with it, but this felt like the only alternative she had. Hell, her kids weren't babies any more. They ate like grown people; grew out of their shoes and clothes so fast it seemed like as soon as she bought them new ones for Christmas, by Easter they needed the next size. Some things just can't be passed down another year. Fuck it, Mildred thought, pulling up to the motel. I'll do this till I can thank of somethin' better.

Her skin felt like little ants and maggots were crawling all over it every time he touched her — a complete stranger, and a white man at that — but Mildred had drunk three stiff shots of Jack Daniel's before she'd opened the car door, and once inside, offered him some and took three more. She told him that her name was Priscilla and she was a widow. That her husband had died of a heart attack and left her with an unpaid insurance policy and seven growing kids. Mildred was so dramatic about it, even she started crying. It took exactly five minutes to make his tiny penis droop with satisfaction. And Mildred went home with one hundred dollars.

She hadn't known just how many people actually crept at the Starlight, but when she started recognizing the cars parked outside her room, she decided to take this fellow to a motel in Canada. Now the kids were going to school in brand new everything and she met him every Sunday for three months, till she couldn't stand it any more. He had started to really like her. Even wanted to meet her kids. Mildred told him he must be nuts. Besides, she was tired of getting drunk every Sunday and lying to her children about a part-time job where she could never be reached by phone. The kids, however, weren't the least bit suspicious.

Ever since Carabelle had moved into Mildred's old house on Twenty-fifth Street, she'd been giving weekend parties — well, not exactly parties; more like a combination casino, restaurant, brothel, and cabaret. Mildred had even gone a few times. Her kids' old bedrooms had been turned into trick stops. The sun porch had little card tables and folding chairs situated so people could eat the platefuls of greens, macaroni and cheese, barbecue, chitterlings, and potato salad that Carabelle sold for $1.50 (the two pieces of white bread were free, she said), and one corner of the living room had been made into a bar. Drinks were a dollar. Didn't matter what proof you wanted, they were all the same price. Folks danced to records in the dining room. There was always a crap game going on in the basement. The serious gamblers came in through the back door and went straight downstairs. The room was always full of smoke and loud voices, and cursing and grumbling and heavy drinking.

Whenever Mildred had run into Carabelle at the dry cleaners or the drug store or the liquor store, Carabelle always flashed a wad of twenties at least six inches thick. Hell, Mildred thought, my house is big enough for a party. And everybody know I make the best barbecue sauce and potato salad in South Park. She made up her mind that she would finally do something that would make her a lot of money.

The kids were excited. They made signs out of cardboard and used bright paint to make sure they could be read at night. Then they put them all over town — in Stinky's Liquor Store, in the Shingle, at the pool hall, at the A&P, in the beauty and barber shops, in the parking lot at the welfare and social security offices, outside the telephone company on a telephone pole, and at Detroit Edison under a streetlight. Mildred's phone was jumping off the hook from folks calling to make sure it was for real. They should've known better, because everybody knew that when Mildred said she was going to do something, she did it.

She had the kids clean up the whole house and she cleared all the furniture out of the way to make room for people and dancing. Freda and Money cleaned thirty pounds of chitterlings and hog mogs — took them almost nine hours — while Mildred had Bootsey and Angel chop up celery, onions, and bell peppers for the potato salad. Doll's job was to roll plastic forks and knives inside napkins and put a tiny rubber band around them. Mildred's sauce simmered for two days, and she hired Dead-man to watch the barbecue grill. When Freda saw him, she couldn't bring herself to say anything, and he acted like nothing had ever happened. Mildred turned her bedroom into the gambling room, but refused to have any whores.

When Friday night came, cars were lined up for more than ten blocks, alongside the railroad tracks and up and down Moak and Thirty-second Streets until daylight peeked through the drawn curtains and Mildred had to make everyone leave. After she paid Deadman, gave the kids ten dollars apiece, and paid Gill Ronsonville for running the crap table, she had made more than seven hundred dollars. She put it in a Tiparillo cigar box and put it on the highest shelf in her bedroom closet. Then she started humming Nancy Wilson's song. "And you don't know and you don't know and you don't know, how glad I am." Mildred knew she was on to something good.

The kids cleaned up the house again the next day, and Saturday night was a repeat performance. For the next several months Mildred had these parties twice a month. She felt like she was on easy street.

Then she got busted.

Carabelle didn't like Mildred taking away all her business, and one Sunday morning, after Mildred had just put out the last of her customers — all except two or three die-hard gamblers and a couple of her friends who were too drunk to move — there was a knock at the door. The police had received a phone call from an anonymous neighbor complaining about the noise. Mildred knew this was bogus because her neighbors had been the first to show up. When they searched the house and found the crap table on the premises, they hauled everybody down town, including Mildred. She was fined two hundred dollars, put on probation for a year, and released. This marked the end of her parties. And even though Baby Franks, the owner of the house, had been one of the highest rollers, when he found out Mildred had been arrested, he suggested it would be better if she found another place to live. Said he didn't want a lot of illegal hanky-panky going on in his house. Mildred didn't hesitate to start looking because she had something she never had before: some money in her pocket.

The city had started excavating to build those housing projects that nobody believed would be built, smack dab in the middle of South Park between Twenty-fourth and Twenty-eighth Streets, and from Moak to Manuel, which was a good ten acres. It had been estimated that about two hundred or more low-income families would have a decent, cheap, and modern place to live. But these dwellings wouldn't be ready for at least another six to eight months. Mildred told Baby Franks she planned to move into one of them, and since he was a righteous, churchgoing man, he said he could wait until then.

Mildred had never learned how to put money in the bank — never had enough to save — so she kept her cigar box hidden in the garage. Then the engine in the Mercury blew up and she had to buy a new one. The gas station attendant told her that if she wanted to go on living, she'd do best to replace the two balding back tires, too. Then she needed snow tires. After all, this was Michigan. Then it was two dollars here and ten dollars there, till the box was empty. So when Prest-o-Lite finally called her, Mildred was glad to take the job. But after she'd been working there a while, she couldn't decide which was worse, scrubbing white folks' floors, waiting on people in a bar, cooking hamburgers and french fries, taking care of dying old people, or winding spools of wire from three-thirty to eleven-thirty at night.

While she sat bent over a conveyor belt, her kids were doing things at home that would take Mildred some time to catch on to. Money and Bootsey had become the biggest rogues in South Park, stealing from the Rexall Drug Store everything they could drop into a pillowcase — candy bars, games, toys, cigarettes for Freda, who was now smoking almost five a day. Angel and Doll were practicing pressing and curling each other's hair, and Angel had talked Doll into letting her cut hers, since it hung down past her shoulders. Angel cut a gigantic plug out and didn't even tell Doll until the next morning when she went to comb it. They were both afraid to tell Mildred.

One Saturday, Mildred was relaxing, watching a rerun of "That Touch of Mink," when a police officer knocked at the door. He was holding Money and Bootsey, one in each hand. When he told her what they were guilty of, Mildred was not as alarmed and angry as she was embarrassed. She thought she had taught them better. Her nerves felt like they were shredding and her temples were pushing against her skin. She wanted to explode, but instead of whipping them, she did something worse. For a solid month, she wouldn't let them leave the front yard, not even to go to the mailbox. They couldn't turn their heads in the direction of the TV, let alone watch it. And they had to be under the covers before the sun went down. For two budding teenagers, this was pure hell, especially when Mildred's shift got changed to days and there was no way they could even think about sneaking.

The kids were squirting each other with the hose in the yard when a coal-black Plymouth pulled up their long driveway and a young man who looked much older than his twenty years stepped out. He had little duck lips and pretty electric-white teeth and he wore a Charlie Chaplin hat on his nappy head. His deep chocolate, almost charcoal skin was so black it looked like it had a film of dust on it.

Mildred had rented out the small upstairs room to him. The room had two entrances, one from outside and the other through a door off Mildred's bedroom. The kids wouldn't be able to play hide-n-go-seek there now.

From the start, Billy Callahan played rock and roll music so loud and had so much company, particularly teenage girls, that after a few weeks Mildred cussed him out, which was how they became friends.

"Look, you little beady-headed niggah," she told him one night. "I know you young and hot and frantic, but you ain't the only one living in this damn house. Some people go to bed at decent hours, you know."

It was three-thirty in the morning and Billy was wearing only his matching red nylon underwear, but he was not embarrassed in the least and said, "I-I'm sssorry, Mildred. I pppromise not to bbblast it so llloud from nnnow on." He didn't stutter as badly as Percy did, and for some reason the kids and Mildred thought that on Billy it was rather becoming. There was something about him that made you trust him instantly and Mildred soon began to rely on him for things that needed to be done around the house, since Deadman always claimed he was so busy these days.

Within a few short months, Billy had become so friendly with all of them that he was like a member of the family. Mildred often cooked a big dinner and sent a plate upstairs to Billy by one of the kids. She felt sorry for him when she saw cans of ravioli and spaghetti in the trash. He could also play a better hand of bid whist than Deadman. Billy tuned up the Mercury for Mildred, let the kids borrow some of the latest records, and when the plumbing broke in his bathroom, Mildred let him take a shower downstairs.

The kids thought nothing about how friendly Billy and Mildred were actually getting, but they did notice that he wasn't the sweetest-smelling young man to be around. In that sense, Billy reminded them of Rufus. "We should tell him," Bootsey said.

They couldn't agree on the best way to tell him, until his birthday gave them an easy way out. They gave him a shaving kit — Old Spice, with soap and deodorant and aftershave lotion. Billy was tickled to death, and for the next few days he smelled real spicy, but it wasn't long afterward that the sweet smell began to mix with funk. This drove the kids crazy.

"Maybe it's just his own personal scent," Angel said.

"Scent, my ass," Freda said. "That niggah just scared of soap and water, is all. He probably don't even wash up, just wakes up and sprays that Old Spice over his old funk. We can't drop no more hints. Let's just let him stay funky."

One night Billy was playing his music so loud that Freda couldn't sleep. She had a civics test in the morning, so she went to Mildred's room to complain. She knocked on her mother's door — a rule Mildred made them abide by — but when she didn't get any response, she eased the door open and saw that Mildred's bed was empty. The door that led upstairs was open. Freda thought that was odd, at this time of night. A pang of fury enveloped her when she realized what her mama might possibly be doing upstairs with that boy. Before she knew what she was doing, she was tiptoeing up the stairs. She stood outside Billy's door and pressed her ear against it. The Four Tops were on the record player, but he had turned it down. Freda cracked the door open. A red glow filled the room. A colored bulb was hanging from a cord. Billy always changed the color to fit his mood. Freda walked through his small makeshift kitchen, and lying there in the middle of an old double bed was her mama, naked, wrapped up in his arms.

Freda felt as if her eyes were full of dirt and rocks and sand and she found herself screaming.

"Get up! Get your ass up! Right now!"

Mildred and Billy both woke up and covered themselves.

"Get up!" Freda screamed.

But Mildred wasn't ashamed and she wasn't about to move. She glared at Freda. "If you don't get your fast ass back down those steps in less than the time it takes me to get up, I'm gon' beat your ass till you won't be able to move again. You getting too grown, Freda. You know that. And if you weren't so damn nosy you wouldn't see every damn thang. Now get on back down those steps, get back in your bed, and I'll see you in the morning."

Freda started to cry. "What are you, some kind of whore or something?"

Mildred went to jump out of the bed, but Billy grabbed her. "Leave her alone, Mildred," he said, "she got a right to be mad. She's coming, Freda."

Mildred turned to him, furious. "And you shut up, blackie. Freda, I'm gon' tell you once, and I'm not gon' tell you again. Get your ass back down those steps."

Freda inhaled as if she were gasping for breath, unable to stop her tears. She exhaled and stormed out of the room.

In the morning, she rolled her eyes at Mildred and would not look her in the face.

"So, now you know," Mildred said.

"Now I know what?" Freda huffed. "That you like young boys?"

"If you don't watch your mouth, I'll smack that smirk off of it. Now sit down."

"I don't want to sit down."

"I said sit your ass down."

Freda flopped lazily into a chair.

"Now, let me tell you something, sister. Since you so damn grown and you want to see so much and you think you can just walk in my bedroom and check up on me when you get good and damn ready. Let me tell you what it's been like for your mama to lay in that cold-ass bed every night and all I do is thank about what's gon' be here for the kids to eat tomorrow. What y'all need. How much I gotta hustle and work my knuckles loose for y'all. I ain't spent an ounce of energy or ten damn dollars on Mildred since I don't know when. And who worries about Mildred? Huh? Nobody! You know who kisses and comforts me when I need it? No damn body, not one goddamn soul!"

Mildred slung her cup on the table and poured hot water into it. Freda was scared she might sling it at her, so she inched away a little.

"One day," Mildred went on, lowering the tone of her voice, "you might understand just what it means to need somebody — no — what it means to need a man. And when you do, maybe you'll understand that age ain't got a damn thang to do with it. Not one damn thang. And I'ma tell you another thang, since you sitting here. I like that man upstairs. And I'm gon' keep on liking him and keep on sleeping with him and I don't care if you don't like it. I don't give a damn who don't like it."

Freda sat there fuming, praying the other kids weren't listening, but they were busy watching "Woody Woodpecker." She sat there staring at her mama like she was beyond disgust.

"You mean to tell me that you really like him, Mama?"

"Yes, I do. And he likes me."

"But Mama, he's young enough to be my boyfriend. What will people say?"

"One day, when you get older, you gon' realize that you have to stop worrying about what people thank about you and what they gon' say about you 'cause they gon' talk about you anyway, don't make no difference what you do. Fuck 'em. Some of these ill-bred niggahs in the streets ain't worth ten cents, and this one, at least he got a good job at Chrysler's and he makes me feel like a woman. Do you know how long it's been since I felt good? Huh?" Mildred reached over and squeezed Freda's cheeks between her strong fingers until they pushed up against Freda's nose.

Mildred was crying and Freda couldn't remember the last time she'd seen Mildred cry. Never.

"I guess I can try to understand," Freda said.

Mildred loosened her grip and stepped back. "Just treat him nice and make sure you talk to them kids so they know what's going on, you understand me?"

"Yes, Mama, I understand you. Can I go now?"

"Yeah, get on out of here," she said, sipping on the hot water that she had forgotten to put the coffee into.

Billy took some getting used to, but Freda tried her best to make the other kids understand what "needs" were all about.

"Mama is lonely. Hard up, really, which just means she needs a boyfriend, especially at night. And we ain't the kind of company she needs all the time. We can't do everything for her and she feels that old black Billy is giving her whatever it is that she wasn't getting before. Y'all understand?"

They didn't, really. So they tried to drive Billy away by treating him badly and making him feel like a damn fool, but it didn't work. He was so nice and spent so much money on them and let them play all of his records and after Mildred married him he was more like a big brother than a stepfather.

The whole town was talking about it, but Mildred ignored them. She held her head just as high as she always had, and Curly Mae was tickled about the whole thang. "Sis'-n-law, he must be a good piece'a ass, huh? All young and spunky and everythang. Ain't shriveled up yet. I bet he can go all night. Wheweee."

"Chile, a man is a man, and a woman is a woman. You know that. I ain't had a man that made me feel this good since Spooky Cooper, and honey, this man wakes up spots in me I thought was long dead."

Curly grabbed her stomach just thinking about it.

And like any young hot-in-the-ass man in his right mind who got swept away by a woman full of experience and twelve years older than he was and who knew how to move her ass like a figure eight and swirl it around like a spinning top in slow motion until he felt close to cardiovascular arrest, the reality of five kids staring him in the face and eating up his paycheck and keeping him constant company when Mildred wasn't there became a little much. When he told them to do something, all they would say was, "Aw, shut up, Billy. You ain't our daddy, you ain't even old enough to be our daddy." Then Billy would laugh and say, "That's for damn sure," and forget about it.

Joy Williams, the same girl who had helped Freda puff on her first cigarette and who lived down the street, was also one of those girls who had crept up the back steps to Billy's room before Mildred had ever set foot in it. And there was something about Billy's blood that made him whorish. He started creeping with Joy when the pressures of marriage and his instant family began to make him feel like he was being swallowed up whole. He felt like he'd aged ten or fifteen years in just the few months that he and Mildred had been married. What did I get myself into? he kept asking himself over and over, and there was bony Joy, seventeen years old, single, with no dependents, no rent, no gas bill, no light bill, and so naturally Mildred's spell started slowly then quickly wearing off. He finally told Mildred that he had had second thoughts about married life and that it was more, much more than he had bargained for, and though there were no doubts in his mind that he loved her, he just couldn't get a handle on all this responsibility. He asked Mildred if she understood where he was comin' from.

"It's that little cripple-looking colt you been fuckin', ain't it?" she asked him.

"No, who you mean?"

"You know damn well who I'm talking about, fool. The one that look like she dying of malnutrition and got polio and enough knees to start a damn forest fire when she walk. Her."

"No, it ain't her, Mildred. I love you and I really like your kids, but I don't feel right trying to be their daddy. Please try to understand. Maybe in five or ten years I'll be ready, but this happened too fast for me."

"Well, go on and leave, motherfucker, but I'll tell you something. When you come crawling back here don't think I'ma be sitting here waiting for you. My behind'll be sweet for a long

long time. Maybe one day I'll meet me a real man who knows how to handle it!"

His feelings were hurt but he packed all of his clothes the same night anyway and returned to what Mildred called his free-flowing, free-fucking life that he had found so habit-forming. Billy Callahan moved all the way up to the North End where most likely he would never run into Mildred. Which was a good thing.

# === Nine ===

IT GOES WITHOUT SAYING that your friends are usually the first to discuss your personal affairs behind your back, particularly in a town like Point Haven, where there was nothing better to talk about over a cup of coffee or a bottle of whiskey in the afternoon, especially if it was raining so hard you couldn't go directly to the source or snowing so bad it wasn't worth putting your boots and gloves on. Mildred's friends thought they had the up-to-the-minute scoop on her. The truth of the matter was, they really couldn't figure out where she got her ability to stay above water.

"Don't you think Mildred cusses too much in front of those kids?" Faye Love asked.

"Honey, she needs to watch more than her mouth, and not just in front of those kids," Willa drawled. "They repeat thangs and one day they gon' repeat the wrong thang and Mildred gon' get her feelings hurt bad."

Janey Pearl put in her two cents. "Chile, them kids gon' be all messed up, just like the rest of them sorry Peacocks, and if they amount to anything, it'll be a miracle before God."

"And since her and Crook split up, has she had enough men running in and out of her house? And husbands? Honey, her and Elizabeth Taylor is running a close race, don't y'all think so?" Bonita laughed. Then they all laughed.

92

"Speaking of houses, girl," Faye Love said, "that place she just moved into on Thirtieth Street should'a been condemned years ago. But then when you can't keep no man, what you supposed to do? That last boy she married done walked out on her. Mildred's behind probably dried up faster than she thought. Hell, she done had five kids, what she expect? And old pitiful-ass Rufus, he was innocent as a flea. Mildred just abused him. Made the man start hitting the bottle again. Rufus had been so mellow up till the time he married her."

"And Spooky is another story altogether." Bonita eyed Faye Love out the corner of her eye.

Most of the time these women were half drunk by the time they'd finished with one person's business for the day, and once in a while the word would get back to Mildred. And if she had one of her nerve pills in her and more than three beers, which she had grown accustomed to these days, Mildred would call up Faye Love, who she knew was the instigator. "These is my kids," she would say, "and this ain't half the shit they gon' see in this world, so they might as well find out from me now what's going on out there before some ignorant ass in the streets gives it to 'em wrong and then they'll really end up catching hell. I don't want my kids growing up all ass backward and stupid and ignorant like some of these ill-bred heathens running around in the streets. I ain't mentioning no names, you understand, but I don't have no stupid kids. They get As and Bs on they report cards. They clean, well-mannered, and they know how to thank for they damn self. I give 'em that much credit."

And everything Mildred said was true, which was what disturbed her friends most. Bonita Bell's son, B-Bunny, was in and out of the detention home. And just last week, he'd been caught stealing a vinyl jacket, some tennis shoes that didn't fit any of his six sisters and brothers, and ten packages of Kit-Kats from K-Mart. Faye Love's oldest daughter, who was the same age as Freda, had just had a baby and dropped out of the tenth grade. And two of Janey Pearl's three were in the "slow" class. But Mildred never said anything about their kids because, she figured, where the hell would it get her?

But they were right about the house on Thirtieth Street. It

*was* raggedy. Mildred knew it, and so did the kids. They were embarrassed by it. But they also knew she was doing the best she could since the time had run out in Baby Frank's house and the projects still weren't finished. Besides that, Mildred had to pay for the divorce. The kids told their friends the reason the front of the house was held up by two-by-fours was because they were getting the front porch remodeled. There *was* no front porch, and there would be no front porch, but since there were so many other things wrong *inside* the house, they defended the first thing a visitor would see.

When Prest-o-Lite laid her off, Mildred's attitude changed. She didn't even bother to look for another job. She went straight to the welfare office and applied without so much as a thought. Her nerves were as thin as tissue paper, and now she was tak- ing two yellow pills — ten milligrams — at a time instead of one because she couldn't feel one any more. Even when the lights got cut off, it didn't seem to faze her. "Fuck it, they gon' be off till I get my check. Here, boy," she said, handing Money two dollars, "go down to the A&P and get some candles. Steal 'em if you want to, I don't give a damn."

The kids worried about her but dismissed it as a phase Mildred was going through. To be on the safe side, they tried to do as much as they could to make things easier. They told her they could live without lights. Wasn't no big deal. Everybody had their lights and gas cut off at some point. They kept the house clean and stayed out of her way.

She was sitting at the dining room table when the insurance man drove up. Mildred had dodged him for the last four weeks. "Tell him I ain't home," she told Freda, and went to hide in the bedroom. Freda tried to lie with a straight face. "My mama ain't home, but she said come back next week and she'll pay you for the back premiums. She know how much she owe."

"But she said that last time, sweetheart."

"I ain't your sweetheart, and I said my mama ain't home, now come back next week or I'll sick that dog on you," she said, pointing to Prince. He was getting old, but he still growled when he heard the word "sick."

Freda had started babysitting for one of the Wigginses' daughters who now had two kids of her own. This was the same family she had planned to stay with when they were going to move to Arizona. She usually made anywhere from four to six dollars, which she would give to Mildred to buy food, except every now and then she'd put a dollar or two on a pair of $6.99 shoes or a Jonathan Logan double-knit dress downtown at Sperry's.

In the winter, Money shoveled snow to help out, and lots of times he'd come home long after dark with his hands almost frozen. In the fall, he raked leaves. He always brought home a can of pork-n-beans, some hot dogs, a loaf of white bread, cookies, and Kool-Aid. Whatever money was left over he gave to Mildred.

One day Mildred was silently watching Freda teach Money how to slow-dance. She suddenly got a startled look on her face. Both of them were taller than she was. These were her babies. Would always be her babies. Each time she entertained the thought that one day soon both of them would be adults, it felt like jolts of electricity passed through her. But right now all of her children needed her, she thought, would probably always need her for something. And Mildred didn't mind. At this point they seemed like the only ones in the world who did.

These days Mildred always wore a scarf around her head because her hair had started coming out in fluffy red balls on her pillow at night and she didn't want the kids to see it. When she stood in front of the mirror, she felt like a cactus whose growth had been stunted. Mildred felt dull and bent, and she was afraid. To avoid thinking about it, she took two pills. When she felt herself quivering and freezing in a room that was almost seventy-five degrees, she just thought she needed more rest and pulled the covers up over her.

Deadman had started coming back over again, and though Freda was severe with him, it appeared as though he had pushed that day completely out of his mind. Freda hadn't. She was still too afraid to tell anyone.

On this particular Saturday, Freda was babysitting for the Wigginses. At Mildred's request, Deadman brought over a fifth of VO. She had told him she hadn't had anything to drink in so

long she couldn't even remember. It had actually been yesterday, but Mildred had forgotten.

When the bottle was almost empty, she sent Deadman to the
store to get another one. They were both pretty near drunk, but
Deadman went anyway. When he returned, Mildred put on Dave
Brubeck. The needle slid across the whole record but she just
laughed.

"Take it easy, Milly, you ain't never gon' be able to play it
again if you don't be careful," Deadman said.

"Ah, shut up, you ugly varmint. What you know about
scratching old records?"

Deadman held the bottle up to his mouth and took a long
swallow. "I know a lot about scratching. Didn't Freda ever tell
you about it?"

"Tell me about what?"

"About the time when you was in Niagara Falls or wherever
the hell it was you went with that white man, and she pulled
her panties down and let me scratch her!" Deadman started
laughing hysterically and couldn't stop.

Mildred picked the needle up off the record. "What did you
say?" She was drunk, but she wasn't that drunk.

"You heard me, woman, your little hot-ass daughter gave me
the first shot at some sweet young stuff and it was good good
good good good. I'm not bullshitting you." Deadman didn't even
know what he was saying. Not only had he drunk almost an
entire fifth of VO but he had smoked one of those marijuana
sticks everybody had started smoking lately.

Mildred walked to the telephone and dialed Mary Wiggins's
number. It felt like her insides were grinding.

"Freda, this is your mama. I'm gon' ask you a simple question and I want a simple answer. And don't lie to your mama,
and don't be scared. What did Deadman do to you when I was
in Niagara Falls?"

There was silence on the other end of the phone.

"Answer me, goddammit!"

"He tried to choke me and he threw me down on the couch
because he was drunk and he tried to rape me but I didn't let
him do it, Mama, I swear. I was too scared to —"

Mildred slammed the phone down, walked back to her bedroom off the kitchen, and reached under her mattress for the .38. She made sure it was still loaded, marched back to the kitchen, pointed it at Deadman, and said, "Here, mother-fucker, scratch this!" And fired four shots at him. With each shot Mildred recoiled another foot, until she bashed into the window in the dining room. Deadman fell on top of the record player, scratching Dave Brubeck forever.

When Money walked through the side door five minutes later and saw Deadman lying in his own blood in the middle of the living room, still breathing but moaning with pain, and Mildred sitting in a chair as if she were in a daze, her elbow gashed open, he called the police and an ambulance. Money tried to get Mildred to tell him what had happened, but she just sat there — did not move, did not blink an eyelid — and simply said, "Get him out of here before I kill him."

When it was learned that Deadman would be okay, that only two of the bullets had actually hit him, one in his groin and one in his side, they released Mildred from jail. She had told them that Deadman had tried to rape her and she'd shot him in self-defense. They believed her, but Deadman denied it, so they let him go free too. As soon as Mildred got home, she called up Minnie, his mama, and told her that if she ever saw Deadman walking the streets of Point Haven as long as she lived there, so help her God, she would put another .38 bullet so deep in his ass that it would be the last step he'd ever take. The next day, Minnie put Deadman on a bus to Alabama.

Crook got sick again and was back in the hospital. This time it wasn't more tuberculosis. It was diabetes. His brother, Zeke, had stopped by to tell Mildred and the kids. "He just got a touch of sugar, ain't nothing to worry about. All he gotta do is change his diet and take it easy. They got him taking sugar pills in-stead of them shots, but he should be all right in about a month. Send the kids over to see him. Make him feel better, 'cause he don't see 'em much, you know."

The kids didn't want to go near the house because of Ernes-tine, but Mildred made them go the same day he got home. Crook was asleep, wound up in a pile of blankets, like he was being prepared for a burial, and his face was a pale peach color.

Money walked over and shook him. "Hi, Daddy," he said.

Crook opened his eyes. They looked like old scratched marbles. He tried to crack a smile when he saw all five of them standing around his bed like surgeons. They had brought him a carton of Pall Malls, some juice, and a new white shirt.

"How's Daddy's little Indians?" Crook asked, trying to sit up.

"We fine, but what's wrong with you this time, Daddy?" Doll asked. "You got some more TB in you?"

"No, your daddy just got a little sugar in his blood. I gotta start eating like the doctor tell me, but I'll be okay." They stared at him, and the look on their faces told him they knew he was lying. To Crook it felt like they were closing in on him, standing around his bed like this, and he had to ask them to step back. Said he couldn't breathe too good.

The kids told him how well they were doing in school. All of them except Money were on the honor roll and Freda was going into the eleventh grade now, and taking driver's education.

"How's your mama?" Crook asked.

"She fine. She say she hope you gon' get better and stop acting like a fool and leave that liquor alone," Bootsey said. Even though Bootsey was thirteen, she still didn't know what the word tact meant.

After a long silence it was obvious that everybody had run out of things to say. They kissed their daddy on his cheeks and forehead and said goodbye, moving past Ernestine as she stumbled through the front door like she was diseased herself.

By the time they got home, it was thundering and lightning. As usual, the house was leaking. Money collected every bucket, every boiler, roaster, jar, and pitcher, and scattered them around the house to catch the splattering drops of water.

"Turn off those lights," Mildred said, "and be quiet till this pass." It was always like this when she was home and there was a storm. Even though Mildred wasn't a religious person, she took what her daddy had said about God doing his work to heart. The kids couldn't figure out why everything electrical had to be unplugged before he could finish his work. Didn't he like a little light too? Besides, they didn't know of anybody who had ever been struck by lightning except Deadman, which was how he had gotten his name. He had told everybody in town that he'd been struck, died, and come back to life. The silence in the house only made everything that much spookier, and, as usual, Mildred sat there sipping a beer.

"How's your daddy?"

"He's all right," Bootsey said. "He say he ain't dranking no more."

"He lying. He still dranking. That sugar'll eat him up if he don't stop. And I want y'all to go see him more often, you understand me? All he got is old sorry-ass Ernestine over there, and Lord knows she ain't no real help to him. Every single time I've seen him, he look lost, and I thank he needs to see y'all more often. I don't care about your cheerleading practice, Freda, or any of y'all little after-school activities. He's you daddy, gon' always be your daddy, no matter what he's done or ain't done and I want you to go see him before something happen to him. You understand me?" Mildred's voice had gotten loud in spite of herself.

"Yes, Mama," they said, and sat silently in the dark until the storm passed.

Freda had made up her mind by now that if something terrible ever happened to her daddy or mama before it happened to her, she wasn't going to the funeral. When she tried to explain her reasoning to Mildred, she didn't seem at all interested. Mildred had just heard it through the grapevine that they were hiring again down at Ford's, and she was trying to figure out which day she could get a ride to Utica to fill out an application. The Mercury had conked out and was sitting on stilts in the driveway. She was not in the mood to be be thinking about dying and funerals, especially her own. Mildred was thinking about work and money.

"I mean it, Mama. I ain't going to your funerals," Freda persisted, " 'cause I don't think I could take it, and I just want you to know it now."

"If you don't get out of my face talking crazy, girl, I'ma smack you clear across the other side of this room. I got a million thangs on my mind."

But Freda had given it quite a bit of thought. When Mildred had shot Deadman, Freda was afraid her mama was going to prison or something awful like that. The thought of her mama's absence had caused Freda to think about death, something she had never really thought about before. It sent chills up and down her whole body. What would she do without her mama? And all winter long, when Freda couldn't sleep because it was so cold upstairs in that attic bedroom, where she and Bootsey had to put the small electric heater on a chair not more than six inches away from the bed and it still didn't do much good, Freda would stare at the crystal formations on the inside of the window and listen to her own thoughts. She had made some decisions and come to several conclusions. She was not going to her mama's or daddy's funeral. She hated this raggedy house, hated this boring-ass town, and when she graduated from high school in two years, she was getting the hell out of here.

Mildred got put on the waiting list at Ford's, and she was so excited that she spent her entire welfare check in anticipation of starting any day now. After a week of waiting by the telephone, she lost her patience and called them. They told her it might be as long as three months before she would get called. Then Mildred started acting even funnier than she had been right before she shot Deadman.

Freda had gotten her first real job, shelving books at the public library for $1.25 an hour. Mildred seemed very excited and proud about it when Freda had told her. That was two weeks ago. This evening, Freda walked in the kitchen door about six-thirty and Mildred was furious.

"Where the hell have you been, Miss Fast Ass?"

Freda looked at Mildred, stunned. She had posted her hours right over the sink last week like Mildred had told her to.

"I was at work, Mama, you know that."

"And since when did you start working? You thank you grown or something?"

"I work at the library, Mama. You don't remember?" Mildred looked at the wall, like she was searching for something, and then it came to her. "Oh, oh oh, I'm sorry, baby. Now I remember. You put up books or something, don't you?"

"Yes, Mama. I put up books."

As the weeks passed Mildred got worse. She wouldn't let the girls wash dishes any more and insisted on doing them herself. Mildred hadn't washed dishes since Freda was nine years old, and that was seven years ago. She would stand, sometimes for minutes, rubbing a single plate and instead of reaching to put it in the dishrack, would throw it on the floor. The kids were scared, but then Mildred would apologize for doing it and start crying. "I can't do nothing right, can I?"

She kept trying to cook, too. Things that none of the kids could even think about eating. She would pour five and six tablespoons of salt and black pepper into a pot of beans, sometimes in addition to a cup of sugar, then taste it, approving of its flavor, and make the kids eat it. They became frightened for her. But the next day Mildred would wake up acting like her normal spunky self again.

It got to the point that she would get excited about something and the next thing you knew she had shut herself in her bedroom and would scream if you so much as called her name. She had even started selling some of her nerve pills to her hairdresser for fifty cents apiece.

When the last welfare check had come, Mildred had taken thirty dollars of the grocery money and bought two horses — a small pony and its colt — that someone who had a small barn had to get rid of. She had come walking down the paved street with these two miniature animals on a leash like they were dogs. The kids couldn't believe it.

"Mama, where you get these horses from?" Money asked.

"Don't worry about it. I got a good deal on these suckers, and besides, it'll give y'all something to do so you can stay out of my hair."

None of them knew anything about taking care of horses, let alone figuring out where the hell to put them, so Mildred kept them in the garage, where a week later they both froze to death and had to be hauled away on a crane. This cost another forty dollars. But Mildred hadn't remembered buying any horses when Freda told her what happened. She looked at Freda like she was crazy.

This morning Mildred woke up cranky and ordered Freda to

bring her a cup of coffee. "And get me two of my pills — no, three — they in the windowsill."

"Mama, you been taking too many of these pills lately, don't you think? And why you still taking 'em anyway?"

"You sure do ask a hell of a lot of questions for somebody who ain't even started her damn period yet — or have you? They for my nerves. N-e-r-v-e-s. How many times am I gon' have to tell you that, every fifteen minutes?" Mildred's voice was high and with each word the tone got higher and louder.

"Are you okay, Mama? You want me to call Granddaddy Buster?"

"Naw. Don't go calling my daddy over here," she said. Now her voice sounded like a tired scream. The anger in it had vanished and so had the hostility. "Get out of here, would you, and leave me alone."

"We're gon' clean up the whole house today, Mama, wood-works and windows, everything."

"Fuck this house, this raggedy-ass hellhole. I don't care if it burns to the ground. And I hope each and every one of you little brats are sitting in here when it does. You know what? I'm so sick of looking at you kids I don't know what to do. Did you know that? The biggest mistake I ever made in my life was having y'all little bastards. Now get out of my face!"

Freda had been sitting on Mildred's bed and she lowered her head so Mildred wouldn't see her tears. "Holler if you need something, Mama," she said as she got up to leave. Maybe if her mama got some rest she would be all right.

Freda decided to clean the house herself and sent the kids outside to play. It would give her a chance to think. She put on a Nancy Wilson LP to keep her company, and when that one finished, she wiped the perspiration from her forehead and put on Sarah Vaughan. For the entire afternoon Freda swept and mopped and washed and waxed and even put on a pot of pinto beans. When the house was as close to spotless as she could get it and the beans were thick and soft, Freda began to stir up a bowl of corn bread, but she couldn't remember how much baking powder to put in it. And since there were no cookbooks in the house, she went to ask Mildred.

To get to Mildred's room from the kitchen she had to go through two doors. The first one led down three steps to a cement landing, where to the right was the hatch that led to the basement and to the left was Mildred's bedroom door. Her room had been an addition to the house and had never been quite finished. There was still no insulation, and in the wintertime, it was a toss-up as to whose room got the coldest, Freda's and Bootsey's or Mildred's.

Freda opened the first door and stopped. Mildred was talking to someone. Freda listened for the other voice, but there was no other voice. Only Mildred's. She walked up to her mama's door and put her ear against it and she knew right then that something strange was happening to her mama.

"Crook, don't hurt me, please I promise, I'ma be good. I'ma be good." Mildred's voice came through the door clearly. "And Mama, stop staring at me. Why don't you stop pulling my hair? Can't I go outside, Mama, please? I'll be a good girl, Mama, please? Lord have mercy. Babies. Here come another one. Whoops. Somebody, hold me, please hold me, here come another one!"

Freda burst the door open and saw her mama hanging over the side of the bed, shivering.

"Where's my daddy?" Mildred squealed. Her face looked mutilated, distorted.

"Who you talking to, Mama?" Freda asked. She saw that no one else was there. This was crazy. Mildred looked directly into Freda's eyes and started talking gibberish. Then Mildred started laughing and asking Freda questions about people she had never heard of.

"Mama!" Freda screamed. "What are you talking about? What's wrong? You want me to get you another pill? You want a pill?"

"Pill?" Mildred yelled, and then started laughing again. Freda suddenly smelled something foul. When she looked at Mildred closer, she saw that her nightgown was soiled from the waist down.

Mildred covered her mouth and said, "Oh, I made poo poo." She lifted the gown up, looked at it, and started laughing again.

Freda didn't know what to do. This had to be a nightmare because this couldn't possibly be happening to her mama. She ran to the telephone and called Buster.

"Granddaddy, you gotta come quick. Something is wrong with Mama. She's talking crazy, she messed on herself and she's mad one minute and laughing the next. Then she start crying. She talking about Grandmama Sadie and cussing out people she hate. Granddaddy! Now she's screaming! What's wrong with her? Please come over here, I'm scared." Buster told Freda to stay with Mildred and keep her warm and not to move her. Not even out of that mess.

Carefully and slowly, Freda walked back into Mildred's room. This time she was afraid of what she might find. But Mildred was just lying there staring up at the ceiling, in a daze. In spite of Buster's orders, Freda filled a bucket with warm soapy water and pulled the soiled sheet from under Mildred. Then she lifted her mama up like a babydoll. "Come on, Mama, sit up. That's a girl." Mildred seemed immobilized and didn't resist or say anything. Freda took her nightgown off and Mildred looked so pitiful and babyish that Freda continued to talk to her like she was a child. "It's okay, Mama. Everything is gon' be all right." Freda bathed her carefully, staring at her mama's thick brown flesh, noticing all the stretch marks. Then she rolled Mildred over from one side of the bed to the other so she could put on clean sheets. Freda put a bathrobe on her, and pulled the blankets up to Mildred's chin.

"Is my daddy coming?" Mildred asked. "Maybe he'll buy me something new. Ain't had nothing new in a long long time, have I? My daddy loves me, did you know that, Acquilla?"

By the time Buster got there, Freda was exhausted. She hugged him, then took his hand and led him to Mildred's room.

"It's all right, Milly. Daddy's here," Buster said, as he walked over to the bed and took her hands. Mildred started crying quietly, and he took her in his arms and hugged and rocked her until she fell asleep. Freda watched them from the doorway. She was trying to remember how many times her mama or daddy had ever hugged her that way. She couldn't remember once.

Instead of taking Mildred to the hospital, like Freda thought he would, Buster took her to his house. Miss Acquilla wasn't thrilled about the idea of babysitting for a grown woman, as she put it, but she didn't want to see Mildred all messed up like this. Buster told Freda this was her chance to prove that she was a big girl. She had to take care of the house and watch the kids until Mildred felt better. "All your mama need is a little rest, baby. Some time to get hold of herself. Put her mind back in order."

It took Mildred three weeks.

# Ten

FREDA WAS ROLLING OUT DOUGH to make cinnamon rolls when she heard a light tapping at the door.

"Money, answer that, would you? I got flour all over my hands," she yelled. Freda had been the mama of the house for these three weeks and had almost done a better job of it than Mildred. She had paid a few bills on time, had forged Mildred's signature on her welfare check at the A&P, and had managed to keep the refrigerator relatively full. She had played hooky from school a couple of days. She told the principal her mother was bedridden and needed her help at home. The other kids hadn't said a word to anybody about what had happened to Mildred.

Freda had made them comply with every single one of her demands. As soon as they came in from school they had to clean up around the house and then do their homework. She even checked it to make sure they'd done it right. She made them brush their teeth before they went to bed at ten o'clock, which was much earlier than they'd been used to, and made them eat a hot breakfast.

They had called over to Granddaddy Buster's to see how Mildred was doing, but she was always asleep. The truth was, she didn't feel like talking. What could she say? Buster had told them to wait until she was ready to come home.

Money pulled the curtains back to see who it was.

"Open this door, boy. It's cold as hell out here," Mildred said in her usual commanding voice.

At first Money was kind of nervous. But Mildred whisked past him, dropped her suitcase on the floor in the dining room, and said, "I hope y'all had enough sense to buy some real food, 'cause I'm starving. Acquilla still can't cook worth a damn. And whoo, did that woman get on my nerves," and Money knew she was back to normal.

The girls were in the living room watching TV when Mildred marched in like a drill sergeant. To their surprise, she looked rather pleased about everything. She had lost some weight, and her eyes looked brighter. And for the first few days, Mildred went out of her way to prove she was her old self again. She started out by being extra nice, which made the kids a little leery. They weren't used to her being so kind. Mildred didn't holler at them at all. Even when she caught Bootsey kissing that boy on the corner, she just told her to step on it and come on inside 'cause it was getting kinda late. Angel dropped a whole carton of eggs on the floor and Mildred almost broke her neck on them, but she still didn't shout. The kids didn't know what to think when they got up Saturday morning and Mildred had starched and ironed all their dirty clothes. That was Freda's job.

So since Mildred went out of her way to be accommodating, the kids reciprocated. They didn't know how long this was going to last but they wanted to drag it out as long as possible. Mildred could barely get their names out of her mouth before they were giving her things she hadn't even asked for — pillows to prop her back up, house shoes when she first woke up in the morning, a cup of hot coffee waiting for her when she came out of the bathroom, and a Tareyton already burning in the ashtray.

Before the month was out, though, Mildred was cussing and hollering at them again. The kids felt relieved. They never thought they'd see the day when they'd be glad to hear that tone in her voice again.

It was a hot, clear summer day. Money had just finished cutting the grass and the air smelled sweet. Mildred's rose bushes were in full bloom and the sprinkler was swerving back and forth like a moving harp. Mildred and Freda were sitting in brand new lawn chairs she'd bought with the fifth check she had cleared from Ford's. They were eating cheese and crackers and drinking iced tea. Every now and then a car would pass by and Mildred would wave. Freda had been waiting for the right moment, and now was as good a time as any.

"You know," Freda began, then she sighed. Her eyes became transfixed by the water swishing back and forth in front of her. It looked like a string of rainbows.

"What, baby?" Mildred asked.

"I've been thinking."

"I hope so," Mildred said, fanning a fly away from her glass.

"When I graduate next June, I want to leave Point Haven."

Here we go again with this mess, Mildred thought. "I don't blame you. If I could get away from here, I'd be out of here faster than you could say boo."

"I'm serious, Mama."

"Where you think you gon' go?"

"I really only have one choice. California. Phyllis lives in Los Angeles. I was thinking of writing and asking if I could stay with her till I find a job. After all, she is my cousin."

"A job?"

"I'm still going to college, don't worry."

"I know damn well you going to college. But what about that scholarship you supposed to be winning?"

"I haven't won it yet, Mama, and besides, I won't even know until sometime next spring. What if I don't get it?"

"You'll get it."

"I got Phyllis's address last week from Lucille."

"You got this already planned, huh? Don't make no difference what I say, then, do it?"

"Mama, I'm tired of this town. It's so boring. Ain't no place to go, and there's nothing to do. I don't want to spend the rest of my life here. I wanna go someplace different. Someplace that's at least interesting, and where everybody don't know all your business."

"Look. I want you to see the world, girl. But you ain't but seventeen."

"I know, I know, but I know how to take care of myself."

"Now don't get me wrong. I don't want none of y'all to end up like me with a house full of babies and then can't go nowhere. That's the honest to God's truth. You *should* meet all kinds of people and see this world."

"So you understand, Mama?"

Mildred took a long sip of her iced tea and then lit a cigarette. She blew smoke up toward the sky. "I guess. Hell, this town ain't going nowhere, and besides, if you don't like it, you can always come back home."

"Want to know something else?"

"What else, girl?"

"When I do finish college, I'ma do something that's gon' make me rich, maybe even famous."

"Like what?"

"I don't know, I got time to figure it out. But you know what I'm gon' do then?"

"Naw, what?" Mildred asked. This chile got some imagination, she thought. Living in a dream world. Rich and famous. But she young, she'll see how hard dreams is to catch.

"I'ma send you on a cruise to one of those islands with palm trees, where they say the water is so clear you can see the bottom. You ain't never had no real vacation, Mama, and the one to Niagara Falls with Spooky don't count in my book. I figure you've done a lot for us and you been through a lot."

Mildred got up to bend the hose back to block the flow of water and pulled the sprinkler over to dry grass.

"Mama, did you hear me?"

"Yeah, I heard you. I heard you," Mildred said, heading for the house. "Sounds good to me."

"And I want to buy you a real house so y'all can get out of this dump. I believe in keeping promises, you know. You believe me, Mama?"

"Yeah, chile, I believe you, I believe you."

Everybody except Freda was home when the phone call came from Money. She was out on Michigan Road at Rene Armstrong's house watching "American Bandstand" and making a dress that Mrs. Armstrong was helping her with. Ruffles and pleats. "Your brother's on the phone," Mrs. Armstrong called down from upstairs. Fletcher Armstrong had just left to open up the Red Shingle.

"Tell him I'll call him right back," Freda yelled back. The needle was piercing the fabric and The Temptations were about to come on. She knew they were going to sing "I Wish It Would Rain," and Freda didn't want to miss them. Besides, every time she came out here somebody from home always had to call and bug her about something stupid. She loved coming over to Rene's. Her house was so pretty. Everything was so modern and brand new. It had three levels and Rene even had her own room. The two of them had spent many a Saturday afternoon lying on Rene's canopied bed, sometimes for hours, smoking cigarettes, and trying to come up with the best plan for getting dates with college boys.

"He said it's important," Mrs. Armstrong yelled again.

Freda pushed her foot down hard on the pressure foot until she came to the end of the seam. The Temptations strutted out in front of a sparkling blue curtain, and Freda bit her tongue, she was so mad. She sucked away the salty taste in her mouth and ran up the steps to the kitchen, two at a time.

"What you want?" she said into the phone. "You better make it quick and it better be important, that's all I gotta say."

"Daddy's dead."

"Don't joke around, Money."

"Prince is dead, too."

"I ain't laughing, Money."

"And I ain't joking, either. Daddy just died in Mercy Hospital and we found Prince across the street in the woods, and . . ."

Freda hung up the phone and slid off the kitchen stool. Everything got quiet and still. But her heart was pounding so loud she could hear it. Her ears started ringing. Dead? She looked out through the sliding glass doors that led out to a cement patio and past the back yard to an open, empty field. Her elbow accidently pushed a place mat from the counter and it fell to the floor with a loud clap. Freda bent down slowly to pick it up, but she couldn't move her fingers. She walked back downstairs.

Rene looked up, snapped her fingers and popping her gum. "Is something wrong, Freda?"

"My daddy just died," Freda said, hearing it as if for the first time. Rene turned down the TV, but in the background Freda could hear The Temptations singing.

"My daddy just died!" she said, louder. Every muscle in her body seemed to melt. She'd never even thought about what death would feel like. Had never lost anybody before. So what if he hadn't been around all that much. He was still her daddy. And she'd just gotten used to seeing him again. He looked like he was getting better. Why didn't he just do what the doctors told him? All he had to do was quit drinking. Give up sweets. Why'd he have to be so stupid? So stubborn. Dead? This isn't fair, Freda thought. He was only forty years old.

On the drive home, Mrs. Armstrong tried to console her, but Freda was too overwhelmed by this new feeling called grief. She was trying to remember everything she could about her father, but the only thing that came to her mind was the time he was teaching her about the birds and the bees. "Keep your dress down and your legs closed," Crook had said, "and you'll make it through high school."

Mildred was saddened by the news but not surprised. She had known it would happen ever since that storm. A coolness had swept through her mind when she had thought about Crook, and that was why she had made the kids go see him every week. She knew this was going to be his last shot at life, and Mildred's instincts were rarely wrong. It just pissed her off that Crook had turned out to be such a damn fool and had finally lived up to the Peacock legend. If only I could turn the clock back, make this shit right, she thought. But I can't. Can't do nothing but remember the way I loved him. And I loved him. Yes I did.

When she was sixteen, Mildred had gone to the dock to take a boat ride up Black River. Crook had followed her when she got off the bus by herself. He stood on the corner for fifteen minutes, biting his fingernails and watching her say hello to the other kids waiting by the railing, and then he made his move.

"Hi there, gal. Going someplace special, or you waiting here to meet somebody?"

"Nope, I'm just going on the boat ride. Ain't meeting nobody except if one of my cousins shows up. You going?"

"Was thinking about it seriously, but don't exactly have nobody to go with. Could use some company. Be happy to buy your ticket if you don't have one already. You won't have to worry about pop and potato chips. I can get all that for you, plus anything else you want, so long as it don't run over three dollars." Crook winked at Mildred and gave her his best grin, showing as many of his white teeth as possible.

Mildred thought Crook was especially handsome. She'd seen him play baseball and knew he was a Peacock, but he wasn't acting like a heathen. What the heck, she thought, folks was gon' talk anyway, might as well give 'em something to talk about.

Within a few short months, their smiles had grown deeper than what was visible on their faces and they couldn't hide how they felt. Started holding hands like they were glued together, sat on the front steps of deserted schools at night, on rotted tree stumps in back yards of condemned houses, on the bleachers of dark baseball fields, hugging, smooching, feeling each other's texture, body heat, heart beat, and professing their love the only way they knew how. And when Mildred realized she was carrying Crook's baby, there was no question about what to do, and they got married, as they would have anyway.

Now, as Mildred watched a raccoon scurry under the shed in the back yard, she realized that she hadn't stopped caring for Crook just because she'd divorced him. She slid her feet into a pair of furry slippers. "Shit," she said, and flopped back down on the mattress.

On the day of the funeral, Mildred sent Money to the store to get her some stockings, but he brought back a pair that were far too light, so Mildred boiled them in black coffee until they matched the color of her legs. She let them dry and was putting them on in the bathroom when Freda walked past and Mildred noticed that she still hadn't gotten dressed.

"What's taking you so long to get your clothes on?"

"I told you I wasn't going, Mama. Don't you remember?"

"If you ain't dressed in five minutes I'ma slap the taste out of your mouth," she said, and slammed the bathroom door in Freda's face. Mildred stood in front of the mirror, rubbing a sponge powder puff over her wet cheeks. "She ain't going," she grumbled to herself. "Humph." She put some drops in her eyes and blotted her peach lips, then she tucked the bottom one in as far as she could.

Even though it was almost ninety degrees, Freda wore an orange wool dress and matching jacket to the funeral. She wouldn't change into something cooler, even after Mildred had warned her. "Burn up, then. I don't care." Freda walked all the way to the church by herself instead of riding in the black car with everybody else. She did not know which route she had taken, but by the time she got there, she had removed her jacket and sweat was running down her temples. She was so hot she felt faint.

She sat in the second row next to Mildred. Ernestine was sitting near the end of the same row. She looked sober and miserable. Lost. Crook was her everything. And the church was packed. There were people there who didn't even know Crook. Sometimes folks went to funerals because it was an event, an excuse to get out of the house and mourn for somebody else for a change.

Mildred didn't even hear the organ, playing "Nearer My God to Thee," or the eulogy. She was too busy thinking about the knot she'd made on Crook's forehead when she had hit him with that cast-iron skillet almost eight years ago. Should'a kept your hands offa me, she thought, wiping the tears from her face. The choir was humming something. Mildred fanned herself because all those flowers were making her nauseated. Mrs. Buckles sang her solo and then it came time to walk up and view Crook's body. Freda couldn't look at him. Neither could Mildred. They squeezed each other's hands so tight that the blood froze.

Just about everybody in town, including Mildred, got laid off at Ford's. Faye Love and Curly Mae tried to convince Mildred to go ahead and move into the projects. It would mean a brand new kitchen and a free washer and dryer. No more mice and roaches. Free heat and electricity. An upstairs and downstairs, tiled floors, a small front yard, and a playground, which Mildred didn't really need anymore. Besides, she didn't like the idea of living so damn close to folks that they could probably hear her whispering or farting in the middle of the night. "Didn't take 'em but a minute to put one up and if a hard wind blow, you mark my words, see if those makeshift rooms don't collapse. This ain't Arizona, this is Michigan."

So even though half of her friends and relatives had moved into pink, blue, and yellow houses, Mildred stayed in her dingy white house on Thirtieth Street, promising herself that with time and luck and a little money, she could still fix this place up, despite the fact that the two-by-fours on the would-be front porch had started to develop dry rot.

During her senior year, Freda had saved close to three hundred dollars, working part time as a keypunch operator at the phone company. Phyllis had told her she was more than welcome to come stay with her and she had made Los Angeles sound so exciting that Freda couldn't wait to go. She had made her reservations to fly out there on August 14.

Mildred tried to act enthusiastic about it, but she wasn't. She still didn't want to believe that Freda was really serious about leaving. But right before graduation, Freda told Mildred she had turned down the scholarship so someone else could use it. Mildred sat through the entire ceremony fuming. She had already told her friends that her daughter was winning a scholarship. Now she felt like a damn fool. Freda had some nerve, she thought. And for the rest of the summer the other kids became go-betweens. Whenever Mildred had something to say to Freda, she told them first and made them repeat it to her. Freda thought this was childish, but went along with it. Hell, this was her life, and she had a right to turn down a scholarship to a rinky-dink college and go on about her business.

And Mildred still hadn't said a word to her by the time they were walking to the gate at Detroit Metropolitan Airport. Naturally, Freda was hurt, but two could play this stupid game, she thought. She handed Mildred a piece of paper with her new address and phone number on it, and bent down to kiss her. But Mildred turned her head so all she got was a stiff peck on the cheek. She said goodbye so low that Freda didn't even hear her. She picked up the pink luggage Mildred had bought her as a graduation present and just looked at her. This felt worse than when her daddy had died.

Buster had been standing there, waiting for Mildred to put her arms around her daughter, but when he saw Mildred step back instead of closer, he went ahead and hugged and kissed Freda himself. "You be careful and don't try to grow up too fast," he said. Freda promised him she would and she wouldn't.

"Bye, Mama," she said, and turned and disappeared down the red-carpeted corridor that led to the plane.

"Come on, let's go, Milly," Buster said. "We parked illegally, you know."

But Mildred couldn't move. Even when he nudged her and pulled her by the arm, she didn't budge. She just stood there, staring at that red carpet for so long that it became a pink blur. And if you had asked Mildred her name, she couldn't have told you. The only thing she did know was that her first baby was gone.

It was hard to get used to Freda not being there, and for the first few weeks, Mildred kept calling the other girls Freda. She had also phoned Freda to apologize.

"I acted worse than y'all kids do," she said, almost biting her tongue. Mildred hated to admit she was wrong, but even harder was being honest about her feelings.

"Mama, I know you were just disappointed, and I'm glad you called. So now can we be friends again?"

"Yeah, we can be friends," she said. Now Mildred was disappointed by the tone of Freda's voice. She didn't hardly sound like she was ready to come home yet. Freda had already found a job, working as some secretary at a big insurance company and making ninety dollars a week!

As a matter of fact, Freda was enjoying herself immensely. She had never had this much fun in her life. She was going to nightclubs, pool parties, and barbecues where the meat was cooked on hibachis instead of oil drums. She went to rock and roll concerts, and for the first time in her life went on real dates. She took herself out to dinner in restaurants where she had to leave tips. And she practically lived at the beach; had four different bathing suits. She took her pick of movies, at least one a week, and saw her first foreign film and was very pleased because she kept up with the subtitles.

In every letter Freda wrote home, she told Mildred about something new she had discovered. "I learned how to pluck my eyebrows and put on makeup. I enrolled in this modeling school because all the girls at work said I look like I could be a model." She'd spent $750 before she realized she was too short to be a high-fashion model and besides that, she wasn't very photogenic and the camera added ten pounds they insisted she shed from her already thin frame. The most important discovery Freda had made was having her first orgasm, which she didn't bother mentioning in her letters.

At first her cousin Phyllis impressed her. She had a wall full of books, mostly about socialism, communism, and black power. She'd been a claims adjuster for seven years at the same insurance company where Freda worked, and was hoping to make supervisor. Phyllis was also ten years older than Freda and wore an Afro that crowned her head like an eight-inch halo. She wore thick glasses and could've been pretty if she had ever smiled. The first thing Phyllis did was make Freda stop using those awful words, "colored" and "nigger," when she referred to black people, which was kind of hard to do since Freda had been saying them all these years. Then she made Freda throw her straightening comb away. "If you want to stay in my house, you ain't gon' be looking like no white woman." Phyllis had thought the whole idea of going to modeling school was ridiculous, not to mention exploitive, and once Freda realized she wasn't going to make any money at it, she quit.

Phyllis also made her feel stupid. "Girl, you can't sit here and tell me you didn't know who Malcolm X was?" she said in amazement one night at dinner. And when Freda said no, Phyllis laughed so hard, she spit out part of her hamburger. It got to the point where Phyllis wouldn't even let Freda watch "McHale's Navy" or "Outer Limits" or "Bewitched," made her sit through documentaries about wild life and everything about Africa, and Phyllis just *had* to commentate the news, which Freda found boring as hell. She had no idea what was going on in the world, and at that time didn't want to know. After three months of living in that two-room apartment, bumping into Phyllis every time she went to the bathroom, and pretending that she liked her, Freda finally decided she'd had it when Phyllis called her a whore because she was spending so many nights out.

She found a studio apartment right down the street and was proud to write Mildred a letter using her very own return address. The first thing Freda did was buy herself a twelve-inch black and white TV and watch everything she wanted to, when she wanted to. The second thing she bought was a brand new straightening comb.

By January, she had enrolled in the community college across the street from where she lived. She went four nights a week. She took an Afro-American history class because Phyllis had made her feel so ignorant about black people. She took sociology because the catalogue had said it would help her to understand social relationships and group behavior. Well, it sounded interesting. She took an English class because she had to if she wanted a degree, and she took a philosophy course because Phyllis had gone on and on about this guy Nietzsche. She was tired of being in the dark about everything. Now she had an ocean of knowledge at her disposal, and it was all within walking distance.

Freda had been living in Los Angeles a whole year before she decided to go back home for a visit. She had deliberately stayed away that long to prove she could make it on her own, though Mildred had never had any doubts about that. Even on Freda's small salary, she'd still managed to send each of them birthday presents.

Mildred went out of her way to make sure everything in the house was clean and cozy. There were new curtains and ashtrays and glasses and towels. Even brand new throw rugs and new sheets and pillow cases on her own bed, where she was going to insist that Freda sleep, instead of upstairs. Mildred didn't want to tell Freda that there were bats up there now. And she hoped Freda wouldn't ask her why the phone was cut off.

Mildred barely recognized her own daughter when Freda stepped off the plane, what with her dark chestnut hair all sunbleached. And Freda had plenty of extra hair with her, too — a cascade, a mound of curls that looked like someone had just taken the rollers out and sprayed them in place. Her skin, which had always been the color of wheat, was now bronzed. Freda had worked hard to get dark after learning that black was definitely in. Mildred didn't like her color one bit and made sure she knew it.

"You need to stay out of that hot-ass sun. You gon' be as black as Joe Porter if you keep it up."

"Mama, there's nothing wrong with being black. We've been made to believe that being yellow makes us more attractive, but it doesn't. It just makes us look more like whitey, so we feel privileged, but we get treated the same as if we were as black as charcoal. Besides, it's beautiful."

"Yeah, well you was born yellow and you gon' die yellow. You laying out in the sun like you white, and just wait till your ass catch skin cancer. You'll wish you had'a listened to me then."

It was amazing to Freda what could happen to a girl's body in just a year's time. Her sisters had blossomed into young women. Bootsey was sixteen, and not only built full like Mildred, she was the spitting image of her too. Her skin was as smooth as creamy peanut butter and her hair was dusty brown. Before Freda could get comfortable, Bootsey had already told her all about her boyfriend, David, who was six years older than she was. Mildred had told Freda she wasn't crazy about the whole idea, but since he worked at Ford's, she knew his mama was in the church, and David always slipped her a twenty when she needed it and kept the refrigerator stocked with ice-cold Budweisers, she said she'd adjusted to him. To tell the truth, Mildred didn't know what the girl saw in him. He had big lips and wasn't much taller than Bootsey, and on top of everything else, he was chubby. Bootsey wasn't satisfied until she had taken one of Freda's suitcases upstairs and tried on some of her California clothes. When she tried on her bikini, Freda noticed a big bruise on her behind. "What's that mark on your butt?" she asked her. Bootsey started laughing. "You ain't never done it on the floor?" Freda was shocked, but said, "Of course I have," even though she had never done it anywhere other than a bed.

And Angel was so feminine it was sickening. She seemed to float when she walked and she whispered when she talked. You never knew what the girl was thinking because she was so quiet and kept to herself. But Freda knew that when Angel got mad or couldn't have things her own way, she could be a real bitch.

Doll was another story altogether. When it came to common sense, Freda had always thought the girl had been left out. She used to have to explain everything to Doll twice, and sometimes Doll still didn't get it. Now, one thing was for sure. Doll was turning out to be the prettiest of them all, just like everybody said she would. She already had hips and little cherrytomato breasts and had stopped wearing those awful cat eyed glasses. And it looked like her eyes had finally straightened themselves out.

Mildred was deeply impressed with Freda, listening to how well she expressed herself, enunciating every word like she had some sense. And she looked so sophisticated, with all those fashionable clothes. Mildred took the credit for teaching her daughter the rudiments of good taste. She had bragged to everybody in South Park about Freda. "Well, you know my oldest is in college. Yeah, she living out in LA. She done met movie stars, Little Stevie Wonder, everybody, chile." Told Faye Love that Freda was studying to be an English teacher. Told Janey Pearl she was learning how to be a sociologist, though neither of them knew what it was. Didn't much matter, it sounded important. And Mildred told her hairdresser Freda was going to be a model, maybe even do commercials on TV.

When Freda had put away all her bags, Mildred made the girls circle around in front of the couch so she could take their picture. Freda felt like a celebrity. Mildred thought to herself that she had raised a stock of fine young ladies, seeing them all together like this.

"Where's Money?" Freda finally asked. Everybody bowed their heads and acted like they were trying to ignore the question.

"You hungry, Freda?" Mildred asked, fidgeting with the flash cubes.

"No, I'm not hungry. Where's Money?"

"Freda, did you make this, too? It's so pretty," Angel said, touching her blouse.

"Come on, you guys. Stop bullshitting. Where's my brother?"

"In jail," Mildred said, in a tone so low it was barely audible.

"Did you say jail?"

"Yeah, I said jail," Mildred said, only much louder this time.

"What the hell is he doing in jail?"

"Watch your mouth, girl. You may be on your own, but you ain't grown yet. Stealing."

"Stealing! Stealing what?"

"A lawn mower."

"A lawn mower? Why the hell did he steal a lawn mower and from whom?"

"He use dope, Freda, and don't ask me why. I've been trying to figure it out myself. He don't listen to me. He just like his daddy, only worse. But he on it."

"What kind of dope?"

"The kind everybody else on around here. Heroin."

"Heroin? You mean Money's shooting heroin? My little brother? Be serious, Mama."

"I'm serious as a heart attack," Mildred said. "We didn't want to spoil your trip before you came home. He been on it for a while. Was probably dipping and dabbing in it before you left. You didn't notice how aloof the boy was?"

"No, I didn't, I can't remember. Besides, what difference does it make? Is he downtown? How long has he been there and when is he getting out? Can I go see him?"

"Slow down, girl, you just got here. He ain't going nowhere. He only been up there two weeks. He waiting for his trial date. Serve his ass right. Ain't nobody tell him to start messing around with that shit. Hanging around Curly Mae's dumb-ass kids, Chunky and BooBoo. Everybody around here is on it. It's like a epidemic. And the way it make 'em look, like they dying on they feet. I can't see why they want to mess with it. And they'll steal anythang from anybody to get some money so they can buy that shit."

"I'm calling down there right now to see what time I can visit him." Freda had already picked up the white receiver and raised it to her ear.

"Not on that phone, you won't," Mildred said.

"Why not?"

"Because it's dead. And you might as well know all of it. He ain't been back to school, either."

"He didn't drop out of school, Mama? He only had a year to go!"

"Tell him that."

"Don't worry, I will."

Freda had expected to see some demonic version of her brother, but Money looked like himself. He was standing on the other side of a partition, puffing so hard on a cigarette that the smoke formed a wall between them. Freda had to ask him to put it out. She hadn't known anybody in LA who messed around with heavy drugs, let alone shot it, and the most she had done herself was smoke a few joints, like everybody else.

"You look good, sis," Money said, looking somewhat embarrassed. He bent over and kissed her on the cheek. Freda was surprised, because her brother had never even touched her before.

"You sure look tall," he said. "Did you grow since you left, or what?" Money grinned, and he looked just like Crook.

"No, I didn't grow, silly. It's these shoes." She stepped back and pointed down to the two-inch pink platforms. When she looked up, Money wasn't looking at her shoes, he was looking at her.

"Money," she said, "you aren't messing with heroin for real, are you? Don't lie to me."

"No, I ain't shooting no dope. I tried it, but it ain't for me. Besides, that shit is too expensive. And don't believe everything Mama tells you. You know how she always likes to exaggerate. I make one little mistake and everybody's gotta make such a big deal about it. You'd think I was a criminal or something."

"Well, you are in jail, Money. What about school? Why'd you drop out of school when you only had a year to go?"

Money frowned. Another lecture. Somebody was always telling him what was best for him. Here his sister had been out in California a whole damn year and now she comes back here on her high horse, acting like she's got everything figured out. "School bores me to death," he said, "always has. Everything except science. You know that, Freda. Remember that time Mama beat me 'cause I got all Fs except that A in science?"

"Yeah, how can I forget it? I had to pull her off of you."

Money started looking nervous, anxious, like he was thinking about a million other things and was just talking to be talking.

"I might go back to night school, really," he said.

But by the look in his eyes, Freda knew he was lying. He would say anything to get himself off the hook. But she wanted to know what he was running from. Wasn't that why people got high? To forget to remember? When their father had died, Money hadn't shown any remorse. After all, Crook had never taken him fishing or to the barber shop or to a baseball game. Had never shaken hands with him or patted him on the back for anything; had never even had a father-to-son talk, at least not that Freda knew of.

And when Mildred and Crook split up Money had become the man of the house at eleven years old. It was Money who picked up the dead mice because everybody else was too scared. It was Money who drained the water from the basement when it flooded. Waded through three inches of water just to put the clothes in the dryer so the girls could wear matching knee socks to school. It was Money who learned how to put a penny in the meter to get the lights and gas back on when they'd been cut off. It was Money who pulled the trash barrels out to the street to be picked up. And when things broke, Money fixed them. No one had taught him; his instincts told him what to do. "I can fix it," he'd said to Mildred when the television went fuzzy, when the electric can opener stopped turning, when the lawn mower died. He'd bend under the hood of the Mercury for hours until he had the engine purring. They all took it for granted that this was his role. He had never had any options.

Now Freda couldn't help feeling that they had treated him like a stepchild, mainly because he was the only boy in the house. Nobody had ever paid much attention to Money, until he got into trouble.

"So, how long you gon' be in town?" he asked.

"A little more than a week. I've got a job, you know."

"I heard. What about a boyfriend?"

"Well, sort of. I don't consider him my boyfriend because I'm not head over heels in love, but we have a lot of fun together."

"When did you start wearing your hair like that?" Money asked, pointing to Freda's Afro, which was crinkled up like a hair sponge. Her fake hair was in her suitcase.

"Oh, maybe six months ago."

"They say it's the latest fad, this Afro thang."

"It's not a fad, Money. It's just one way of outwardly showing how proud you are of your heritage."

"Yeah, where'd you hear that?"

"I read it in a book. *The Autobiography of Malcolm X*."

"I heard of him. Ain't he the one who says the white man is the devil or something?"

"Yes, he's the one. But there's more to it than that. He'll tell you why you're behind bars instead of working at a summer job, and he'll tell you why you dropped out of school. You're doing just what the white man wants you to do, you know that. They love to see young black men ruin their lives by not getting an education and wasting away on dope."

"I told you I don't use dope. You know, you haven't changed a bit, Freda. You still don't listen to me. Don't believe nothing I have to say, do you?"

"I want to believe you, Money, but I didn't expect to come home and find you here."

"Yeah, well, I'm sorry to disappoint you." Money looked over at the clock. "You gotta go," he said. "It was nice to see you. I know you gon' be busy, so you don't have to come back. I'll see you next time you're in town." He turned his back to her and she left.

After a week of being home, having seen that absolutely nothing had changed, at least not for the better, Freda couldn't wait to get back to LA. She knew she hadn't made a mistake by leaving this hick town. And she also knew she was never coming back here to live. Most of the girls she had gone to high school with were living in the projects with one or two babies, and they were big and fat and quite a few of them needed dental work. The guys seemed to spend all of their waking hours in front of the pool hall, drinking wine or nodding over cigarettes, or parked in the field next to the Shingle, honking their horns at anybody who drove by. Freda couldn't even recognize some of the folks who said hi to her on the street. What's going on around here, she wondered? It couldn't just be dope. It had to be something more debilitating, more contagious. It was this town. This termite of a place, which would sooner or later eat away her mama and the girls too. It already had Money. The thought itself alarmed her. Her sisters stuck in front of a TV all day watching soap operas, on welfare, with a house full of babies. And what about Mildred? Freda knew she couldn't sit back and let this happen to them.

The morning she was leaving, she was standing in front of the mirror in just her panties and a black lace bra, filling in her eyebrows with pencil. Mildred had been watching her from the doorway in silence. Freda saw her, but didn't say anything.

"That school taught you how to pluck your eyebrows like that?" Mildred finally asked, coming in and sitting on the bed.

"Yep."

"Next time will you do mine?"

"Yep."

"Just when is that gon' be, anyway?" Mildred asked.

"I don't know, Mama. I've got a full load of classes next semester. There's a good possibility I can go to school full-time and work part-time, and if I do, I won't have any money to come home. But it shouldn't be more than a year, two at the most."

"Two! I could be dead in two years!"

"Mama, you will not be dead in two years. Let me have a drag of that cigarette, would you?"

"Don't you thank that brassiere is just a little big on you?" she was joking.

"If you like it, you can have it, Mama."

"Naw, naw, naw. I don't want to take nothing off your back, girl, damn."

"Mama, you can have it, it's just a bra. Here," she said, unhooking it. "Wait a minute, I've got something else I wanted to give you." Freda opened one of her suitcases and handed Mildred four fifty-dollar bills.

"For me?" Mildred asked, surprised. "Oooo, yum, yum, yum. Thank you, baby. You sure you can afford all this? You know I can use it, but I don't want you to go home broke."

"I'm not broke, Mama," she lied. "You like these?" Freda held up a pair of silver earrings shaped like long teardrops.

"For me too?"

"If you want 'em."

"Want 'em! I don't like to be greedy, chile, but I've been watching them dangle in your ears since the day you got here. This is real silver, ain't it? Put 'em on me, right now, would you? Curly gon' be sick when she see these." Mildred was already admiring herself in the mirror. "How much you pay for 'em?"

"I don't know, Mama. Ten or fifteen dollars, maybe."

"I always knew you would grow up to have good taste. If you don't use nothing else I taught you, don't ever lose that. Don't waste your time or your money on cheap shit, baby, 'cause all you'll end up doing is paying for everythang twice."

# Eleven

"**D**O I WANNA COME to Los Angeles? Is the sky blue? Do a bear shit in the woods?" There was no doubt in Mildred's mind whether or not to accept Freda's invitation. Hell, she'd seen a rat the size of a cat run under her bed, the front porch had finally caved in and torn off part of the roof in the living room, and to top it off, the septic tank had backed up and the toilet wouldn't flush. Mildred had felt so hard-pressed that she went ahead and moved into the projects. And Money had almost driven her crazy. He had stayed in and out of trouble and was just finishing six months at Ionia Men's Facility, which was a nice way of saying prison. He was coming home next week, but Mildred was glad she wasn't going to be here.

She asked Faye Love if she could borrow two of her good suitcases. Mildred never was one to let a man come between friends, although nothing ever came of Faye and Spooky. Faye, who had been to California before, was extremely jealous when Mildred told her. "You won't like it. I can tell you that right now," she said. "It's too damn hot, too big, and everythang is so spread out, you gotta ride in a car just to go to the grocery store. You better pray on your mama's grave there ain't no earthquakes when you get out there. Be just your luck, wouldn't it, Milly?"

"Chile, I'm ready for a earthquake and a hurricane and a tornado, if it'll get me the hell away from here for a few weeks. And you can keep your thoughts to yourself, Faye. A herd of cattle couldn't stop me from getting on that plane. And don't let me hit the number before I leave. Hot damn!"

Mildred dipped into her rent money to buy a decent pair of white pumps and matching purse, a half slip, a couple of cotton panties, and a push-up bra. She knew she wouldn't get evicted from the projects. Everybody was always behind anyway.

Curly Mae let Mildred borrow four of her best summer dresses. "Chile," Curly said, rummaging through her closet to find something else Mildred might want to take with her, "if one of my kids was to get near a college and send me a one-way ticket to hell, I'd be out of here so fast, you wouldn't see nothing but the trail of dust behind me! You ought to be proud, Milly, you raised them kids right. I can't understand what's happened to old knuckleheaded Money, but you know how boys are. You hit the jackpot with them girls, though. Just keep it up."

What Curly had said about the girls was almost true, but not quite. Mildred thought Bootsey was getting too grown, and it was getting so that Mildred had to smack her every now and then just to let her know she wasn't as grown as she thought. She was always trying to prove she could do things better than Freda. Always sewing something or being creative in the kitchen. But her meals were usually too creative to be edible, and the clothes she made really did look homemade.

Angel, on the other hand, was still too damn quiet. She was like a cat. Look up and she'd be standing right next to you. Mildred thought of her as sneaky. She knew that behind Angel's gentle and sweet exterior, she was a slick number. Mildred didn't trust her out of her eyesight. To tell the truth, Angel was the only one who truly eluded her. She didn't know what to make of her. She'd just have to wait and see, and hope for the best.

Doll was already boy crazy. Every time Mildred turned around, she was drawing hearts with her and some new boy's initials in the middle, with an arrow darting through it. She talked on the phone nonstop. Mildred's instincts told her that Doll was probably going to be hot in the ass, and she dreaded the day when the girl found out about sex, if she hadn't already. Doll was too pretty; it was already going to her head. Thought she was gorgeous because her hair wasn't kinky and it didn't have to be straightened. It got so that Mildred made her wear ponytails to stop her from sweeping it away from her face like those white girls did in shampoo commercials.

"You gon' send me a postcard, ain't you Milly?" Curly asked.

"If my name is Mildred Peacock I'll send you a postcard. I might just call your old silly behind." Mildred had stopped using Billy Callahan's last name because she had never liked it anyway. Besides, she felt like a Peacock.

She'd been packed for three days now, and the night before she was leaving, Mildred could hardly sleep. She was too excited. Couldn't remember the last time she'd been this anxious about anything. She had put a fresh red tint in her hair so that it shone like copper, and Connie James had pressed it hard and curled it tight. She had had Angel polish her fingernails because she was too nervous. And she had even given herself one of those oatmeal facials, like Freda had showed her.

In the morning she took two nerve pills, ran her bathwater extra hot, and poured an excessive amount of bath oil in it to make sure the bubbles rose higher than the tub. She soaked until the last bit of suds disappeared, and when she finally got out, she talcumed her body down and misted it with Emeraude. She put on too much makeup because she was trying to hide the dark circles under her eyes. She wore bright orange lipstick, which complemented her skin and hair, and blotted her lips on a Kleenex. She tucked the bottom one in.

The airplane ride made Mildred giddy. A double shot of bourbon on top of another nerve pill helped to relax her, but not so much that she was able to fall asleep during the four-hour flight. Besides, she didn't want to miss a thing. "Just thank," Mildred said out loud, as she watched the clouds float by her window, "I'm going to visit my daughter in California."

When she spotted a copper-colored Freda at the arrival gate, Mildred hollered out, "Here I am!" And Lord have mercy, the girl had on skintight blue jeans. And she was wearing a man's sleeveless undershirt that had been dyed like a bleeding rainbow, and above and beyond everything else, the girl wasn't wearing a brassiere! But hell, it had been over a year since Mildred had seen Freda, and she told herself she wasn't going to start out by telling her how tacky she looked.

She kissed her oldest daughter real fast, getting lipstick all over her cheek, and pushed Freda away so she could get a good look at her.

"Since when did you stop wearing a brassiere?"

"It's too hot out here to wear a bra, Mama."

"Yeah? It can't get that damn hot. And when we get to where we going, you better find one. I ain't running around here with you bouncing around like some jumping beans." Freda hadn't forgotten her mama's bossiness, but decided she would comply this once to avoid any more arguments.

As the taxi drove out of the airport, Mildred thought she was dreaming. Row after row of palm trees lined both sides of the streets, and the sun was piercing through their leaves.

"So, these is palm trees, huh? Lord have mercy. Don't look like they give off much shade, though, do it?"

Freda just laughed.

Mildred didn't say anything for the longest time. And even though the taxi driver had his air conditioner on, Mildred rolled her window down and let the ninety-degree heat hit her in the face. She didn't even know how hot it was. She was too busy looking at the mountains, the beautiful houses, the tall buildings, and the people driving all these brand new cars, many of which she'd never seen before in Michigan. When the taxi finally pulled up in front of a white stucco building, Freda dragged the suitcases from the car.

"This damn sure ain't nothing like Point Haven, is it?" Mildred asked. "Everythang is so clean and bright. Look at these streets, they all paved. And everybody must sweep their sidewalk every day or something, huh?"

"No, Mama. The city keeps it clean like this. Did you bring enough clothes, or what? You're only staying two weeks. Looks like you brought enough things to last at least a month."

"If I like it, I might stay longer than two weeks, so shut up. I swear, if you knew how you looked without no brassiere. It looks downright nasty. Gon' get your little fast ass raped again out here if you don't stop thinking you so cute."

Now why'd she have to go and say that, Freda thought. She had done such a fine job of forgetting that awful day. Mildred interrupted her thoughts.

"How far are we from Hollywood?"

"This is Hollywood, Mama."

"No shit," she said, grinning.

"No shit. Look. Over there through the smog. See those hills? That's Hollywood, where the movie stars live. On a clear day, you can see the sign. As soon as you get some rest, we'll get on a bus and go see some of it, okay?"

"Rest? Girl, I ain't tired. You thank I'm some old woman or something. I'm only thirty-seven. I probably got more energy in my baby finger than you got in your whole body."

They opened the wrought-iron gates that led into the courtyard of Freda's building. A calm and empty swimming pool stood in the center. There were two floors of apartments surrounding it like a motel. Rock and roll music was drifting out of open doorways, and a few people were barbecuing on hibachis. Some of Freda's neighbors waved and welcomed Mildred to LA. Invited her to stop by for at least one drink before she left. Said they had heard all about her and told her she didn't look old enough to be Freda's mama. Mildred felt like a celebrity.

"Is that a real swimming pool or am I still dreaming?" Mildred asked.

"It's real Mama. I thought I told you I had a pool."

"You did, but I thought you meant the kind you had to fill up with a hose."

"Just about everybody has pools in LA."

"Some people really know how to live, don't they, baby? How much rent you paying for all this? I bet you picked the most expensive building in town, didn't you?"

"It's pretty cheap, Mama, believe me."

"Yeah, I betcha," Mildred said, blushing. Her daughter had already started to move up in the world, and Mildred was proud, but she didn't know how to say it without sounding corny.

Once they had settled into Freda's apartment, Mildred walked to the picture window and looked up into the hills. This sure was pretty. And this glittery ceiling was too much. Mildred didn't much care for the pea-green carpet, or that monstrosity of a plaid couch, but she wasn't going to say anything about it.

"Did you pick out this furniture?"

"No, this apartment was already furnished," Freda said.

Then Mildred started scouting around. She was looking for dust, spiderwebs, anything that looked amiss, but she couldn't find anything. "You keep this little place pretty clean, huh? How much did you say you were paying for it?"

"I didn't say."

"Well?"

"A hundred and ten."

"Really," was all she said.

Mildred picked up a brown and green plaster-of-paris vase Freda had bought in Tijuana. "You collect some nice creative art," she said. Iridescent posters of Jimi Hendrix and all the signs of the zodiac hung on the wall, along with a few other atrocities splattered with psychedelic paint that glowed in the dark. "This place ain't bad, ain't bad at all. I'm proud of you, baby." There. She'd said it. And that's all Freda had been waiting to hear.

"Thank you, Mama. I'm glad you are."

Freda had worked overtime for the past three months so she could pay for Mildred's trip and finally buy some new glasses, dishes, towels, throw rugs, and a real chenille bedspread. She had also stayed up half the night making sure everything was spotless.

During the next two weeks they walked block after block down Sunset Strip and Hollywood Boulevard. Mildred kept gloating about how Curly and Faye would just die if they could see her. She snapped her Instamatic, using up two whole rolls of film the first day. They went to Grauman's Chinese Theatre, where Mildred stepped on the stars' footprints and reminisced about the old movies, to the Wax Museum, and to a taping of a Dionne Warwick special, which almost floored Mildred. She couldn't wait to get back home and tell Curly about this. They took buses to Beverly Hills where they window-shopped because Mildred was hesitant about going inside. Freda told her that this was America, that her money was as good as anybody else's, so Mildred spent three dollars and bought Curly a lime-green ashtray with a gold map of the movie stars' homes painted on it. They went to Century City and had lunch in an outdoor café. They went to a market, where Mildred had to touch the oranges and lemons and grapefruits and limes just to make sure they were real and bought a grocery bag full of them to take home. She'd never even heard of an avocado, and didn't much care for them when Freda made her that guacamole. By the end of two weeks, Freda had spent almost every cent she had put aside for her mama's visit, but she couldn't remember having had this much fun with anybody, and it had been well worth every penny.

On Mildred's last day, she finally pooped out. Freda made bacon-lettuce-and-tomato sandwiches, put potato chips in a plastic bowl, and set out two long-stemmed glasses and a bottle of wine on the kitchen table. Freda had seen a documentary about winemaking and had jotted down the French name to remember it for moments like this. Bordeaux.

"Mama," she said, "let's go swimming before lunch."

"Swimming? Girl, I ain't been swimming in damn near twenty years."

"I thought you said you could swim."

"I can, but I don't have no bathing suit. I didn't bring one. Didn't know I was gon' be this close to water."

"Put this on," Freda said, going to her closet and handing her a one-piece Hawaiian print. She had bought it for Mildred because she knew her mother was going to have some excuse. Mildred took the suit into the bedroom and Freda followed her. They both removed their clothes and tried not to notice each other's bodies. They couldn't help looking. Mildred's breasts looked like someone was pulling them down. But aside from the stretch marks and a few too many pounds, for thirty-seven, Freda thought, Mildred still looked pretty good. Not like she'd had five babies. And peeking over at Freda, Mildred remembered that her own hips used to be that narrow and her waist used to clench like that too. Damn, Freda's skin was so smooth and firm. Mildred pulled the straps of her suit across her shoulders and didn't bother looking in the mirror.

They took turns diving and doing laps and relaxed on the

lounge chairs. Mildred didn't like the wine. "Oooh, this stuff is so bitter, ain't a drop of sugar in here, is it?"

"It's not supposed to be sweet, Mama. It's a dry wine. They say the drier it is the better quality it is."

"Is that right," Mildred said, sipping it slowly, after watching how gracefully Freda drank hers. And the more she drank, the better it tasted. She leaned her head back and stared up at the clear blue sky. I could get used to living like this, she thought. But she didn't dare let Freda know what she was thinking. She didn't know how Freda would feel about her and the kids moving out here. Freda was so independent, now that she was on her own. Maybe she would think her mother was following her, or moving out here just to check up on her. Which would be half true.

Freda pulled up another lounge chair beside her and put her sunglasses on. Her dark skin looked glazed against her white bikini, but she massaged another layer of suntan oil on top of the latest coat of color anyway.

They were both silent for almost ten minutes.

"You probably gon' stay out here, then, huh?" Mildred asked.

"I don't know, Mama. It's nice out here, and I'm getting a free education."

Mildred nodded her head up and down in agreement. Freda stared at her through her dark glasses. Her mama looked so relaxed. She wished she had enough money to move the whole family out here. But all Freda had in the bank was $234.

"There're opportunities out here for all kinds of people, and it doesn't seem to matter what color you are. As long as you've got a skill, you can find a job." Freda felt like she might as well have just bit her tongue. She knew Mildred had only done day work, cooked in restaurants, and worked in factories. There weren't any factories in LA. And she also knew Mildred wasn't getting back on her knees again. And working in a restaurant? Well, she'd see.

But Mildred hadn't taken it that way. The way she figured it, she could get qualified for damn near anything. Hell, if Freda wasn't but twenty years old and could come all the way out here and make it, surely, she could come out here and learn how to do something worthwhile. LA. wasn't that big of a deal.

"Everybody miss you, Freda."

"Who is everybody?"

"Me. And the kids."

"I miss all of you too, Mama. But I swear, I can't go back to that place. A person could rot away there."

"You got a boyfriend?"

"Not really."

"What's wrong with you? You can't tell me you on your own and you ain't screwing."

Freda was embarrassed. She had never talked about this kind of stuff with her mama before. "Well, yes, I'm going out with someone, if that's what you mean."

"Chile, please, you know exactly what I'm talking about. Is he good?"

"Mama!"

"Aw, you can stop that little innocent act with me. I saw that diaphragm in your bathroom."

"You've been rambling in my drawers?"

"I was looking for some bobby pins," Mildred said, laughing. "At least you know how to protect yourself. It's a relief to know that." She took another sip of her wine. "You ever want kids?" she asked, seemingly out of nowhere.

"Of course I want to have kids, Mama."

"How many?"

"I don't know. How am I supposed to know?"

"Well, you should have some general idea. One, two, three, how many?"

"Two."

"That's all! You'd hardly even know they was there."

"Two is enough to keep you busy."

"What about a husband?"

"What do you mean, what about a husband?"

"You want to get married, don't you?"

"Well, of course, if I want to have kids, most likely I want to get married."

"Just when you plan on doing that?"

"When I meet someone I love and someone who wants to

marry me. I'm going for a swim," Freda said and dived back into the pool.

Mildred watched her baby swimming back and forth through the turquoise-blue water. She refilled her glass, but left it sitting on the cement. She wiped the sweat from her forehead. The sun was blinding. Then she put on Freda's sunglasses and closed her eyes.

Freda was still just a child, Mildred thought. And Mildred had always worried about her. She remembered one of those hot muggy summer nights when Freda was a baby. Crook was supposedly at the Shingle. She had put Freda in bed with her while she watched TV because she was lonely. Crook had warned her that the baby would get spoiled, too used to sleeping with them, and he had insisted that she sleep in her crib. But how would he know when he wasn't here? As Mildred was watching the television, a mosquito swerved past the screen. Freda already had two purple bruises on her tiny arms where she'd been bitten a few days ago. Mildred wasn't about to let her get bit again. She pulled the top sheet up under Freda's chin and got up from the bed. Then she closed the bedroom door and made sure the window screens were secure. Mildred lay down on top of the sheets and waited. If it was going to bite anybody it was going to be her. She waited some more. She was tired, but kept her eyes wide open. Finally, Mildred felt something soft land on her arm and she slapped it so hard she hurt herself. She walked over to the window to use the light from the moon, and sure enough, she had smashed the damn bug. There wasn't a drop of blood in it, either. With relief she slid under the sheets next to her baby and wrapped her inside her arms. Something Mildred had not done since.

Now, whenever the phone rang late at night, Mildred's heart would pound like crazy because she just knew it was somebody calling to tell her that her baby had drowned, had been hit by a car or was in a horrible accident. Something tragic. And for the past two years Mildred had to keep reminding herself that that baby was a woman now, just like she was.

"Are you seeing someone, Mama?" Freda asked, startling her. She was standing in front of Mildred, blocking the sun's rays and drying herself with a light blue beach towel.

"Like who?"

"Come on, I mean, are you in love with anyone?"

"Chile, the only thang worth loving in that town now is your dog or cat, and I ain't got neither one."

Freda could hear Mildred's bitterness. And she wondered what it felt like to have had five kids, three unsuccessful marriages, and have nothing to do now but sit around and watch your children grow up and leave you one by one.

"You ever thought about what you would do when all of us are gone, Mama?"

Mildred suddenly felt like she had a migraine headache. She never got headaches.

"Girl, Doll ain't but fifteen, I got at least four or five years to be worrying about something like that."

"But have you ever thought about what you're going to do?"

Mildred did not like being put on the spot like this. Do? She wasn't prepared for this kind of question. She hadn't ever thought about what she would do when her kids grew up. She didn't know what she was going to do. Shit. How in the hell was she supposed to know?

"I might go back to school," she said on the spur of the moment, just to get an answer out. Now that she'd said it, it didn't sound bad at all.

"School?" Freda was just as surprised to hear it as Mildred had been saying it.

"Yeah, school, I might just go back to school."

Freda wasn't about to ask her exactly what she would go back for. "That sounds great, Mama. I sure hope you do. It's not too late, either."

"I'll put it this way," Mildred said. "If Money keep his act up, he gon' either be dead or in prison for the rest of his life. He still on that shit, and ain't nothing nobody say to him works. He hardheaded and act like he doing this to get back at me or something. And that Bootsey. She getting so grown I could strangle her sometimes. I don't have no trouble out of Angel. And Doll, if I could pay somebody to give her an ounce of common sense, I would."

Freda started laughing, but not because what Mildred had

said was funny. God, Freda thought, how can you save your family from itself?

"I don't want to get as black as you, chile, I'm going upstairs. You coming?"

"Nope, I think I'm going to do a few more laps and swim off some of this wine. I don't like to drink this much, and this sun is giving me more of a buzz than I wanted."

That night the two of them stayed up drinking until almost three o'clock in the morning. Then they crawled into Freda's double bed and said goodnight to each other, but Freda was too wired up to fall asleep. A yellow glow from the streetlight filtered throughout the room. It was so quiet, to Freda it felt like they were the only two people in the world.

She was thinking about all the times she used to sneak in bed with Mildred. Crook was still in the sanitarium then. Freda loved nestling up next to Mildred's warm body.

"Is that you, Freda?" Mildred always asked, knowing full well it was.

Freda always had some excuse. "Mama, Bootsey keep taking up all the room, and she likes to push her knees against mine and —"

"Get on in here, girl," Mildred would say, and she'd lift the covers back and act like she was shuffling around to make room for her, but really wouldn't move an inch. She loved the way her daughter felt against her skin.

"Mama, you asleep?" Freda asked Mildred now.

"Almost. One more drank and my head would be spinning."

"If you can scrounge up the plane fare for everyone to come back out here, I'll help you find a job and a place to stay."

"That's sweet, Freda, but I have to thank about it. You talking about making a pretty big move. Now go to sleep, we'll talk about it tomorrow." Mildred closed her eyes and tried to wipe the grin off her face. She had made up her mind this afternoon that she was coming back. Shit. She wanted the other kids to get the same introduction to the good life that Freda was getting. And Freda had sure changed. She was so much sharper and alert, even sounded wiser. And she wasn't just her daughter any more, this person was her new friend.

They overslept.

"Aw, shit, Freda," Mildred said as she was hurrying to pack the next morning. "You forgot to remind me!"

"Remind you about what?"

"You were supposed to pluck my eyebrows this time like yours!"

"Oh, Mama. I thought it was something important."

"It is important. I want to look different when I get home."

"You do look different. You're two shades darker, and you look rested."

"I sure do, don't I?" Mildred said, smiling to herself in the mirror. "I sure do." If this place and this lifestyle could make her look this good in just two weeks, Lord, what would years do?

"Here, Mama, take these," Freda said, handing her a pair of earrings. They were shaped like half moons.

Mildred took them gladly.

"Thank you, Freda. I didn't want to tell you this, but you know that pretty red brassiere you had in your drawer?"

"Had?"

"I borrowed it. I ain't never seen a brassiere that red before. Okay?"

"It's quite okay, Mama. I put it there so you would see it."

"Do me one favor, though, would you, baby?"

"What's that?"

"Promise me you'll start wearing one regularly so they won't be hanging down to your navel."

"I promise, I promise, I promise!"

They were announcing the last call for Mildred's plane when they reached the ticket counter. She kissed Freda on the cheek, but there wasn't any time to hug. Mildred was already inside the entrance gate, running, waving, and yelling. "Just give me a minute to get my money together, baby, and we'll be back out here so fast it'll make your head swim."

# Twelve

*P*OINT HAVEN HAD SHRUNK. Seemed like Mildred had been gone a year instead of just fifteen days. The streets looked narrower and shorter, the houses old and rickety. Even the people in South Park looked like they had aged and their clothes looked like they were from another era. Mildred's front yard was nothing more than a patch of grass to her now. Hell, she'd seen rolling hills and green mountains, mansions hanging off cliffs, had eaten Chinese, Italian, and Mexican food, and had shopped in Beverly Hills. Mildred felt like she'd stretched out like a rubber band and now she'd been snapped back into reality.

"So, how was it?" Bootsey asked, "I bet Miss Show and Tell went all out for you, huh?"

"You know, you got a smart-ass mouth. One day it's gon' get you into trouble. I had a ball. Angel, get those clothes off the line, would you? And where's Doll?" Mildred asked.

"She went to K-Mart."

"With what and with who?"

"I don't know," Angel said. She was busy reading a teen magazine with the Jackson Five on the cover.

"Where's Money?"

"Upstairs, asleep, where else?" said Bootsey.

"Wake his ass up. And them clothes better all be ironed. I

told you before I got back I wanted everythang in this house cleaned and pressed."

"They almost finished. God. What you want me to do, go wake Money up or keep on ironing?" Bootsey had her hands on her hips, a smirk on her face, and all of her weight on one leg. Mildred got on her nerves. Always ordering her around like she was her slave or something. Ever since Freda left, seemed like Mildred just picked and picked at her. And if Bootsey could have hauled off and smacked her and gotten away with it, Mildred's face would've been purple by now. But she couldn't, and the closest she could get was aggravating the hell out of her. Bootsey was glad Freda was gone, because it made her the oldest. She had tried to fill Freda's shoes by bossing the other two girls around in Mildred's absence, but most of the time they just ended up arguing or shoving each other. Bootsey was sick and tired of all of them, and was even more tired of listening to Mildred bragging about Freda day in and day out. That's all she talked about. Freda this and Freda that. But Freda wasn't all that hot. She had knock knees and a wide face and a lead lip, and only had one boyfriend the whole time she was in high school and he dropped her for a college girl. Just 'cause she done moved to California, Bootsey thought, she thank she Miss It.

"Bootsey, don't stand there all day lolly-gagging, girl, 'cause I'm tired and ain't in the mood to be tested."

Bootsey marched up the steps, stomping her feet and mumbling something under her breath.

"Mama said wake up, Money." He was a mess. Still had his clothes on and wasn't even in his own bed. Sometimes when he came home at daybreak, he'd fall asleep downstairs in the middle of the living room floor. Now he was in Angel's twin bed. He was always so high these days that half the time he didn't know where he was when he woke up. He lifted his head slowly and rolled over.

"You better get your ass up before Mama come up here and see you like this."

"I'm coming," he said, dragging himself out of bed. He walked into the bathroom and threw some cold water on his face. He looked like he'd been beaten up and he felt even worse.

Mildred was on the phone when he came downstairs.

"I want to know how much it cost to rent a U-Haul one way to Los Angeles." She was waiting for the answer when she noticed him in the doorway. She shook her head back and forth, as if to say, "pitiful."

"I said one way. Oh." Then Mildred hung up the phone.

"Boy, if you know how you look."

"How you doing, Ma?"

"Better than you are, that's for damn sure."

"What's with the U-Haul."

"We moving to California."

"What?" he asked.

"Not me," said Bootsey, walking into the room with a pillowcase in her hands. "I'm not going noplace."

"What do you mean you ain't going? You go where I tell you to go," Mildred said.

"I'm getting married."

"You getting what?"

"You heard me, I said I'm getting married."

Money flopped down on the couch. He knew this was going to be yet another episode in their long-running drama. He was fed up with all of them and their little troubles. He was the one who was going through real changes, but nobody wanted to hear his problems. They didn't want to know that he was sick inside, that he couldn't get a grasp on himself, and the sad part was, he didn't know why. The only time he found relief was when he pushed that needle into his veins. Usually it made the turmoil and confusion stop scrambling around in his head. But sometimes it did just the opposite. Made him think too much about everything. And to put his thoughts in reverse, he got higher and higher. He kept hoping he would reach a plateau where everything would become transparent. Just clear up.

Angel put her magazine down so she could hear this too.

Mildred was eyeing Bootsey. "You pregnant?"

"No, I am not pregnant. I love David and he loves me."

"Love? You ain't but seventeen years old. What the hell do you think you know about love? You done got your first piece of ass and it done got so good that you thank it's love. You just

like the rest of them Peacocks. Your brains is all in your behind."

"We ain't done nothing like that." Bootsey lied with a straight
face. But the truth was David had given her everything she hadn't
gotten from Mildred or Crook. He was affectionate, kind, gentle,
and spoiled her rotten. Anything Bootsey wanted, he gave it to
her. All she had to do was sort of bat her eyes at him and give
him one of Mildred's most cogent smiles, and he was hooked.
Bootsey was his Barbie doll.

David had let Mildred know his feelings about Bootsey from
the start. He knew he was too old for the girl, but he promised
Mildred he wouldn't do anything to hurt her daughter. "Yeah,
you better not," she'd warned him. "And don't send her home
pregnant, either, or I'll blow your brains out."

Mildred sat looking deeply into Bootsey's big black eyes. It
wouldn't make any sense to drag her all the way out there with
them. Bootsey would only make her miserable anyway. Be one
less mouth to feed, Mildred thought.

"Marry him, I don't care. We'll leave you in this dead-ass
town to wither away like everybody else. Just when did you
plan on doing all this marrying, anyway?"

"After graduation. We haven't set the date yet. We wanted
to tell you first. See what you thought."

"Well, it ain't like he no hoodlum, and I wouldn't have to be
worrying about you. You got my blessings one way or the other.
But we'll be out of here in the next six to nine months, so if
you expect me to be there, you better do it before then."

During the next few months Money developed a special passion for equipment. He had burglarized somebody's house up
on Strawberry Lane and had over three thousand dollars' worth
of power tools in the trunk of his Nova when he was pulled
over for a smoking muffler. They threw him in jail and Mildred
bailed him out. She told him that if he didn't get his shit together by the time she was ready to go, she would leave his ass
standing in the middle of Twenty-fourth Street.

Money promised her he would try to stay out of trouble. He
even began going to one of those new rehabilitation programs
they had started. But this didn't do him much good, because
the methadone was about a mile short of soothing him, and

that poppy had already grabbed hold of him like a steel glove. It was squeezing Money's will so tight that he began to think the only place he would ever find complete solace would be inside death's arms.

Angel and Doll were upstairs asleep one night when he quietly opened their door and unplugged the color TV. Angel opened her eyes — she had always been a light sleeper — but she didn't say a word. She just watched. Money inched the TV through the doorway and tiptoed downstairs. Angel eased out of bed, stood at the top of the steps, and heard drawers and cupboards opening and closing. She knew what he was looking for. Mildred's silverware. The set she'd gotten as a wedding gift when she had married Rufus. She had never even used them because they had never had an occasion special enough. Money found the case under the china closet and was putting it into a pillowcase when Angel came downstairs. He didn't know she was watching him and she startled him.

"You low-life, stupid junkie. Put the fucking TV back where you found it, and I'd appreciate it if you would put Mama's silverware back, too. I mean it, Money. Right now!" It hurt Angel to see her brother stoop this low. She had busted him once before, when they had lived on Thirtieth Street. He had pawned the diamond wedding ring that Billy had given Mildred, and for three days Mildred couldn't figure out where she'd put it. "You took it, didn't you?" Angel had said. "You can't lie, Money. I'll tell you one thing. You got twenty-four hours to get it back in this house." Money was so high when she confronted him that he fessed up. He begged her not to tell. But this time, he was pushing his luck.

"I wasn't *stealing* it, Angel. I was just borrowing it until tomorrow. Mama won't even miss it. I'm gon' return it."

"Put it back, now, goddammit, or I'll go upstairs and wake her up. So help me God," she said, pointing to the stairs.

"All right, all right, all right!" Money was flustered. "But what am I gon' do?" He sounded so pitiful and helpless, as if he didn't have a solitary friend in the world, and he looked at Angel as if she were his only salvation.

"Suffer. Like the rest of us," was all she said. Angel waited until he had put everything back, then she went back to bed.

Money went into the downstairs bathroom and closed the door.

Angel couldn't sleep. Almost an hour had passed and the sun was coming up. She got up and went back downstairs to see what Money was doing. She didn't see him, but she hadn't heard him leave, either. The bathroom door was closed. She knocked but got no response. She knocked again. "Money, you in there?" She tried to turn the handle but it was locked. When she still didn't get a response, she walked outside in her bare feet to go around to the bathroom window. The frost on the grass was so cold she had to hop up and down. The window was too high, so she went back inside and got a pair of Mildred's old shoes from the closet and took a kitchen chair back out with her. She pushed it up against the house. When Angel peeked through the foggy window, she saw Money lying on the floor, unconscious. A needle lay on the linoleum and blood was dripping out of his arm. She pushed the window up and slid through it, then grabbed Money and shook him ferociously. At first Angel thought he was dead, but she was relieved when she felt his pulse. She threw handfuls of cold water on his face and screamed out for someone to help. Money still hadn't opened his eyes. Angel unlocked the door and opened it. "Mama! Doll! Bootsey! Somebody call an ambulance. It's Money!" Everybody rushed downstairs to see what was going on. Mildred called the hospital.

Before the day was over, Money was back home, acting like it had been no big deal. And before the week was over, he was back in jail. He had stolen another color TV, but this time from Howard Johnson's. There was a real question as to whether or not he'd go to the state penitentiary since he'd already been convicted of two felonies, and if the court deemed Money a habitual criminal, they could give him life. For some reason, they set his bail at only $375. Mildred went ahead and forfeited the rent and phone bill money to get him out. If she could just get the boy out to California, she thought, maybe he'd have a chance.

"I'm warning you," she said, as she drove him home. "This is the last damn dime I'm spending to get your retarded ass out of jail. I don't care about your sick-ass drug habit. You can shoot all the dope in the world but if you behind bars when we get ready to leave, you'll rot in there. Do you understand what I'm saying?"

Money nodded his head.

By the end of August, Mildred still hadn't figured out a way to come up with enough money to cover all her expenses. Time was running out on her. She had already told half the town she was leaving before Labor Day. Then she came up with an alternative plan. She pawned her silverware, both wedding rings, and the record player, and sold the washer and dryer (they did not belong to her) and the stove and refrigerator, which still only added up to $409.

Mildred always could lie with a straight face, and that's exactly what she did when she told the U-Haul people that she was only going as far as Detroit.

To her surprise, Money kept his word. He made it through the treatment program at the methadone clinic, and when Mildred told him that all of them couldn't possibly fit in the U-Haul, he even managed to get his 1960 Chevy in running condition. Angel and Doll would ride with him. In spite of the fact that Mildred had shot Deadman all those years ago, she and his mama, Minnie, were still friends, and Minnie's oldest son, Porky, offered to help Mildred drive the U-Haul if she promised to send him back on the bus. (He was afraid to fly.) "A deal," she had said. Mildred knew Porky didn't have anything else to do and he had never been farther than Toledo.

Curly and Buster were about the only two people Mildred knew she would miss. But Curly was happy because it meant she would finally have somebody else to visit instead of her dull relatives in Alabama. And Buster, who had retired and now spent most of his idle time in the summer cultivating his crop — moonshine and potato wine and corn liquor — was glad to see his favorite daughter finally get a real chance to live. Nothing special could happen to Mildred in Point Haven, and Lord knows she needed a husband. Miss Acquilla didn't care one way or the other. She just sat on their front porch, spitting out snuff, rocking in her favorite chair, and listening to the Detroit Tigers losing on her transistor radio.

Bootsey decided to get married on Labor Day.

"I'm sorry," Mildred told her. "You had all winter and spring to do it. I told you when we was leaving, didn't I?"

"It's okay. His mama and daddy will be there," Bootsey said. Mildred told her she would be happy to come back to help celebrate their first anniversary or first child, whichever came first. The truth was, Mildred couldn't stand the thought of sitting in a church full of flowers — which always reminded of her funerals — and watching another one of her babies get away. She wanted Bootsey to feel like she was losing a mother instead of gaining a husband. And that's exactly how Bootsey felt when they backed out of the driveway.

It took them four days to get to Los Angeles. Between keeping herself and Porky supplied with liquor, feeding the kids, and putting gas in the truck and Money's gas-guzzling, oil-burning Chevy, Mildred's cash got so low she was surprised they made it.

Freda met them at her front door. She had moved into a larger apartment, and, to Mildred's disappointment, this building didn't have a swimming pool.

"Girl, I hope you got some money in this house, 'cause we broke. I had to spend every dime I had on gas and food, and I need a drank." This was the first thing Mildred said to her daughter. But Freda didn't care, she was just happy to see everybody. It felt weird, though, knowing that Bootsey was married and staying back home.

Mildred never was big on living in cramped quarters. Even as a child, when she had had to share a bed with her two sisters, she sometimes took a pile of old clothes and slept on the floor just to have some room to herself. And Freda's little one-bedroom apartment wasn't much different. Six people were living in this place. And Mildred was too broke to send Porky back to Point Haven.

After a week of living among boxes and clothes scattered all around her living room, Mildred and Porky arguing over who had the last drink, Angel and Doll yelling about which TV show to watch, and Money bored with everybody and everything, spending most of his time looking lost and pathetic, Freda decided to lay down her house rules. She sounded exactly like her mama.

"Now look. This is my house and I'm grateful that all of you are here" — she looked at Porky — "well, almost all of you, but all this bickering and screaming and carrying on like slobs is getting on my damn nerves. When I come home from work and school, I'm tired. You guys are eating me out of house and home and I'm spending every dime I have on you as it is. Money, tomorrow I want you to get a paper and start looking for a job. Vacation's over. And Mama, you aren't helpless either. It wouldn't hurt you to look. You guys can stay here until I can find a decent place for you to live, but as long as you're under my roof, you're going to have to act more civilized. Does everybody understand me?"

And each of them, including Mildred, said a low yes.

But nothing changed. By the second week, Freda thought she was going crazy. Maybe having all of them stay with her hadn't been such a bright idea after all. And why did Mildred have to come more than two thousand miles with no money in her pocket?

"Where's all the colored people?" Angel wanted to know.

"How many times am I going to have to tell you? We're black, not colored," Freda said.

"Aw, what difference do it make?" Angel said.

Freda shrugged her shoulders in frustration. Angel and Doll were flipping through magazines looking for new hairstyles. Freda was ironing, and Mildred and Porky had both passed out. No one knew where Money was.

"Don't tell me you haven't seen any black people around here," Freda said. "There's lots of us in this neighborhood."

"Show me where, 'cause all I've seen are white people and Chinese people."

"What do you have against white and Chinese people?"

"Nothing, but I just like colored people better."

"Doll," Freda said, "when are you going to take those rollers out of your hair? You've had 'em in for three days now."

"When I go somewhere. Everything out here is so expensive. You can't do nothing if you ain't got no money, can you?"

"That's true anywhere," Freda said.

"No it ain't. At home we didn't never have no money and we did a lot of things."

"Name one."

"We went over to people's houses and ice-skating and —"

"You've only been here a week and a half. How do you expect to go visiting when you don't know anybody yet?"

"Like I said. I'll take these rollers out when I go somewhere."

Freda was coming home from work when she noticed the U-Haul wasn't parked outside her building, at least it wasn't in the same spot it had been parked in for the past two weeks.

"Mama, did somebody move the truck?" she asked when she got upstairs.

"What you mean, did somebody move the truck? It's not outside? That truck ain't outside? I know you lying," Mildred said, getting up from the couch and walking over to the window. "Please tell me you lying, Freda."

"What happened to it?" Freda asked. She knew something was fishy. "What's going on, Mama?"

"Shit. I told them I was going to Detroit. You know how much it would'a cost if I had'a told them we was coming way out here? I'd still be sitting in that damn town right now. Shit, I never thought this would happen."

Freda picked up the telephone and dialed the nearest U-Haul company and asked them what had happened. They told her they had the truck and wouldn't release it or its contents without a certified check for $328. Mildred was even more hysterical after Freda told her that.

"Shut up, would you, Mama? When are you gonna learn that you can't get away with trying to be so slick all the time? Shit, sometimes it pays to tell the truth and do things right for a change."

"You can stop all that damn cussing and telling me what to do. I'm still your mama." Mildred started to cry. She didn't know what they were going to do. We shouldn't have come out here, she thought. I'm always trying to be so quick, and now look.

"Stop crying, would you? Don't worry, I'll think of something, 'cause y'all getting out of here if I have to pay for it myself. I'm not gonna let y'all put me in the nut house," Freda said.

The next day Freda didn't go to work. She went to her bank and applied for a personal loan for seven hundred dollars. She withdrew all but one hundred of the five hundred dollars she now had in her savings account. Three days later her loan was approved and in the meantime she had dragged Mildred and the girls on the bus to an area called the "Jungle," where a lot of black people lived. Freda found them a three-bedroom apartment, complete with swimming pool.

She handed Mildred's new landlord a money order for $550, took a certified check to the U-Haul company, and gave Mildred the rest after they put Porky on a bus back to Point Haven. That night, sitting alone in her apartment for the first time in three weeks, Freda pulled a joint of Colombian grass from a shoe box top beneath the couch and smoked the whole thing. She ate two bowls of strawberry ice cream and fell asleep, alone, in her own bed. It was nice.

Life became simple again, especially since her family was a forty-five-minute bus ride away. Freda had planned it like that. It was true that she loved every single one of them, but she was also glad to see them leave. Besides, they thought they were in seventh heaven after they moved into that building. There were blue and red lights surrounding the pool, and big banana plants, and Angel and Doll were going to an all-black high school, which thrilled them. Teenage boys hovered around Mildred's door and the phone was always ringing off the hook. Mildred found her neighbors to be quite friendly, and to her surprise they weren't even nosy. This was nothing like the projects, she thought, although Mildred didn't know just how long she'd last, living in an apartment. She already missed working in her garden.

Money didn't like LA at all. He didn't even try to find a job. He had told Freda that LA was a little too sophisticated for him. He couldn't get used to walking up and down the streets and nobody knew who he was. The real reason he didn't like LA was because it was harder for him to find dope. Heroin wasn't that popular in Los Angeles, and it wasn't until they had moved to the Jungle that Freda realized all but two of her Darvons were missing. She didn't bother mentioning it to him. She was tired of talking to Money about his problems.

Mildred was having a pretty rough time finding a job. Seemed like every ad in the paper called for some kind of expertise, the one thing she didn't have. There were no factories in Los Angeles — at least they weren't advertised in the paper — and when Mildred did see one, it was way out in the San Fernando Valley. She'd need a car to get out there but she decided to keep it in mind for the future. She had driven out to the Valley with Phyllis once, and was impressed by the nice homes that black people owned. Mildred had told herself that when she got on her feet, that's where she wanted to live. But today was today, so she did the most sensible thing to help her get through tomorrow. She signed up for aid at the county welfare office.

To help lower her expenses, Mildred tried to talk Freda into moving in with them, but Freda told her she was applying to Stanford University and most likely would be leaving Los Angeles.

"But you just got here."

"I've been here three years, Mama."

"Well, *we* just got here."

"So?"

"What you mean, so?"

"Mama, look. They've got a special minority program at Stanford, and it's one of the top universities in the United States. I've got the grades and I can't pass up an opportunity like this. They might give me a grant and pay my tuition too, if I get in."

"Where is this Stanford place?"

"It's in Palo Alto."

"That ain't telling me nothing."

"You know where San Francisco is, don't you? It's near there."

"All the way up there? That's at least a seven-hour drive from here, ain't it?"

"No, it's really six, but it's only an hour by plane."

"Is this how you gon' spend the rest of your life? Just hopping around from place to place?"

"Mama, please. I'm going to go to college, it's not the same thing."

"Yeah, I wanna know how you expect to find a husband when you can't sit still."

Freda just shook her head.

In April she got her acceptance letter and couldn't wait to move up north.

Mildred was happy and disappointed, again. "I don't know why you didn't thank about going to UCLA. They got all kinds of smart basketball players down here. That's what you should'a been thanking about, finding you somebody with some brains in his head and some money in his pocket. You be twenty-two before you know it, girl, and all the education in the world ain't gon' make no babies or make you feel good at night. Keep that in mind when you up there studying."

Mildred was sitting by the swimming pool in her shorts. The sun sure felt good on her legs. She was feeling pretty good about life in general. Freda loved it up there in Northern California and was doing well in school. Money had gone back to Point Haven and, as far as Mildred knew, hadn't been in any trouble. Bootsey was pregnant. Angel had gotten so involved in high school politics that she'd been elected class president, and Doll was named the prettiest girl in the tenth grade. Mildred's bills were pretty much paid. She hadn't taken a nerve pill since she didn't know when, and even though she hadn't met that perfect somebody yet, right now this water was giving her all she needed. A little cooling off.

"Hi, Milly," her neighbor, Sheila, called out. She had just had a baby and was still walking around like she was nine months pregnant.

"Hi, girl. What you know good?"

"I want to show you something. Me and William and the baby is moving. Got us a house in the Valley, on this special program for low-income families. You gotta check it out, Milly, 'cause I know you qualify. You still on the county, ain't you?"

"You better believe it, sister. I can't find no job out here to save my life. Y'all got a house, huh?"

"Yep, and look at this." Sheila showed Mildred the brochure that spelled out all the details. All Mildred needed was five hundred dollars. Five hundred dollars. For a whole complete house?

She used her next two checks for the down payment.

# Thirteen

"Ouch! Damn, Freda. Take it easy. What you trying to do, pull my brains out?"

"Well, be still, would you? You're the one who's trying to be so cute. You gotta pay the price if you want to look good. I told you it would hurt. Now be still." Freda pulled Mildred's head back, spit on her index finger, then smeared it across Mildred's eyebrows to keep them moist, even though she had already slicked them down with Vaseline.

Mildred had finally cornered her to make sure she got her eyebrows plucked this time. It was Angel's high school graduation, and she had told Freda she wanted to look as glamorous as possible. "There could be some nice divorcés there, you know. These days, by the time kids get to college, most likely the mama and daddy ain't together no more."

"Open your eyes and look up," Freda told her. She was staring at her mother's face as if it were her own creation.

"I know you thank you slick, Freda, but I saw you hiding them earrings with that big blue rock in 'em. Ouch! Don't worry, I don't want 'em, I just want to wear 'em today. Is that that turquoise stuff?"

"Yes, and don't move." Freda raced to the bathroom and brought back the plastic bag. She pulled out the silver and turquoise earrings. "Here," she said, handing them to Mildred,

153

"but I need them back." Mildred sat them on the table and leaned her head back like she was in a dentist's chair.

Freda couldn't even count the number of earrings and bras she'd already given her mother. She knew how good Mildred was at conning her out of the things she cherished most. But she wasn't parting with these earrings.

Since Freda had moved, they had still seen a lot of each other. Some weekends, she would drive down to the Valley in the car Mildred had bought her with part of her settlement money. Last October, some drunk man had hit Mildred while she was crossing the street in front of the drug store. She had suffered a pinched nerve in her neck, and thanks to the advice of her friends, was awarded four thousand dollars for the discomfort and aggravation. Mildred paid off a lot of bills, got the shutters painted, the front door sanded and stained, landscaped the front yard, and bought Freda a used car. She would've bought herself one, but driving in a big city made Mildred nervous, plus she didn't have a driver's license any more.

They'd been living out in the Valley, in this olive-green house, for almost a year now. There were rose bushes and banana plants and palm trees and an oval swimming pool in the back yard and a panoramic view of the mountains. Mildred finally felt like she had moved up in the world.

A lot of times Freda's friends would drive the thirty-two miles from LA to see her when she came down, and sometimes even when she wasn't there they'd still come to visit Mildred. They envied Freda for having such a down-to-earth mother. Mildred was like their surrogate mom. She made them feel at home. She let them smoke their reefer in peace in the back yard, and in exchange for Mildred's hospitality they usually supplied her with liquor. Every holiday, they showed up with boxes of expensive Scotch or sealed envelopes of money for her. They had migrated to LA from small towns all over the United States to escape the mundane life at home and get an education.

When Freda came to visit, she usually spent half the day lying by the pool, drinking gold tequila, smoking cigarettes, and rubbing cocoa butter all over her skin until she looked like fresh baked bread. After she'd been assigned to read fourteen books in fourteen weeks, she gave up marijuana. Figured it was time to start remembering things for a change.

"You thought about what you want to be yet?" Mildred had asked her the last time she was there. "I mean, shit, you pushing twenty-four and you should know by now, don't you thank?"

"Well, I'm considering sociology. I can't save the world, but I want to make a difference somehow. You've read some of my poetry, haven't you, Mama?"

"Yeah, and it's beautiful, baby. I show it to everybody," Mildred said. "I got all of it in a big brown envelope up in the closet with the rest of my important papers."

"I can't make a living being a poet, though. Did I tell you I wrote an editorial for our campus newspaper?"

"A what?"

"An editorial. That's an article where you give your opinion about something. I enjoy writing. Helps me get things off my chest. Who knows, maybe I'll go into journalism. I don't know. I have to decide by next semester, though."

"Yeah, well, you better step on it, sister. You ain't exactly got the rest of your life to find no husband. You be thirty before you know it, and I didn't exactly see men swarming around your place last time I was up there."

"Mama, I've got plenty of time to find a husband."

"Yeah, well I'm gon' be waiting for the day when you brang somebody home to meet me."

On this trip, that's exactly what Freda had done. Mildred had heard all about this Delbert over the phone. His name was usually the first word out of Freda's mouth.

"That's kind of a country name for a city boy, ain't it?" Mildred had asked. "Is his teeth white and straight? What kind of hair he got? Don't be bringing me home no nappy-headed grandbabies. I couldn't stand it. I hope he ain't got no skinny legs, neither. Just what we need in this family. Bones. And I know he got to be at least six feet tall and black as night, ain't he?"

Mildred knew her daughter all right. Delbert was tall and thin. His skin was Hershey brown and every feature on his face was so distinct and separate that at first Freda didn't think he was all that handsome. But with Delbert, Freda had discovered complete ecstasy: multiple orgasms. And after that first time, Delbert started looking better and better to her. As time went by, Freda thought he was the most handsome man she'd ever seen in her life. He told her he was a photographer and was studying film, but Delbert didn't tell her he was an epileptic. When she found out, it didn't change her feelings toward him. Freda thought he had charisma. And then there was that red Porsche he drove, and the control he exercised when he shifted gears, doing 80 mph around curves, and those leather gloves he slid on his long fingers, and the way he looked at her with those sad raccoon eyes. Freda found him irresistible.

Delbert thought Freda was beautiful, sexy, smart, and luscious, and he was madly in love with her. He felt lucky to have found her. Even though she went to an uppity school, she still knew how to have a good time. As a matter of fact, all they did was have a good time. Delbert had introduced Freda to cocaine and she had taken quite a liking to it. She was always full of pep and energy, and when he said, "Let's go . . ." she already had her hand on the doorknob. They spent most of their waking hours in bed, staying up until daybreak, doing lines, sipping gold tequila, playing backgammon, and making serious love.

Mildred couldn't stand him the minute she saw him. She tried not to show it, but it was obvious. At first, she ignored him, which made Delbert so uncomfortable that he could hardly finish the breakfast she'd cooked for him and Freda the first morning.

"You look like you could stand to put on a few pounds," she'd finally said to him.

"It doesn't seem to matter how much I eat, Miz Peacock, I've been the same size since I was in high school."

Mildred just looked at him, as if to say, "You must thank I'm some kind of fool or something." She knew the boy used drugs, anybody could see that. She just hoped Freda wasn't that stupid or so easily influenced. Mildred continued making small talk with him, but Delbert knew he wasn't making such a big hit. When he offered to clear the table, Mildred told him not to worry about it and to go on about his business since he wasn't going to the graduation.

"Bye, sweetie," he said to Freda, giving her a slow, wet kiss. Mildred swallowed hard. She felt as though she was getting ready to gag. As soon as they heard him pull out of the driveway, Mildred had poured herself another drink and sat down so Freda could pluck her eyebrows.

"He must be fucking your brains out, ain't he? I can tell he a freak. He look like a freak. That's what your problem is. That's what Bootsey's problem was, too. Get a taste of some good dick and go crazy. Thank it's the only action in town. Well, take it from your mama, there's always something better out there if you keep your eyes open for it. And this thang you done brought home, looking like a fresh-born colt. He's downright homely. Tell me something. You couldn't do no better than this?" Mildred turned to Angel and Doll for support. Angel was blowing her fingernails dry, and Doll was busy teasing her hair.

"I wouldn't say he was homely, Mama. But why don't you ease up before you hurt Freda's feelings? After all, it's *her* boyfriend. So be cool," Angel said.

"At least he drives a tough car," Doll interjected. She was hung up on this type of thing.

"Mama, I've never said anything about those poor excuses for men you married, have I? I like Delbert. As a matter of fact, I love him, and most likely I'm going to marry him, so *you* might as well get used to him."

"Yeah, you like him all right," Mildred said. Then she started laughing. "I ain't never believed that something was better than nothing, but I guess I can learn to like the little monkey. He better not mistreat you. That's all I gotta say about it. If he ever do one single thang to hurt you, you pick up that phone and call me. And I swear, I'll blow his brains to kingdom come. Pour me a drank."

Mildred was rather anxious about Freda bringing home a man for her approval for the first time, and her other daughter graduating, all in the same day. But it wasn't just all the excitement that was taunting her. It was Money. She didn't want to spoil everything by telling the girls he was back in prison, doing one to three years for parole violation. And from the time Mildred had gotten up this morning, every fifteen minutes or so she had been filling her jelly jar with VO.

She cried so hard during the graduation ceremony that her makeup ran even though Freda had made her wipe off a layer because she had overdone it. When they got home, Mildred rushed around the kitchen, heating up all the food she'd spent half the night cooking. Sweet-potato pies, black-eyed peas, collard and mustard greens, fried chicken, even a pot of chitterlings, which nobody was going to eat but her. None of the kids ate pork any more, not after what Freda had told them about pigs.

Freda had invited all of her friends out; Delbert had come back buzzing on coke and couldn't stay in one place but a few seconds; Angel's boyfriend, Willie, sat in a chair, looking totally out of place because he wouldn't take off his gangster hat and he was being as unsociable as always; and Doll had brought her latest boyfriend, Richard, whom she'd been going out with for the past few months. He was darker than Delbert, but Mildred liked him. He had straight white teeth, jet-black wavy hair, good manners, and he went to church every Sunday. Mildred prayed that Freda wouldn't end up marrying that creature from the black lagoon. Freda deserved better. In one regard, Mildred was glad that Angel was following her big sister's footsteps. She'd been accepted at UCLA.

Everybody was having a good time, swimming, dancing half-naked in bathing suits, smoking reefers and drinking wine, and the music was blasting so loud you could hardly hear the person sitting across from you. Mildred sat on the patio, sipping more VO. She couldn't take her eyes off her three daughters. She just sat there grinning until the whole scene started getting to her.

She slipped away from the crowd, after asking Freda to keep an eye on the ribs that were sizzling on the hibachi. She walked inside the house to the bathroom and closed the door behind her. Mildred looked in the mirror. She couldn't understand why she felt sad. Her eyes were glassy. Then she spotted a gray hair so she yanked it out. "Two babies left," she said to her blurry image, "and I started out with five. Shit."

Mildred had forgotten all about that typing class she was supposed to start and took a job instead at a makeshift factory where they made household appliances. Stoves and refrigerators, washers and dryers — all kinds of things. She was hired as an inspector. Her job was to check every part to see that it was attached properly and soldered according to the picture that sat next to her arm. And since she was entitled to a twenty-five-percent discount, Mildred bought herself a brand new range. She also took advantage of the friendship of her boss, Big Jim. She had gathered he was attracted to black women by the way he went out of his way for her. Sometimes he bought Mildred lunch or coffee and doughnuts and let her stretch her breaks. He was always offering her a ride home.

Big Jim was six foot six and not what you'd call fat, but he was huge. Looked like a bigger-than-life version of Wayne Newton, mustache and all. Angel and Doll had never given him much thought until he gave Mildred a ride home one day and she invited him in. They were both suspicious when Mildred introduced Big Jim as her friend instead of her boss. At first they thought he had come to fix something around the house, which was somewhat true, but it wasn't any of the appliances. Big Jim didn't stay long, only long enough to slip Mildred a hundred-dollar bill to help her with whatever it was she had told him she needed help with. She walked him to his car and gave him a soft kiss on the cheek, which influenced him enough to say that if she ever needed anything, anything at all, please don't hesitate to ask. Angel and Doll couldn't believe that Mildred had gotten this hard up.

"Mama, I know you aren't crazy, are you?" asked Angel.

"Crazy, how?"

"That man is white! What do you think Freda's gon' say about this? You know how she feels about white women and black men, what you think she's gon' say about her own mama messing around with a white man? You're disgusting sometimes, you know that?"

"You can watch your mouth. I don't care what Freda thank. I let her go on about her business with that paraplegic she so in love with, and do I say anythang? No. And who the hell is she? Big Jim is nice, and I'll tell you something. Color don't make no difference. That's what's wrong with this world now. Everybody too damn color-conscious. And if it weren't for him, y'all would be standing here in the dark today, so just shut up and pour me a drank."

Big Jim paid for Angel and Doll's first trip back to Point Haven. They liked him now, and had had a sudden revelation. Just because he was white didn't mean he wasn't human. He talked just like any other man. He acted like any other man. He even had a sense of humor and he had one thing that none of Mildred's other men had ever had in the past: lots and lots of money. And he was generous with it. Big Jim gave them each fifty dollars for spending money.

"Shit, if she wants to go out with a white man, that's her business," Doll had said to Angel, as they were about to land in Detroit. "Who knows, we could end up with one ourselves. You never know."

"Speak for yourself. I wouldn't even consider going out with a white man. Just the thought of kissing one gives me the heebie-jeebies. Skip the subject, would you?"

They stayed with Bootsey, naturally, and felt quite at home despite the fact that her two little boys didn't give them a moment's peace. And Bootsey had turned into a regular little Susie Homemaker. She was working ten hours a day at Ford's but was managing home, work, and family quite well. She made sure she let her sisters know right off the bat that she didn't have any misgivings about getting married, staying in Point Haven, and not going to college. "I like doing just what I'm doing and the way I'm doing it," she said. And Bootsey went out of her way to prove it. She cooked them elaborate meals, meals she had finally learned how to prepare accurately, and Doll and Angel could've sworn they were eating Mildred's cooking. Bootsey's house was decorated like a picture in a magazine. All she talked about was buying furniture and crystal and a chandelier and carpet for the home they were going to build. Angel and Doll couldn't contain themselves.

"Are you for real, girl? The way you talking, you sound like some old woman. You only twenty-one. Damn," Doll said. "What about having a good time, partying sometimes?" But just looking at Bootsey told Doll that she had bypassed all that.

"Age don't make a bit of difference; it's all a state of mind. I'm a married woman with two kids and I love it. And I like the idea of making my home as pretty and as comfortable as possible. Y'all know I always liked to cook." Angel and Doll started laughing.

"Yes, how can we forget that you liked to cook," Angel reminded her. "You've gotten a helluva lot better, thank God."

Bootsey continued rambling. "And I love decorating, and wait till you see this French provincial couch I'm getting. It's so, so plush."

Angel and Doll shook their heads. This wasn't even worth debating.

Bootsey drove them out to Fortieth Street to see her land. Doll and Angel hadn't been on a dirt road since they had left Point Haven, but they didn't feel any bump, sitting in the soft cushions of Bootsey's Seville. The property was right across the street from where their Uncle Jasper lived. He was now a preacher and had so many kids he had to keep adding rooms onto his house so he could have somewhere to put them. They didn't want to go see him, because he'd never been very friendly, and they knew he was going to make them go to church before they left. While they sat in the car, Bootsey described in the utmost detail what her house was going to look like, but the girls couldn't picture anything so lavish sitting in the center of this green and gold field.

They visited Curly Mae, who had had a stroke. She looked like a different person. The right side of her jaw was caved in, and when she talked, it sounded as if her gums were full of Novocain. She couldn't even move one side of her body. The girls had chipped in and brought her a dozen yellow roses. Curly was tickled by their thoughtfulness, but wasn't able to say it.

They stopped by to see all of their relatives and friends and watched a lot of TV. They had wanted to go roller-skating but the McKinley rink had been closed — too many fights. There wasn't much else to do. They'd already seen *Battle for the Planet of the Apes*, and the only other thing that was playing downtown was *Pinocchio*. On the last day, Doll managed to reactivate an old junior high school romance, and Angel babysat for

Bootsey and David while they went to the drive-in.

The two sisters didn't have a chance to talk about what they'd done until they were back on the plane to LA.

"Was it boring, or what?" Angel asked.

"Sort of, but Bryan wasn't, that's for damn sure."

"You are just too fast, you know that. And Bootsey got on my nerves. She sounded like the Old Woman in the Shoe, didn't she?"

"Honey, Mama don't even talk about furniture and shit the way she did. I swear. What she gon' be like at thirty?"

"All I can say is that we should thank our lucky stars that our big sis got the hell out, or we'd probably still be sitting there in the projects like everybody else," Angel said.

"Give me LA any day," Doll said.

Then they slapped each other's palms in agreement and ordered two ginger ales.

Things got pretty much back to normal real fast. Angel fell in love with that boy Willie, whom Mildred liked about as much as she liked Delbert, and Doll completely immersed herself in Richard. Everybody was in love, and when Mildred showed them the 1.5-carat diamond that Big Jim had given her, Doll and Angel almost died.

"Mama, puleeze. Have you completely lost it?" Angel asked.

"I'm marrying him. Why not? Black women deserve a little happiness too, you know. Especially since ain't nary a niggah been by here to so much as light the pilot on the dryer or buy me a beer. And this man is extremely nice. Treats me like a queen, and I'm marrying him. I don't care who don't like it."

But the wedding had to be put off because Doll started putting on so much weight that Mildred guessed she was pregnant. She knew her daughters very well, almost as well as she thought she knew herself. And Mildred's instincts were hardly ever wrong.

"You pregnant, ain't you, girl? Don't lie. You can't lie."

Doll started crying and admitted it. She'd been too scared to tell Mildred. She had pushed her lovemaking too close and in two different directions, here and in Point Haven.

But Mildred didn't care who the father was. "Keep this baby, girl. Have it and love it. If you grown enough to fuck like a woman and stupid enough to get pregnant and not leave enough time between men, then you old enough to carry the responsibility that goes with it." Then Mildred chuckled. "And to tell you the truth, a baby ain't such a bad thang. I had five of 'em and I survived, didn't I?"

Doll dried her eyes.

"I been wanting another grandbaby anyway, since Freda is taking her sweet time about it."

As the weeks passed, Mildred's maternal instincts took over. Every other day, she came running in the door with something in her hands that would make a baby's life comfortable. She bought rattles, teething rings, booties, and receiving blankets in all colors: white and yellow, mint green, light blue, and lavender, just in case. Mildred didn't know what she wanted, a boy or a girl. It didn't matter, so long as it was healthy and had ten fingers and ten toes.

Big Jim started pressuring her about setting a date, but Mildred kept postponing it. She told him she had too many other thangs on her mind to be thanking about marriage right now. Of course she hurt his feelings, but Big Jim was so in love and so stupid and so desperate that he went along with it. He didn't even know she was stalling.

Mildred hadn't been this happy in so long that Doll had a hard time telling her she was thinking of getting rid of it.

"You what?"

"I want to go to college, Mama. I can still make graduation without showing, but I don't know how I'll ever get my B.A. with a baby."

"Look. You know how many women out here done had a house full of kids and kept on living like it wasn't nothing? Millions. And I'm just talking about the black ones. A baby don't stop no show. It may slow it down, but it don't stop it. You just have to learn to do for somebody else. That's all. And if you want to go to college, you'll go. I'm so sick of people always coming up with excuses about why they can't do this and why they can't do that. You can do anything you want to do. Look. This house is big enough for all of us. I can take care of this baby and you can graduate and take your college classes.

Don't worry about it, damn. And I'll tell you another thang. All these women running around here having abortions ain't gon' do nothing but end up messing their insides all up and when they want to have one, they ain't gon' be able to. And ain't nobody having no damn abortions under my roof, I can tell you that right now. So what you gon' do — piss or get off the pot?"

Doll decided to have the baby, and as her day approached, she worried more and more about who the child would look like and whether she should tell Richard and Bryan the truth. But Mildred was of the belief that what you don't know won't hurt you. "Look. You yellow and Bryan is yellow and Richard is as black as tar. It's gotta come out either bright as hell or somewhere between brown and black. Wait and see and keep your damn mouth shut before you end up putting your foot in it."

Richard believed the baby was his all along because Doll had never given him any reason to suspect her infidelity. And when she gave birth to a seven-pound nine-ounce baby boy who was so pale he looked white, they went ahead and named him Richard anyway.

With the new baby, Mildred was in her own world. She had changed her mind about marrying Big Jim. She had too much to do now. It was as though the clock had been moved back for her and instead of feeling the angst of her forty-first birthday, Mildred felt like she was twenty-three again. She quit her job at the plant and told Big Jim he could have his ring back if he wanted it, but he told her to just keep it, which she did.

And Mildred, a brand new mother, left little for the real mother to worry about, so Doll enrolled full-time at a junior college. The washer was always soaking diapers and baby clothes, and although Doll was of the generation in which Pampers had become a convenience, Mildred had insisted on cloth diapers. "Pampers are a waste of damn money. You spend a fortune and don't do nothing but throw 'em away." Her electricity bill was twice as high but Mildred didn't care. She bathed the baby in the kitchen sink and talked to him like he could understand her. She oiled him down and lay him on a blanket in the back yard, stark naked, so he could get some color while she pulled up the weeds in her flowerbed or cleaned the swimming pool.

Richard never questioned that this baby was his son, despite his color. He had never known who his own parents were; he had been adopted. He was proud to have brought something into the world he could claim. Even though he had just started working, he gave Doll money every week to supplement her welfare checks and food stamps. His parents saw to it that little Richard had everything Mildred couldn't afford to buy him. They never questioned the color of his skin either. Thought he looked just like Doll, really, and maybe the next one would favor Richard more.

Doll and Richard hadn't seriously discussed marriage. He had brought it up casually when she had first told him she was pregnant, but Doll had said that she wanted to wait and see what happened, that she wasn't sure just how she felt about everything.

Mildred didn't care one way or another if they ever got married, so long as her grandson was there with her, and when Doll and Mildred started bickering over what was best for him — when to pick him up, when to let him cry, when to burp and feed him, how often his diaper should be changed, and who had spent how much on what — Mildred would start getting on her nerves so bad that Doll would threaten to leave. But Mildred didn't want that to happen and quickly smoothed things over.

Doll knew Mildred not only loved little Richard's company but had also started depending on her to pay half of the house note (sometimes all of it). Doll also bought most of the groceries and gave Mildred booze and cigarette money. Mildred had started drinking more heavily and more often, but Doll didn't feel that she could say anything about it yet. Mildred was doing too fine a job taking care of her son.

Angel moved in with Willie, not because of the space problem, but because she was spending so much time at his place anyway and it was closer to campus and he had been badgering her about doing it for so long. Mildred was glad to see her go because it meant she could fix her room up for little Richard. But Mildred didn't trust this Willie. First of all, he was a low-rider. He drove one of those cars that didn't have any handles on the outside, and the windows were tinted too dark. And

Willie had no intention of going to college. He had told Mildred that. He said college was all hype. The last thing Mildred wanted was for some homely boy from the ghetto to make her daughter forget all her smarts and scruples. But she couldn't stop her. Mildred figured that after being around so many intelligent and high-class people at UCLA, the girl would come to her senses.

"Just don't forget that you ain't no cheap thrill," she told Angel. "You worth every dime that a niggah spend on you and more. You deserve the best of everything. And as long as you use the brains God gave you, instead of letting them fall by the wayside, you won't steer too far off the track. And I don't care what that slew-footed boy try to talk you into. Don't you come in here talking about you tired of school or it's a waste of time and you gon' quit and settle down. I don't want to hear that shit."

By the time Richard was two, Doll had graduated from the two-year college and had been accepted to one of the state universities. Her grades weren't high enough to get her into UCLA, so it looked like she was going to have to move. She wasn't sure what she was going to college for, but her other two sisters had gone and Doll didn't want to look like the dummy in the family.

"I'm moving," she had said to Mildred one day out of the blue.

"Now, how you gon' watch this boy, go to college all day long, pay for an apartment, and live like you got some sense? You might as well stay here till you get a job and at least till the boy is old enough to know how to act. Damn. I told you I'd watch him. You been coming and going as you please all this time, what's the big hurry now?"

"Mama, I'm old enough to be out on my own. I'm twenty years old! Jesus. I would like to have some privacy. What's wrong with that? You did it, didn't you?" And to that, Mildred couldn't say a word. Her face felt as if it was swelling up and she was perspiring, which she'd been doing a lot of lately, for seemingly no reason at all.

"Hand me that bottle under the sink, would you?" Doll opened the cabinet and pulled out a half point of VO. Mildred poured it in her coffee cup.

Doll kissed little Richard and left for school. Mildred sat at the table and watched him playing with his toys on the floor. She took a sip from her cup. "Baby," she said, "Granny's down to zero now."

Mildred wasn't used to being in a house with no people in it. There was no noise to complain about. Nothing was ever out of place, so she couldn't blame anybody when she couldn't find something. She had told Doll that now she would finally have some time to do all the things she'd been meaning to do. But she had already cleaned out every drawer, closet, and cabinet, and there wasn't a weed left in her flower garden. She looked at Freda's old sewing machine, but Mildred hadn't sewn since high school, and she was not in the mood for mending.

It occurred to her that she could look for another job, even though the welfare checks kept her going. But doing what? She remembered that flier she had taken off the bulletin board in the grocery store about a training program for middle-aged women who wanted to reenter the work force. Mildred hated that word "middle-aged." She applied anyway. They were going to pay her to learn how to type, file, and take shorthand. But before the first class was even over, Mildred realized she didn't have the patience for it. At lunch time, she punched out and never went back.

The house seemed to grow. She couldn't find enough to keep her busy, and she got tired of bugging Angel and Doll on the telephone three times a day. She got irritable. Worse than bored. And so tired, tired of doing nothing.

She was lying on the couch one afternoon, watching TV. When the commercial came that said, "How do you spell relief?" Mildred sat up and said, "D-R-I-N-K." She pulled up her tube top and went to the kitchen and poured herself another glass of VO. Then she opened the sliding glass door that led to the patio in the back yard and sat down by the swimming pool. She stuck her bare feet in the cool water and kicked at it. She looked around the yard, then up at the sky. The clouds floated through it like a backdrop against the green mountains. It was so pretty it was disgusting. She splashed her feet up and down and looked at her fat brown hands clasping the glass. They looked hard. Housework, she thought. "Everythang," she said. She clinked her ice cubes around and lowered her head. It felt so heavy. Her tears began splashing into the pool like rainfall. She was afraid to look up again because Mildred didn't want God or anybody else to catch her whimpering like some baby. But she couldn't stop. She felt so empty, like somebody had dug a hole inside her.

"I hate it here!" she screamed out. What did she care about, here? Not these flowers. Not this swimming pool. Not this house. Her kids were gone. And a man? That was the biggest joke of all. So what's the point of staying out here in the desert by myself? In this big-ass house, collecting dust? My kids don't need me no more, she thought, but my daddy might. His arthritis been acting up, and he can't depend on Acquilla for too much of nothing. And Curly done had that stroke. She could probably use some decent company for a change. I could cheer her up. And Lord knows Bootsey could use some help with them kids. "Hell," Mildred said, setting down her drink and easing into the shallow end of the pool, "what good is roots if you can't go back to 'em?"

# Fourteen

*F*REDA HAD TRIED to talk her out of it, but Mildred's mind was made up. And once Mildred's mind was made up, wasn't a thing you could say to change it. She rented her house to a neighbor's daughter who had two kids and was in the middle of a divorce. The girl couldn't decide whether to move back up to Bakersfield or stay in the Valley near her mama and daddy. "You got three or four months to decide what you gon' do," Mildred had said to her. "And don't let them wild-ass kids of yours tear up my house."

When Mildred got to Point Haven, she stayed with her daddy, but she didn't know how long she'd be able to stand Miss Acquilla's nagging. After only three days, Acquilla was already complaining that Mildred was having too much company and too many phone calls and Buster was staying up too late, stinking up the whole house with his nasty cigars, and he was drinking too much moonshine. Mildred knew Acquilla was just jealous because Buster hadn't laughed this much in years.

She hadn't been home a solid week when old stuttering Percy dropped by. He sure looked good. Better than she had remembered. His hair was still black and wavy, just a touch of gray in it now, and his mustache was thick and shiny. She couldn't see his lips, but when he smiled, Mildred saw he still had all his own teeth. Percy wanted to take her out for a drink, but at first she hesitated.

"Where's your wife?"

"We been separated for a year and a half now. Getting divorced as soon as I get my income tax return. You getting prettier with age, you know that, Milly?"

She tried not to blush, but hell, when was the last time somebody told her that? Even if it was only Percy, a compliment was a compliment. Mildred got her jacket from the closet and told Buster not to wait up for her. Miss Acquilla, who was sitting in front of the TV in the living room soaking her feet in a roasting pan, merely rolled her eyes at Mildred as she was leaving.

Once outside, Percy ran to open the passenger door of his station wagon for Mildred. She got in and he tried to slow his feet down as he galloped around the front of the car to his side. He backed the car slowly out of the driveway, and Mildred looked over at him. She had no intention of sleeping with Percy, if that's what he had on his mind.

"I don't want to go to the Shingle. I was in there a few days ago, and it's about as exciting as sitting up talkin' to Acquilla about her bunions."

Percy just laughed and headed toward the North End. They rode in silence for almost ten minutes, along a zigzagging road that exposed the Canadian shoreline. Mildred looked out at the glistening black water. She rolled her window down some, and Percy turned on the radio. Aretha Franklin's voice was soft and soothing. The fall air felt just right. Mildred leaned back in the seat and watched the green lights twinkling on the Blue Water Bridge. Aw shit, she thought, when she felt that twitching between her legs. She'd been celibate against her will for damn near a year now, and block after block, her body was filling up with lust. Percy had just flipped his blinker up to turn into the Golden Eagle Tavern, when she put her hand on his knee.

"Percy, why don't we stop by the liquor store and get us a bottle, then make our way up to the Starlight. What you say?" Mildred was looking him in the eye.

"For real, Milly? Sounds like a good idea to me," he said, "a real good idea."

What the hell, Mildred thought to herself, maybe this knot in my stomach will go away. All she needed was to feel a man again, and right now she was just grateful it was somebody she knew.

When they got to the tiny room, she wasn't a bit nervous, but she poured them both a drink anyway. Percy had brought his transistor radio and had already put it on the jazz station. Mildred flicked off the ceiling light, and turned on the lamp next to the bed. They took off their clothes without saying a word. Nancy Wilson was singing, "You can have him, I don't want him . . ."

"You thank it's cold in here, or is it just me?" Mildred finally asked. She felt obligated to say something.

"Don't worry, Milly. I'll make you warm. I been waiting a long time to make you warm."

They slid under the covers and Percy kissed her. Mildred was already on fire. She slid her tongue in his mouth and wrapped her arms and legs around him like an octopus.

"You feel soooo good, Milly," Percy whispered.

And so did he, much better than she remembered, but then again, Mildred had only slept with him once, and that was twenty-five years ago.

Her body was still tingling when Percy rolled over. She sank deep inside his arms like he was quicksand. He held her tight. Mildred felt twenty pounds lighter. Revitalized. This would definitely get her through the rest of her visit.

After two weeks, Bootsey suggested that Mildred stay with her, David, and the kids. Took her long enough, Mildred thought. One more minute, and she was going to strangle Acquilla.

Bootsey and David had built one of the finest houses in South Park, right across the street from Mildred's brother Jasper. It looked like a mansion to most of the black folks who drove by it, and Mildred was truly impressed, if not a bit jealous. All she'd ever wanted in life was to live in a nice home with a nice husband who had a nice income and could afford a house full of nice kids.

"What you need with a house this damn big?" she asked Bootsey.

"Mama, I got a growing family," Bootsey said, as she gave Mildred a tour.

Mildred flopped in a cushiony chair in the living room, puffed on her cigarette, and drummed her fingers on the arm. She was already bored as hell. "What y'all got to drank around here?" she asked. Bootsey knew Mildred drank VO, and had bought her two fifths. She poured her mama a drink and sat down at the dining room table. She held her chin in her palm and looked out the picture window, daydreaming.

"Mama, me and Dave gon' put a swimming pool out there one day, and not that plastic kind, either. I'm talking about a real one, that go in the ground."

"I know what kind you talking about, girl. You thank I was born yesterday or something? I got one in my own back yard. Y'all making that kind of money around here?"

"Well, between the two of us, we made fifty-two thousand last year."

Mildred's eyes lit up.

"Yeah, we worked a lot. I worked a lot. Overtime. Ten hours a day and six days a week."

"But when you spend time with these kids?"

"Nights and weekends. I cut down my hours a lot since we got the house. I'm gon' go back to school too, Mama. I wanna start my own business one day. I don't want to retire at Ford's, and I don't believe in having ideas and not making 'em real. You know what I mean?"

"Of course I know what you mean, girl. But if you and David is working like mad scientists, when y'all gon' have time to enjoy all this?"

"As soon as we get thangs the way I want 'em. If I could get Dave to get off his lazy ass and help me more . . . He getting lazier by the year, if you wanna know the truth. I have to beg him to do anythang around here. He was supposed to have the front yard leveled. But he say his back been bothering him. He blames all his ailments on Vietnam. He got an excuse for everythang and you'd swear he had amnesia. I gotta remind him to do the tiniest thangs."

"He can't do everythang, Bootsey. Men get tired too, you

know. Y'all ain't been in this house a good six months. Give it time."

"I am, I am," Bootsey said returning to her original thoughts, "but we gon' have one of those circular driveways. Like the white people got on Strawberry Lane, only ours is gon' be longer and wider. And Dave is gon' get these trees to run along the edge of it. It's gon' be so pretty, I can't wait."

Mildred sipped her VO and lit another cigarette. She stared out at the straw-filled field. Then she looked around at all this space, this furniture, this thick carpet, that dishwasher and microwave in the kitchen, and shook her head. This girl ain't gon' never be satisfied, she thought. Bootsey want too much of everythang.

Mildred knocked on Curly's screen door, which was hanging off the hinges.

"Come on in. It's open," Curly yelled. She sounded like herself, which was a relief to Mildred. She had bought Curly a fifth of Scotch, which Mildred had already opened. She'd been nervous about seeing Curly, which was why it took her almost three weeks to make it over here. She didn't want to spend all day talking about Curly's stroke; Mildred didn't want to make her feel self-conscious about it. Hell, Curly was only forty-five, three years older than her.

"What you know good, good-lookin'?" Mildred asked.

Curly got a grin on her face a mile wide. "I heard you was in town, girl. Every time I call down to Buster's, you in the streets." Curly was sitting on the couch. It had an old bedspread thrown over it, which was sliding down behind her back. She was trying to pull it up, but her body wouldn't let her. Mildred bent down and pecked her on the cheek, and knocked Curly's cane on the floor. Mildred picked it up like it was an umbrella, and leaned it against a chair. Then she saw that Curly's eyes were dull and her skin looked dry. Curly had lost her sparkle.

"Girl, I had to take care of some business before I could start socializing. How you feeling for real, Curly?" Without waiting for her answer, Mildred walked back to the kitchen to get two glasses. When she opened the cabinet, roaches were crawling all over the place. Made her skin itch. She slammed the door and went over to the sink to wash them out. On the way back, she saw that Curly still had those same dark drapes up to the windows, only now they were hanging on a rope with clothespins.

"I'm feeling much better, now. Girl, you know I couldn't talk for a while, don't you?"

"Yeah, I heard," Mildred said, "but you sound good now."

"I'm still in therapy, and it's helping. I can move my arm pretty good now, watch." Straining, Curly lifted her elbow upward about three inches, and smiled. Mildred looked at her and smiled too.

"How's the kids?" Curly asked.

"They all doing good. Angel going to UCLA, you know. Claim she gon' teach English. Something. And Freda, you know she graduated from Stanford University. Every week that girl sending me clippings she done wrote for some newspaper. And that Doll, she in college too, but as far as I'm concerned, all she majoring in is being cute. What she really want is a husband — won't settle for Richard — and a daddy for Little Richard. And chile, you should see that boy. Getting just as big and handsome. And smart? Can out-thank you and me put together. I ain't got to tell you where Money is."

"Money gon' be all right if he can just get hisself together. He ain't no criminal and you know it. He just young and mixed up. Give him time."

"He's a fuck-up. He blame everythang and everybody for all his problems, but that's bullshit. Let's skip the subject, please."

"Well, I'll tell you. I don't know what happened to mine. They take after they no-good daddy. After I had this stroke, chile, I didn't give a damn what they did. I got tired of telling 'em to keep out of trouble. Leave that dope alone. Finish school. Get a job. I was in the hospital for two whole months and couldn't move. And you thank they kept this place clean? Naw. Now Shelly in prison, done went and had a baby in there, too. Every week she writing or calling me collect, begging for something. Chunky and Big Man is just hopeless, and BooBoo, I'm surprised he ain't up there with Money. And that husband of mine," she sighed, "he still dranking and screwing everybody in the streets." Curly took her good foot and stomped on a roach. "My kids is some of the most ungrateful bunch of bastards I ever seen in my life. And sometimes I don't want to believe I even gave birth to 'em."

"Well, Curly, it's your own damn fault. If you'da stayed on their asses a little more, maybe they wouldn'ta turned out so damn bad. And you should'a done divorced that rogue you married. He ain't brought you nothin' but misery and you know it."

"I know, girl, I know. But Milly, I ain't had the strength or the guts to leave him. Anyway, enough of me. How is Buster? Is he bad?"

"Naw, girl. Just his arthritis acting up. I took him to the doctor, got him some new prescriptions. I thank he just miss me, if you wanna know the truth. As long as he take that medicine and Acquilla don't drive him nuts, he'll be all right."

"You like it out there, huh, girl? I can see it all in your face. You look a hundred times better than when you left. And honey, you better be glad you did. It's miserable here. Worse than Peyton Place, and you know they took that off the air." Curly scrunched up her shoulders and giggled. "I sure wish I could go back to California with you."

"Why you thank they invented airplanes, girl?"

"What the men like out there, Milly?"

"Shit," Mildred said, gulping down her drink. "I wish the hell I knew. They act like faggots if you ask me. The few I been with must'a been retarded, and none of 'em over forty is good for more than ten or fifteen minutes. But I'ma stick around. The kid here got a few thangs up her sleeve. I'ma make it out there in California. Or somewhere. You can believe that."

"When I get up and at it, I wanna come visit you for a week. Would that be okay, Milly?"

"Girl, please. You know I got three bedrooms, a pool in the back yard, and honey, you can see up in the mountains from every window in the house. And palm trees? I got 'em on three sides!"

"You lying, Milly?"

"If I'm lying, I'm flying."

Mildred had been in the Point a little over a month and couldn't stand it any longer. She'd grown even more restless here than she'd been in LA. She had enjoyed being with her daughter and grandchildren but had refused to go see Money. He was on her shit list. And Buster, he was acting like his old spunky self again.

The Sunday before she was leaving, Bootsey asked Mildred to go to church with her.

"What for?"

"Mama, that's a terrible question to ask."

"All right, all right," Mildred said, and went to take a shower.

They sat in the eighth row of St. Paul AME Church. The same church where Crook had lain in a casket and below the very same pulpit where Mildred's brother the reverend was now trying to spread God's word. Her girdle was too damn tight, but she tried to concentrate on the sermon anyway.

"We all have problems," Jasper yelled out. "*Sometimes*, they can make you so discouraged and panic-stricken, that you feel destined for *gloom*. Destined to *suffer*. Destined for *misery*. Am I telling the truth this morning, brothers and sisters?"

A few voices called out from the congregation. "You telling the truth, Reverend." "Tell it."

"*Sometimes*, you can get so full of sorrow and so heavy-hearted, that you feel like you in a jail run by Satan."

"Let me out!" somebody yelled.

Mildred turned to see who it was, but she didn't recognize the woman. Bootsey elbowed her, and Mildred turned back around to face Jasper.

"*Sometimes*, you confronted with situations that feel so threatening, feel like misfortune is your middle name. You feel so downcast, so weary, so spiritless, and you don't know which way to turn. Am I right or wrong, this morning, y'all?"

"You right, Reverend, you right."

"And it seem like the harder you try, the less progress you make. Sometime, do it feel like you in a boat rowing backwards when the island you trying to get to is up ahead?"

"All I see is fog," yelled a fat woman with a tall white hat on. She was fanning herself with white gloves.

"But wait a minute. So you rowing backwards, but thank

about this, this morning. Who is it you thank give you the strength to row? Satan? No. It's the devil causing all that fog. It's the devil making you feel discouraged, making it so hard you don't even feel like rowing no more. Y'all want me to tell you the answer? It's our Lord Jesus Christ that gives you the strength to row."

"Amen."

"But what can you do, brothers and sisters, what can you do to turn your boat around?"

Reverend Jasper looked out at their blank faces.

"You can pray."

Pray, thought Mildred. Shit. Was that what she was supposed to do when she couldn't pay her house note? When she needed a man to put his arms around her? Pray.

"Once we reach an understanding with God, every last one of our problems can be solved. Know ye not that ye are the temple of God, and that the Spirit of God dwelleth in you?"

Did that mean God was supposed to be inside you, Mildred wondered? If it did, then where the hell was he? She'd already been here a half hour and didn't feel no different.

"The Bible is full of promise," Jasper declared.

"Ain't that the truth," Mildred said to herself.

"Let me tell you a story," he said.

Mildred eased her red pumps off. This was gon' take all day. She sure wished she could smoke in here.

"Know this first. Desire is prayer. Did you hear me, brothers and sisters? I said *desire* is prayer. And in order to find God, you must first have discernment." Mildred did not know what that word meant. But it sounded like something quiet. She took off her gloves.

"*Sometimes,*" Jasper yelled, "God demands mental strength in his children, before he heals. Take the case of the teenage girl who injured her ear. For two years she couldn't hear nothin' but a roaring sound. For two years she slept in her bed on that bad ear, and she slept so very sound. But do you know what she did every single night for those two years? That little girl prayed to hear like normal again. She had faith in the power of Almighty God. And then one day. I said, *one day*, sisters and brothers, after praying persistently to our God, that little girl's hearing was completely restored."

Reverend Jasper lowered his voice.

"A miracle, you say? To human view, yes, it is a miracle. But that's how our God works." Now his voice was rising again, and he was clapping his hands. Then he started laughing. "The power of Almighty God is *swift. Immediate.* His healing powers are *dramatic.* And *perfect.* Can I get an Amen?" he asked, waving his black-robed arm up into the air. Sweat was pouring down his face now, and he patted it dry.

"Amen," roared the congregation.

"Preach," someone said.

"Teach us the truth," someone yelled out.

Jasper continued to tell healing stories for what felt like hours to Mildred.

Finally, he said, "I leave you today, my brothers and sisters, with the *belief*, not in *superstition*, but *knowing* that the power of *God* is within you. We must *wake up* and wean ourselves from Satan. Have no *fear* of the mountain, brothers and sisters, because the *spirit* of God, the *faith* in *God* alone lessens the sum total of all evil. Let us bow our heads."

As Reverend Jasper prayed, all heads looked toward the floor until they heard him say Amen. When the organ music began, he asked for donations. Mildred heard the sound of rustling in pockets and pocketbooks and she dropped one of her last five dollars into the brass plate.

She could hardly get her feet in her shoes because they had swollen up, but Mildred told Bootsey she wanted to walk home anyway. She shook hands with folks she hadn't seen in years and told Jasper how much she enjoyed his sermon. He was on his way to somebody's house for dinner and thanked Mildred for coming.

She stood outside on the church steps and could see her daddy's rusty brown house. It looked like it was on its last legs, like most of the houses around here. Mildred was glad she was going back to California. She fastened her coat and started down the steps, and there was Percy, pulling up along the curb.

"Need a ride?" he asked, as he leaned over to roll the window down farther. Mildred looked at him for a minute. He was so nice, it was too bad she couldn't force herself to love him.

"Naw, but thank you, Percy. For some reason, I feel like walking today."

"You sure, now?"

"Positive," she said, and started walking down the sidewalk. The yellow, orange, and red leaves were dropping from the trees. The October air was crisp and Mildred felt it stiffening her hands. She slid them into her pockets and continued to walk. Mildred was thinking about some of the things Jasper had said, but she was disappointed. She did not feel an inch closer to God.

## Fifteen

"**H**ERE," DELBERT SAID, passing Freda a mirror with eight hefty lines of cocaine spread out on top. She took it carefully, pressing her thumb on the straw so it wouldn't fall into the water.

"I don't know if this was such a bright idea, Delbert. We could have a heart attack in here. This water is a hundred and seven degrees, you know." She set the mirror on the redwood floorboards surrounding the hot tub and wiped the sweat from her forehead.

"We won't have a heart attack, sweetie. We can get out now if you want to."

"For fifteen bucks an hour, I'm staying."

They'd been up two nights in a row, and had walked here, a new establishment called Shibui Gardens, that rented individual saunas and hot tubs and gave Swedish massages. "Let's cool out tonight," she had said to him earlier.

Delbert lit a Sherman cigarette. Freda picked up the mirror and snorted a few lines. Then she lit a Kool. They always smoked lots of cigarettes when they did coke. Delbert raked his long fingers through his dreadlocks, moving them away from his eyes. He had stopped combing his hair almost a year and a half ago, right after he and Freda had moved in together.

"I gotta get out of here," she finally said, and got up. Delbert didn't move, but he watched Freda's wet and shining body move gracefully out of the water. He loved looking at her naked, and under these yellow lights, her brown body glowed. Freda's hair was now short and curly and she didn't have on any makeup except lipstick, most of which Delbert had kissed off. She opened the adjoining door, and closed it behind her. Then she stood under the shower and turned on the cold water. It felt like someone was throwing electric darts all over her body and the next thing she knew, Delbert was rubbing up against her, cupping her breasts inside his hands.

"I'm too high," Freda said, breaking free and lying down on one of the wooden benches. Delbert followed her and then lay down on top of her, but she pushed him away. He went back out the door to get the mirror. When he returned, he walked around her to another bench. The ceiling was made of redwood strips, and through it Freda watched the leaves on the trees, which were swaying and making a whispering sound. Pretty, she thought. But then again, everything in Marin County was pretty, and everything seemed like it was made out of redwood.

Freda was buzzing.

"When are we gonna stop this, Delbert?" she asked, staring up through the cracks of wood. Most of the time she loved the sensations she got from cocaine. It made her feel perceptive, sometimes so perceptive that the real condition of her life was as clear as glass.

"Stop what, sweetie?"

"That," she said, pointing. Delbert was bent over the mirror with the straw in his nose. Freda was getting tired of this whole scene. Staying up three and four nights a week, partying. Her neck was always full of tension, like it was now, and it felt like someone was plucking guitar strings up and down it. She rarely ate a decent meal. And her skin was sallow. They never relaxed, which was why Freda had wanted to come here tonight.

"Didn't I promise you I'd only sell on the weekends, and I'm keeping my promise, right?"

"Yeah, you're keeping your promise, Delbert. But you also promised me that you'd get a real job, but you haven't. You just had to take up auto-body repair. But when was the last time you went to class?"

"It's hard getting up at six-thirty every morning."

"Tell me about it. What time do you think I get up to go to that stupid secretarial job?"

"You didn't have to take that job, Freda."

"Yeah, well a lot of good a B.A. in sociology has gotten me. When I met you, Delbert, you had all kinds of plans about what you were going to do with your life. That was one of the things I really liked about you. Your energy and your drive. I've got ideas too, you know, and my mama didn't raise me to live like this. Drinking tequila, snorting cocaine, and hanging out every night till the crack of dawn."

"Nobody's making you do this, Freda, so don't blame me."

"I'm not blaming you, Delbert. Let's get out of here. I want to make us a nice dinner tonight."

"I'm not hungry," he said.

When they got home, their Doberman pinscher greeted them at the front door. Freda had decorated this house to suit the rustic atmosphere, using plenty of reds and purples and whites to complement the woodwork. She patted Dane on the head and went to the kitchen, where she took out a thick steak and slid it under the broiler. Then she made a salad. By the time she walked into the bedroom with a plate in each hand, Delbert was sitting up in bed doing more lines. He had set up the backgammon board and he had a guilty look on his face.

"How about a quick game?" he asked her.

"Sure, why not," Freda said, setting their plates on the headboard. The bed was wooden too, and whoever had made it had started to carve a monkey on one of the bedposts but had stopped before they could chisel out the eyes. Freda's heart was beating so fast and she was already so bored that she needed to do something to stop from fidgeting. "Any more lines?" she finally asked. Delbert took a small Baggie from the table and poured about a tablespoon onto the empty mirror. Freda got the razor blade to chop up the rocks.

They played five straight games and when she finally looked at the clock, it was two in the morning. The plates of food were still untouched.

"You feel like it, now?" Delbert asked, looking desperate.

Even though Freda was far too high to feel anything, she took her clothes off and lay down beside him. Delbert was a good lover — a slow, considerate lover. But each time she felt herself on the verge of coming, something blocked it. It didn't stop Delbert. Under normal circumstances, he would have waited for her, but tonight he couldn't help himself and Freda was glad. He fell asleep instantly. But she couldn't sleep. She got up and went into the dining room.

Now it was three o'clock, and Freda still wasn't sleepy. She found the half pint of gold tequila and drank some from the bottle. It burned her throat. What the hell, she thought, it was tomorrow already, so she walked back into the bedroom and lifted the Baggie from the table. She tiptoed back into the kitchen and took out about a teaspoonful of cocaine, putting some flour back in its place. Who would know the difference out of a whole ounce? She put the Baggie back, then sat at the dining room table in front of her typewriter. She put a piece of paper in, then took out enough coke to make two lines. Her mind was already into next year. "Things I Have to Change" headed her list. Quit smoking. Exercise. Apply for *real* jobs in my field. She put a question mark after the word field. Stop getting high (at least during the week). Apply to graduate schools. Write something every day. She chopped up more coke and typed "Article Ideas" on a separate sheet of paper. By five o'clock, Freda had used up seven pieces of paper and felt like a zombie. She went to lie down, but each time she closed her eyes, it was hopeless. Delbert was snoring.

When she heard the birds chirping outside their bedroom window, Freda realized she must have finally dozed off. It was six-thirty, so she got up. She didn't bother to wake Delbert. She took a hot then a cold shower, hoping she would feel invigorated, but it didn't work. She got out her stash and did a few more lines to perk herself up.

When she got to work, Freda called Berkeley and New York University to ask them to send her their journalism brochures. This vacation had lasted a whole year.

When the brochures came in the mail, she didn't try to hide them.

"I know you don't want to move all the way to New York, Freda," Delbert said.

"I don't really know, Delbert, but I gotta get away from here. I'm falling apart."

"You mean you would leave me?"

"If that's what I have to do to get my life back on the right track. Yes," she said, swallowing the huge lump in her throat.

"Did I tell you I've been thinking about ways I can start my own business after I finish school?"

"No," Freda said sadly. This wasn't the first time Delbert had done a complete about-face to prove to her that he loved her and didn't want to lose her. But even though she was six weeks pregnant, it was still too late for that now.

When Mildred had gotten back to the Valley, she moved in with Doll and Little Richard. The girl renting her house said she'd leave, but Mildred had already spent the two months' rent she'd paid her in advance. And to Mildred's surprise, Doll was still doing quite well for herself. She had taken two leaves of absence, one from Richard and the other from college. She had gotten a full-time job driving a truck for UPS. Doll had told Mildred that she needed to make some real money, and this job paid very well. Not only that, but she got a chance to meet all kinds of people.

Doll had bought herself a white convertible Volkswagen, and always wore short shorts and tight T-shirts whenever she went out.

"You must thank you Marilyn Monroe or somebody," Mildred told her. "You need to stop prancing your behind around here half naked or you gon' get more than you bargained for."

Mildred decided there was some kind of trend going on with the Peacock girls. Freda was leaving Delbert, thank the Lord, Doll had quit Richard for the umpteenth time, and now, here was Angel with her suitcases.

"You finally came to your senses, huh?"

"You could say that, Mama. But if Willie calls over here looking for me, don't tell him I'm here."

"What happened? He didn't hit you or nothing, did he?"

"No, nothing like that. It's just over."

"This is kind of sudden, ain't it? Just last week y'all was over here acting like two lovebirds. What happened between then and now, girl?"

"I met someone else."

"And . . . ?"

"Willie found out about it."

I knew it. I knew it, Mildred thought. That girl was not to be trusted. Something always told me she was sneaky, and would grow up to be the kind of woman that would take your damn husband and not thank twice about it.

"Is he married?"

"No, he's not married. What would make you ask that?"

"I'm gon' tell you something. I know all y'all young girls is moving in with these boys like it ain't nothin'. But as far as I'm concerned, it's just like being married. You sleeping with him every night. Splitting the bills. But out of all the men I ever went with, and that includes my husbands, I ain't never snuck behind they back to be with no other man. Well, just once, but I had my reasons."

The phone rang, and Angel jumped. Mildred went to answer it.

"Don't tell Willie I'm here, Mama. I know it's him."

Mildred picked up the telephone. It was Willie, all right. "No," Mildred said, "I haven't seen Angel. Did I know what? No. White? No, I didn't. I can understand that," she said, looking down at Angel who was pulling piling up out of the carpet. Mildred didn't know how many times or how many ways to tell Willie she was sorry, but finally she said her clothes were on rinse and she had to put the softener in. She hung up the phone and looked at Angel, who was scraping the polish off her fingernails.

"This boy is white?"

"I don't need a lecture, Mama. Yes, he's white."

"White?" Mildred asked again, "Well, I'll be damned. I hope he got some money."

"Mama, what a tacky thing to say."

"Well, shit. If you gon' be going around with a white boy, at least get one with some money. It's enough poor-ass niggahs around here to choose from."

"Well, he's not poor."

"Do he have any money? Answer that question."

"I know you've got something to say, so go ahead and say it. Let's get this over with."

"Do you really like him or is this just some fling?"

"I love him."

"Love him? Damn, how long you been seeing him?"

"Six months."

"You sneaky little cunt, you. Why didn't you just move out of that boy's apartment and come on home, instead of creeping like some little whore?"

"At first it wasn't anything. He was in my French class."

"Yeah, so he parlay-voo-français'd your behind, then, huh?" Mildred said, laughing. "When can I meet him?"

"You really want to meet him?"

"Why not? Anythang gotta be better than that skunk you been living with."

Angel sighed with relief and smiled. "I'll bring him over this weekend." She thought Mildred was going to fall over when she found out. Maybe even disown her. But Mildred never ceased to amaze Angel. Now all Angel had to deal with was the rest of the family. She knew Doll would find it thrilling — so long as he was handsome — especially when she saw that Mercedes he drove. Bootsey would think it fit right in with the whole Hollywood syndrome that she swore they lived by anyway. But Freda, she was going to be a problem. Even though she wasn't a so-called militant any more, Angel knew Freda wasn't going to accept this. And Money, she'd tell him in a letter.

Mildred was happier about Freda getting away from Delbert than she was about her going to graduate school and moving all the way to New York, and that's exactly what she told her when Freda got to LA, plus a few extras.

"Why didn't you learn everythang the first time around and come out of there able to get a regular job? You gon' be going to college the rest of your life if you keep this up. What you need to be doing is looking for a damn husband. Writing for newspapers and thangs sound glamorous and everythang, but when you gon' slow your ass down?"

"Mama," Freda said, "how many times do I have to tell you.

When I meet the right man you'll be the first to know about it." She didn't want Mildred to know that she had every intention of coming back to Delbert.

"And no husband means no babies," Mildred added.

"Mama, you've got enough grandbabies now, so get off my case, would you!"

"Watch your mouth, I done told you that a million times."

"You just don't seem to understand what it means to be black and female and be accepted to these schools, do you, Mama? They don't let just anybody in! I can have a baby any time," Freda said. She hadn't told a soul that she had had an abortion. She had told Delbert she had a yeast infection and couldn't make love for two weeks. "I could've been married at least three times by now, if you want to know the truth."

Mildred decided to skip the subject. This wasn't worth arguing about.

"What you gon' do again? Write for some newspaper or go on TV and be like Lisa Davenport on Channel 7?"

"I don't wanna be an anchorwoman, Mama, that much I do know."

"What's wrong with sitting in front of millions of people every single day and making all that money? You tell me."

"Mama, those people are puppets. Most of them don't even write the news, they just sit there and read it. I want to use my brains."

"What you dranking?"

"Tequila."

"You still dranking that shit? Yuk. Don't know how you can drank that mess."

The night before Freda was leaving, Doll and Angel sat up with her, talking and sipping tequila long after Mildred and Little Richard had gone to sleep.

"What about this guy Tony Mama's been telling me about, Doll? Is this serious, or what? I mean, the way she rants and raves about how handsome and respectable he is, I swear," Freda said.

"I'm gon' marry him," Doll said.

Angel was quiet. She still hadn't told Freda that Ethan was white. She figured she would wait a little longer.

"You love him?" Freda asked.

"He loves me to death, that's for damn sure."

"But that's not what I asked you. Do you love him?"

"Well, shit. I don't know. All I know is he's got a good job at a men's shop where's he's the manager and most likely will get promoted to buyer. He drives a Datsun and takes me all kinds of fancy places, not like old dead-ass Richard."

"Can he fuck?"

"Freda!" Angel said, who would never dream of asking anybody a question like that. Besides, it was none of Freda's business.

"Girl, you so damn nosy," Doll said, "you sound just like your mama. Of course he can fuck. You think I'ma marry somebody who can't?"

"No telling. You sound like you're more hard-up than anything."

"Mama likes him."

"Mama's not gonna marry him or fuck him either, is she? And at a weak moment, Mama would marry damn near anybody."

"I'ma tell her if you don't shut up. Dig this. We're planning the wedding for the end of September. I know it's right around the corner, but I can't get married without my big sis being there. Can you fly back for it?"

"That's next month! Damn, I'll just be getting to New York. Where am I supposed to get all this money?"

"If you can pay one way, we'll sport you the other half. I mean, shucks," Doll said, putting her arms around Freda's shoulders. "We gon' party hard, girl."

"I'll see what I can do."

In the morning, Mildred refused to ride to the bus station with them because she said she was too tired, too busy, something. Truth was, she was tired of saying goodby to her kids. It had become too much of a ritual and she still couldn't get used to it. She didn't know how to show them she would miss them. "Write me," she said, pushing Freda out the door. "Now get on out of here. You make me sick sometimes with all this kissing and hugging." Freda kissed her on the forehead anyway and

Mildred sucked in her lip and lowered her eyes as if she was
embarrassed. Mildred couldn't stand all this mushiness. But no
sooner had the door closed behind Freda than she sat down and
cried as if her daughter had just died. Little Richard stood there
staring at her for a few minutes. "What's wrong, Granny, you
getting sick again?"

"Naw, Granny ain't sick. Granny just keep losing all her kids.
You the only baby Granny got left now."

And as if he knew what would comfort her, Little Richard
handed her a glass of VO. "Here, Granny, here's your drink,"
he said in his proper five-year-old voice. Mildred looked at him
and took it from his small hands, trying to stop her hand from
trembling. "Thank you, baby," she said, and took a long swallow.

Freda's new landlady, Mrs. Flowers, was a nice old woman,
pushing seventy. Freda was a friend of her granddaughter's, and
Mrs. Flowers had agreed to let her stay with her in Queens
until she could find housing closer to school. Freda never knew
a room could be so small, and why did she pick this olive green
for the walls? She tried not to think about California or Delbert
because it would only depress her.

As Freda learned quickly, it was easy to get depressed in New
York. It took her three subways and a bus just to get to campus,
and all her classes were at night. She had heard so many stories
about people getting mugged and raped and killed that during
the first week, she came straight home from school, after picking up a pint of Courvoisier, since most of the stores, as she
learned even quicker, didn't sell her brand of tequila. Freda
thought nothing of drinking the entire bottle before going to
bed, which was the only way she was able to get to sleep. She
felt like shit in the morning, and that was one reason why she
liked tequila — it didn't give her a hangover.

As it turned out, she was too late to be included in the in-
ternship program, but Freda's adviser had told her she would
have enough to do during her first semester as it was, without
working. She had gotten a fellowship, which was a nice way of
saying loan. And her adviser was right. She spent the first few

weeks running around New York, getting lost, covering stories that her professors had picked and racing to get assignments in on time.

Before Freda knew it, it was time to fly back out to LA for Doll's wedding. Thank God, she thought. No subways for four days, no Mrs. Flowers asking if she was okay when she stumbled into the house at midnight after stopping off at a bar with a few other students, no library, no editing, and no fieldwork.

Mildred had moved back into her house and had painted the entire inside. She spruced up the back yard, too. Bought new lawn chairs and special lights to hang around the bar, and recovered the bar stools.

Doll was a gorgeous bride. Freda and Mildred had stocked up on film to capture the girl in white, but by the time the ceremony began, they were both so high and shook up by the reality of the baby in the family getting married that neither of them could see through the view finder.

The weather couldn't have been more perfect for an outdoor wedding. Doll and Tony stood between the two giant banana trees, while a girl sang a Billie Holiday song. Angel stood beside her sister. By the time Doll said "I do," the birds were singing like crazy and Freda had put the camera down because she couldn't stop crying. Mildred stood up the whole time in front of the patio window, and after the bride and groom kissed, she slipped away to the bathroom. The thought of all of her kids belonging to somebody else hit her and made her feel like she was breaking into a million pieces. Finally, she wiped the smudged mascara from under her eyes and forced herself to join in.

The reception was loud and rowdy, but also elegant and civilized in a manner characteristic of most black folks when they've got something to celebrate. By eleven o'clock, Mildred and Freda had passed their champagne limit and had slid off into the bedroom, where they fell asleep on Mildred's bed, side by side.

Not even two months after she'd been married, Doll started calling Freda to complain that Tony was already getting on her nerves.

"But you just got married, girl! Give the man a chance to really get on your nerves," Freda said, but Doll wouldn't let her get in another word. She said Tony was smothering her to death. She couldn't move two feet, and there he was, breathing all in her face. He always wanted to kiss and hug and screw her all the time. And the money. The little bit he made selling those clothes was a joke. Said he was spending half his check in the store and on that damn Datsun. And jealous? Doll said she couldn't leave the house for more than fifteen minutes and Tony was asking her where she'd been.

Finally, Freda butted in.

"Look, Doll, give this thing a chance. Everything takes some getting used to."

"I'm trying, girl, I swear I'm trying, but if he don't ease up and get his shit together, this ain't gon' work. I can tell you that right now. And if you thought Mama was quick to leave a man, you ain't seen nothing yet."

Freda got a part-time job as a legal secretary in spite of what her adviser had told her. Hell, after she paid her tuition and bought books, she didn't have enough money to get her own apartment. By February, she found a rent-controlled six-month sublet near campus and was happy to leave Queens.

School wasn't so hot. She found most of the students to be incredibly snobbish and cliquish. A lot of the first-year students were working as interns at some of the major networks and newspapers. Freda thought it strange that she hadn't been given the same opportunity. She also learned that most of them already had jobs lined up after they graduated.

Freda had covered everything from political debates and campaigns to garbage strikes and murders, and now she had to get her thesis approved. She waited outside her adviser's door, smoking a cigarette, before he called her in.

Mr. Bernstein barely turned around to look at her.

"So, Freda, how's it going?"

"Fine, I guess."

"I've read over your proposal. So you want to expose some of our so-called slumlords."

"Yes."

"You realize this is an awfully big topic, I'm sure."

"I do."

"Why this particular issue?"

"Why?" She looked at him like he was crazy. "Because, I think it's downright sickening the way all of these rich people who own apartment buildings in poor areas of New York are taking advantage of poor people. There are apartment buildings in this city not fit for animals to live in. And most of those places don't even have heat or hot water. Not to mention rats and roaches that are all over the place." She sat back in her chair. "I think it's disgusting that they violate every housing code in the book and get away with it. They need to be exposed for what they are, greedy and insensitive to the plight of other human beings who don't happen to be rich, white, or Jewish."

Mr. Bernstein glared at her.

"Tell me something, Freda, what do you plan to do with your master's in journalism?"

"I'd like to do investigative reporting for a newspaper, at least that's how I feel now."

"And is this how you think you're going to make your living?"

"Yes."

"I'm not trying to discourage you, young lady, but do you have any idea how much a writer makes?"

"No."

"Well, I'll tell you. The average, and I say average, writer makes around six thousand a year. Everybody wants to work for the big city dailies, but it's not easy to find jobs there. When you finish here, your classroom and fieldwork won't count for much. I suggest you give writing a long hard thought. If nothing else, if you're dead set on reporting, I'd at least consider going to a small town, anywhere but New York."

"I've got time to decide. Are you going to approve my thesis?"

"Yes, and I wish you the best of luck." He signed a piece of paper and handed it to her. Freda closed the door and went directly to her favorite bar.

Tanya, the hostess, was on duty. Freda often chatted with her when she stopped in here after work. Tanya was black, but had freckles and sandy brown hair. She wore false eyelashes and batted them at male patrons when she seated them. But Freda thought she was pretty down-to-earth. She worked here between singing gigs. As a matter of fact, she told Freda, she'd just landed a sweet one up in the Catskills for the whole summer.

"Look, girl," Tanya said, "I've got a one-bedroom a block from Central Park. It's nothing fancy, but it's clean, and it looks like I'll be away at least four days a week, so if you want to, you can stay with me a few months."

"Are you sure you wouldn't mind?"

"Yes, I'm sure. You'll just have to sleep on my little raggedy couch when I'm there."

"No problem, Tanya. I'd pay half the rent, you know. Is it expensive?"

"I'll tell you what. You give me five hundred and that'll cover half of two months' rent."

Two weeks later Freda moved into Tanya's dark basement apartment. The furniture was old and cheap, and Freda thought the place needed some artwork. But Tanya, who said she thought she'd be leaving in just a few days, told Freda she didn't want her to hang anything on her walls. She had a large portrait of herself, holding a red apple, on a wall by itself. On another wall was a scratched mirror. Opposite that was the kitchen, and to the side, the entrance to the tiny bedroom.

A week later, Tanya still hadn't received word as to when her gig started. After three weeks, the only notes she'd sung were in the shower and the farthest she had traveled was to Bloomingdale's. Freda knew she'd been taken, but didn't feel she was in any position to complain.

Freda started eating out almost every night, and drinking even more. She did everything to avoid seeing Tanya, because Freda didn't know how to come right out and tell her that she was full of shit.

One night, she stumbled home and Tanya was waiting up for her.

"I need to talk to you," she said sternly. "I haven't said anything to you about eating my tuna fish or using my milk to put in your coffee in the morning, but something even worse has been bothering me."

"I've got a few things that's been bothering me too, like why you haven't gone to the Catskills."

"I'm leaving next week for sure, but that's beside the point. I didn't know when you moved in here that you were an alcoholic. I should've known by how much you drank at Chili's. Still, you seemed like a mature woman, working on your master's, and I just thought you were in a bad way."

"I'm not an alcoholic. I'm just depressed."

"No, honey, you need help, and I can't live with anybody who stumbles in all hours of the night. Last week half the contents of your purse were outside the door. You know how embarrassing that is? I want you out of here by Friday."

"But that's the Fourth of July!"

"I know what day it is," was all she said.

Freda put her coat on and walked back down the street to the bar.

She moved into a woman's hotel, which was worse than living in Queens. It was full of old ladies who never wore anything except a slip and always had rollers in their hair. There were also young girls who had just graduated from secretarial school or had come to New York to make it as high-fashion models. They were always so full of zest and energy it was sickening.

She hadn't told Mildred or anybody how miserable she was or about her new living conditions. But she had made two decisions. She was not going back to NYU, and she was going to finish her thesis and try to sell it to a real newspaper.

Tonight, Freda sat on the bed in her dingy room, on a mattress that must have been a hundred years old. She could feel the springs on her behind. She poured herself a shot of tequila, picked up the phone, and waited for an outside line.

"Hi, Mama."

"Hi, Freda, how you doing? We ain't heard from you in almost a month. You get my letter?"

"Yes, I got it. I'm fine, Mama. How are you?"

"Couldn't be better," Mildred said, lying. She was sitting in a dark house, burning candles for light since the electricity had been getting too high. But why mention it now? She took a sip of her VO. "What you doing? How is school?"

"School is fine, keeping me busy. Last week I had to cover a story on arms control and some demonstration they were having up in Harlem."

"Don't get yourself killed, girl. Ain't no newspaper article that damn important."

"Heard from Money?"

"Naw, but Bootsey have. Say he be out soon."

"How's Angel and Ethan?"

"Fine, they in Hawaii. Doll and Tony still tripping. That girl is as nutty as a fruitcake. Don't know a good man when she see one. How's your love life, by the way?"

"So-so. Could be better. I've been going out with a nice guy at school," she lied.

"What's his name?"

Freda had to think quickly, and took a name from one of her textbooks on the night table.

"Norman."

"You in love?"

"No, it's not that serious yet, Mama."

"You don't sound so hot if you ask me. Ain't no pep in your voice. You sure ain't nothing wrong?"

"No, Mama. I'm just a little tired."

"Then, take your behind to sleep. Write me a letter."

They said goodbye and Freda lay down on the lumpy mattress. She lit a cigarette and stared up at the cracks in the dingy beige ceiling. She started to cry, but then she stopped abruptly and sat up. For some reason, Freda remembered that once Mildred had said women were just like queen bees. Could do everything except fly.

# Sixteen

**M**ILDRED COULDN'T SLEEP. Even the pint of VO she'd drunk didn't make her drowsy. She lay there considering getting up. But for what? The house was so quiet, the only thing she could hear was the refrigerator humming, the clock ticking, and some crickets in the grass in the back yard. Then she remembered she'd forgotten to turn off the pool pump. She pulled herself up out of bed, walked out into the cool night air and just stood there for a minute. It felt good. She flipped the pool light on, and as if she'd been given an order, threw her nightgown on the bar stool and dived in. In all the years Mildred had lived in this house, and all the years she'd dreamed of having a swimming pool, this was the first time she had ever dived in. The water felt like it was running through every pore in her body, gliding through her veins, and Mildred felt like mint. She swam as if she were in the Olympics, and with each turn, her heels pushed off the cement and her body wiggled like a small whale through thick blueness. After eight or nine vigorous laps, Mildred walked up the side steps of the shallow end of the pool and sat there. Out of breath, she pulled her sagging breasts into her hands and cupped them. What good were they? She let them drop flat against her chest.

The air was causing her to shiver, so Mildred jumped up and

ran inside. She toweled her face and body like a rich woman would — pat pat pat — and dabbed herself softly here and there. Then she wrapped a bathrobe around her tingling body and poured herself a drink. Straight. Now what? she thought, looking around the room. She was not sleepy. She slid over on the gold sofa and stared at the telephone, then the clock. It was one o'clock in the morning. Four in New York. She hadn't spoken to Freda for weeks. If she had called, Mildred would have discovered that Freda was having a hard time getting to sleep too. Freda had just poured herself another shot of tequila and was contemplating whether or not to call her mama. But she thought it was too late.

Mildred walked around the living room, looking at the pictures of her daughters. Her grandchildren. All of their faces, just smiling at her. Freda had turned out to be a fine young woman, and so damn smart. All she need is a good man. And Bootsey. Just like me, too much like me. Stubborn as hell, and can't nobody tell her nothing. Living good. And Angel. In love with a white boy. He better watch her like a hawk, too, or she be gone. And Doll, she a little on the dingy side but she still my baby. Mildred let out a deflating sigh. Why couldn't Money's picture be up here and make everythang complete? Who knows? Them bars might just turn his head around straight.

Her hands moved to her stomach. It was sticking out like a woman four months pregnant. All that junk food she swallowed with her daily fifth of VO was catching up with her. She had also started dying her hair more often, because the gray that kept coming up at the roots scared Mildred.

She walked into the bathroom and stood in front of the full-length mirror behind the door. The crinkles of skin and sacks under her eyes weren't lying. I'm getting old, Mildred thought. It's right there in that mirror. And what have I done with my life, besides giving birth to five kids? What the hell have I done? Here I am in sunny California in this house by myself with no kids no man and not even a damn dog. Nothing but these birds Doll and Little Richard gave me for Mother's Day. Yeah, I got these fucking birds.

She heard a car door slam, and went to the front door and

flipped on the porch light. It was Jimmy, across the street, pulling into his driveway. A nice man, married to a woman who had never spoken to Mildred.

"Is that you, Milly?" Jimmy called out.

"Yeah, it's me, Jimmy. Out kinda late, ain't you?"

"Yep, went bowling. What you doing up so late?"

"Couldn't sleep."

"What you got to drank over there?"

"VO."

"Want some company?"

"I need something."

Jimmy put his bowling bag back in the trunk of his car and walked across the street. Mildred closed the door behind him and tightened the belt on her robe, then decided to let it hang loose.

Shit.

It had been so long since she had even touched a man — not since Percy — and Mildred hardly knew how to contain herself. She just about devoured poor Jimmy. "Hold on a minute, baby," he finally said. "Take it easy. I ain't used to so much at once."

Mildred slowed down, reluctantly, because he felt so good inside her and she realized that she wasn't as old as she thought. And with each stroke, she regained another year of life.

She got up and went to the bathroom. Now her face had some color to it and the wrinkles seemed to have disappeared. Her eyes were sparkling like fresh-cut diamonds and Mildred could've sworn it was morning. She heard the birds twirping in the living room, and damn, she loved those birds. She cleaned herself up and walked back into the room, where Jimmy was still trying to catch his breath.

"Damn, Milly, you kind of spunky ain't you, gal?"

"That ain't all I am," she said, as cool as she could be now.

"I thank I better be getting on home, wouldn't you say?"

"I would say so too, Jimmy."

In the morning, Mildred was trimming her shrubs in the front yard and pulling up weeds along the sidewalk when Jimmy came outside to water his lawn. They said their usual hellos, and

Mildred gave him her regular neighborly smile. Jimmy looked disturbed.

"How *you* feeling this morning, Milly?"

"Fine, and yourself, Jimmy?" she asked, without stopping or looking up. Mildred didn't want to look at him. Didn't need to. She felt fine now and would be for months.

She was sitting at the kitchen table, sipping VO'd coffee and whistling, when Angel walked in.

"What you so happy about, Mama?"

"That's none of your business. A woman got a right to feel good every once in a while, don't she?"

"Yes, and it sure is nice to see you so up in spirits."

"Ah, baby," Mildred said, snapping her fingers and shaking her hips as if she were dancing to music only she could hear. "If only you knew the half of it."

"We set the date, Mama."

"You did? Oh! You did!"

"April third."

"That's five long-ass months from now! I hate long engagements."

"Long engagements! Mama, do you have any idea how much a wedding costs?"

"Naw, how much?"

"Five or six thousand. And you remember what happened at Doll's, don't you? All those last-minute expenses. I want mine all planned out and paid for in advance."

"Well, I can understand that."

"Mama, it's customary for the bride's parents to pay for the wedding, you know. I know you can't afford that much, but can you help us a little?"

"How much help?"

"Like a thousand dollars?"

That didn't sound impossible. "Yeah, I guess I can help you. I'm your mama, ain't I?"

Mildred's mind was already clicking like a stopwatch. How in the hell was she going to come up with a thousand extra dollars in five short months? She had already taken out a second mortgage on the house, and the note was two months behind as it was. But she hadn't bothered to tell anybody this time. As a matter of fact, Mildred had started to keep a lot of secrets lately. Her period came irregularly and she was getting hot and cold chills all the time, but she didn't want her kids feeling sorry for her. Hell, she could come up with the cash. All she needed was a little time.

Mildred did not appreciate Acquilla dying a month before Angel's wedding, especially since she hadn't come up with her part of the money yet. Her daddy had asked if Mildred could come back just to help him get things back in order. Said he couldn't depend on his other kids. Mildred thought about it and thought about it. He was her daddy, but this time around, somebody else was going to have to carry the weight. Her sister, Georgia, lived right down the street.

She did not go to Acquilla's funeral. Mildred was glad she was dead. It was a terrible thing to say, but it was the truth. About a week later, Bootsey called Mildred to tell her things had gone haywire around Buster's house.

"Mama, Aunt Georgia done went through every closet in the house, staking her claims on all Grandma Acquilla's thangs. You wouldn't believe all the stuff Grandma had packed in the attic and in all those closets. Boxes and boxes of sheets, pillowcases, curtains, canned goods — you name it. Granddaddy said she was saving all this stuff in case we had another depression."

"Has Georgia helped clean up around there?" Mildred asked.

"Nope. I've been branging him food and washing all those dirty clothes, but the house is a mess. The kitchen got pots and pans and roasters with old food stuck inside, and Mama, some of it is so moldy, I can't touch it. Dirt is everywhere and them windows, they so dusty, you can't even see out of 'em."

At first Mildred felt guilty for not having gone, but then she got pissed off. Why should she have to get on a plane and fly all that way when all those relatives were right there? The lazy no-good bastards, she thought. She picked up the phone to call Georgia but decided to wait a few more days. She wanted to see just how slick Georgia thought she was.

Georgia was six years older than Mildred, and they had never been close. Georgia had always been jealous of her, because Mildred got all the attention. Mildred never could stand her. True, Georgia had had a mastectomy, and didn't have any breasts. True, her second husband had left her for the hundredth time. And true, her four kids didn't provide much comfort. Her oldest son, the smartest of them, had run away to join the air force, married a white girl, and was living somewhere in California. Georgia's oldest daughter, who was the same age as Freda, was an alcoholic, lived in the projects with three babies by three different men, and had never worked a day in her life. The other one, who was Bootsey's age, had been the homecoming queen, and had married someone else's husband. Georgia's youngest son was in love with his first cousin from Arizona, Leon's oldest daughter. But despite all Georgia's misery, Mildred could never bring herself to feel sorry for her sister.

Georgia had turned her soul over to God. Claimed she was saved. She'd told everyone about the spiritual awakening she had had driving down the street one night, on her way up to see some man. (That much everybody knew was a lie. Didn't nobody want her.) Anyway, she had stopped at the light on Twenty-fourth and Oak, and when she pressed down on the gas pedal, the car wouldn't move. The motor was still running and she got scared. Then she noticed there wasn't a car in sight besides hers. Out of nowhere, Georgia said, her dead husband told her to turn that car back around and go home, and she did. When she turned onto her street, her house was on fire. But Mildred didn't believe that shit. She knew Georgia was broke and had probably set the fire herself to get the insurance money.

And now, Mildred figured, since her husband and all her kids had abandoned her, Georgia was trying to mooch off Buster. After all, he did have his pension and that big old house to himself now, and Acquilla's insurance money was bound to be coming soon. So when Bootsey told Mildred that Georgia was selling that little shack she had lived in for twenty-seven years and was moving in with Buster, Mildred hit the ceiling and grabbed the phone.

"Who the hell do you thank you're trying to fool, Georgia?"

"Mildred, please watch your mouth, the Lord —"

"Lord my ass. Look, whore, you can cut out this saintimonious act with me. God took your titties, didn't he? Took your sorry husband and gave you them pitiful-ass excuses you call kids, too. I'm your sister, been knowing you all your damn life, and I want to know who do you thank you are, going down to Daddy's, taking all of Acquilla's stuff without so much as lifting a holy goddamn finger to clean up some of that mess? Now, if you thank you gon' bring your no-tittied fat black roly-poly ass down there and move in with him 'cause you ain't got no money or nobody, you're wrong, sister. If I have to come back there and put padlocks on the doors myself, you ain't using my daddy."

"Lord forgive you, Mildred, you don't know what you're talking about."

"Shut *up!* If you thank you're moving in with my daddy so you can spend up all his money, you're a goddamn lie. If you were going down there with good intentions, that would be an altogether different story. I could see it. But you going down there for your own selfish-ass reasons, and the whole thang stanks. Now what does your Bible say about that, huh?"

"Mildred, he's my daddy too. Jesus —"

Mildred slammed the phone down in Georgia's most religious ear.

When Money first got back in town from the state penitentiary, he only saw two people: Candy — the girl whose picture he'd been making love to for the past year and nine months — and the dope man. Shit, he'd been locked up for two whole years, away from the two things he like best: pussy and heroin. But not in that order. He figured he would get himself a nice buzz before he started getting down to business. He had to think of a plan, a way to get his feet back on the ground. But he needed to stretch out, kick back, and enjoy himself a few days first.

Bootsey didn't even know Money was out until she saw him standing out in front of the Shingle with their cousin BooBoo and some other guys she didn't recognize. She was on her way home from K-Mart. She honked the horn and pulled up into the parking lot. Money recognized her Cadillac, and walked over and leaned against the window.

"When you get back, Money?" Bootsey asked.

"A few days ago. I've been tied up, looking for a job, you know. I was coming by tomorrow."

She could tell he was high. "Sure, you could've called somebody. Damn."

"I know, I know." Money looked down at her big stomach.

"You pregnant again?"

"Eight months."

"You talked to Mama and them?"

"Yeah, you know Angel's getting married in a few weeks, don't you?"

"Yeah, but I ain't going. She never wrote me one single letter. You going?"

"I can't get on no plane in my condition. I'm too close to my due date. Why don't you at least call Mama?"

"She didn't bother coming to see me the last time she was here, why should I?"

" 'Cause she's your mama, Money, that's why. You pissed her off. She went all out of her way to get you away from here, so you could clean up your act, and what did you do? Went all the way out there to California and then came running back here. And just like everybody thought, you went straight to prison."

"Don't remind me. I know where I've been."

"You know, if you don't stay out of trouble, you ain't gon' be able to get no job nowhere, especially with a prison record. Then where you gon' be, and what you thank you gon' do?"

"I can always work construction. Most of those dudes got records worse than mine. Some of 'em are murderers and real felons. I ain't done nothing but petty larceny."

"Money, who wants to work at a job just 'cause it's the only thang available?"

"You mean to tell me that you graduated from high school just so you could work at Ford's?"

"That's different, Money!"

"How?"

" 'Cause it's easy work. And I'm not gon' be doing it for the rest of my life. I'm gon' open up my own business."

"Yeah, right," he said, holding up a finger to BooBoo, indicating that he would be ready in a minute.

"I am. I'm gon' open a bridal shop on the North End."

"More power to you," Money said, standing up.

"Look, why don't you come over for dinner tomorrow or something. And we can really sit down and talk, then. I gotta go to the bathroom something terrible."

"I can't make it tomorrow."

"Next week, then?"

"Yeah, all right. Tell Dave and the kids I said hello. I'll see you next week."

Money's hand brushed the top of the trunk as Bootsey sped off.

# Seventeen

*T*HERE'S ONLY so much juice you can squeeze out of a lemon, and all Mildred's lemons had dried up. She had thought of everything she could pawn to help with Angel's wedding, but even if she pawned one of the televisions or the record player or her old silverware, or Big Jim's engagement ring, it wouldn't come close to a thousand dollars.

Mildred felt bad. So bad that she stayed drunk so she wouldn't have to think about how she was going to tell Angel. There wasn't a soul Mildred could borrow from, not even Big Jim, who had come to her mind first, but she had treated him so badly, she balked at the thought. And her daddy . . . she couldn't ask him. Not after she'd accused Georgia of trying to use him for his money. And her other kids, none of them had any extra. She couldn't think of walking into a bank, with no job and her credit being so bad. The house was on the verge of foreclosure. She'd been toying with the idea of selling it, thinking she would probably be ahead about ten thousand, but she couldn't do that in a week.

And that son of hers. Calling her collect every other day for the past two weeks. Trying to get her to send him a ticket. When was that boy going to stand up on his own two feet? Got on her nerves, just listening to him.

"Ma," Money had said, "I want to come to Angel's wedding, but I ain't got no money. You know how hard it is to find a job in this town?"

"Have you looked?"

" 'Course I've looked. I don't expect nobody to take care of me. I thought I could get on with Uncle Zeke's construction company, but he say he been laying people off left and right."

"You should'a kept your ass right out here in LA and you wouldn't be in this situation. But I don't want to pour salt on an open wound, so let me shut up."

"What's this guy like that Angel's marrying?"

Mildred bit her lip. She forgot Money and Freda still didn't know. Nobody had had the heart to tell them yet. All Doll had wanted to know was if he had any brothers. Bootsey was thrilled about the whole idea of it. "Ooooh weeee!" she'd said. "So now we know who's coming to dinner!"

"He's nice. His name is Ethan."

"What kind of work does he do?"

"He's in dental school at UCLA."

"I knew he had to have some money."

"Yeah, and he's white, too."

"He's what did you say? White?"

"You heard me."

"You gotta be kidding, Mama."

"Naw, and don't give me no long-ass speeches about the shit. I don't want to hear it. He's a good person, and he loves the hell out of Angel. I wouldn't care what color he was, so long as he make her happy."

"This really takes the cake. A whitey? Do you realize what she's about to do? She's a traitor. If it weren't for whiteys do you think I'd have gone to prison, among other things?"

"Don't try to hand me that bullshit. The white man didn't tell you to get hooked on no damn heroin, did he? He didn't make you rob no Howard Johnson's, did he? Naw. That's your own stupidity, and the white man damn sure ain't responsible for that."

"I knew you were gon' say that. You know what? I wouldn't come to Angel's wedding if you sent me a ticket right now.

And you know something else? This whole family is fucked up."

"Yeah, well you in the starring role, that's for —" and there was a click. Fuck the little retard, Mildred thought. One day, that boy gon' realize he got to grow up and face everythang head on. Just like the rest of us.

A few days before the wedding, Freda showed up, claiming she was going to use this time as a long-overdue and much-needed vacation. The Courvoisier and tequila had made her blow up to a size twelve, when all these years she'd been a firm eight. Her face was puffy, her cheeks round and fat, and she even had a gut, something no one had ever envisioned her having.

"Damn, Freda, what are you eating in New York?" Angel asked, when she first saw her.

"You look good, girl, don't listen to this bag of bones," Mildred said. "It's about time you gained a little weight. You look like you could stand to do some sit-ups, though."

Freda had learned something from her mama — how to lie — and had switched around the last two digits of her social security number, added a few years to her length of employment and a zero to the end of her income, and had managed to get some credit cards. The week before she flew out to California, she went on a shopping spree at Macy's and Bloomingdale's. Bought Mildred two lace Christian Dior bras with underwires and bought herself one with matching panties. Of course, she had to have the perfect dress and had spent over a hundred dollars for it. She also bought Angel and Ethan four red long-stemmed hand-blown wine goblets.

Angel had asked her if she wanted to be one of the brides-maids, but Freda had told her she wasn't sure what day she was going to arrive and she'd rather not hold up the show, what with all those rehearsals and fittings and everything. The truth was, Freda felt the same as Mildred did about big church weddings. They reminded her of funerals.

"I can't wait to meet this Ethan," Freda hollered from the kitchen to Mildred and Doll. "What does he look like?"

"He's real light and his hair is straight," Doll said, laughing under her breath. Mildred, who was sitting on the floor, picked up the brush and whacked her on the knee. Then Doll pulled Mildred's head back so it fell in her lap, took the comb, and zigzagged it against Mildred's scalp.

"I asked you to scratch my head, not dig my damn brains out. Pour me a stiff one, would you, Freda?"

Freda poured some VO into one glass, and tequila into another. She went back into the living room. "Did you say he's got straight hair? Is he mixed with something?"

"Yep, white and white," Doll said, cracking up.

"He's white!" Freda almost spit her drink out on the carpet.

"Angel didn't tell you yet?" asked Doll. Mildred was very quiet. It was almost as though she wasn't in the room.

"No, Angel didn't mention a thing about this. I just assumed he was black. What the hell. It's almost the twenty-first century, and things are changing. If she wants to marry somebody white, that's her business."

Mildred and Doll looked at each other like they were in shock. They'd expected Freda to have a fit. What Freda didn't tell them was that she had slept with a white man herself, out of sheer curiosity. He was in her broadcasting class. Had taken her for a drink, then invited her up to his apartment. Without even thinking about it, she went, and without giving it another thought, spent the night. What she learned was that white men made love the same way black men did. She wouldn't have known he was white if she had closed her eyes. As a matter of fact, he had made her Christmas bearable. So now, what could she possibly say about Angel marrying one?

"What does he look like?" Freda asked.

"He's . . ." Mildred began.

"He's rich and drives the baaadest peach Mercedes, and —"

"He's handsome," Mildred said, cutting Doll off and sipping her drink, "and he's tall and got light brown hair. He's gon' be a dentist in a few months."

"Do you guys like him? Is he friendly?"

"Yeah, we like him. Of course he's friendly, especially after I told him if he mess over my daughter I'd blow his brains out."

"Mama, you didn't!"

"I tell all y'all boyfriends the same thang, and I mean it. What difference do it make if he white, he still a man."

"Are you gon' ask Angel the same thang you asked me, Freda?" Doll asked, giving her the eye.

"About what?"

"You know, personal thangs."

"It's none of my business."

"Since when?"

"I just hope this won't be one of those stiff and dry weddings," Freda said.

"Girl, puleeeze. It's still gon' be a lot of black folks there who know how to party," Doll said.

They heard Angel's car pull up and she walked in without knocking. She said hello to everyone and Freda gave her a wicked grin.

"Mama," Angel said, "can I talk to you outside for a minute?"

Doll thumped Mildred on the head, then stuck the comb into a mound of red hair and pushed her away. "I'm finished anyway," she said, and flipped one leg up and over Mildred's head, leaving Mildred sitting on the floor like a Raggedy Ann doll.

"I'm coming," Mildred said, in a tired voice. She was not only tired but drunk. She and Freda had been drinking all morning. Freda got up and went into the bathroom to change into her swimsuit. She wanted to work on her tan. Doll went into Mildred's room to wake up Little Richard for lunch. Mildred followed Angel outside and within minutes they heard Mildred's voice getting louder and Angel screaming. What Freda didn't know and Doll did know but had kept her mouth shut about, was that Mildred hadn't come up with the money. When Doll and Freda heard the front door slam and Mildred stormed into the living room with Angel trailing behind her, no one moved an inch.

"Look, you little ungrateful wench. I don't care if you never get married. I told you I don't have no money, not one damn dime. And I don't. He ain't worth all this trouble and I don't know why you had to have such an expensive-ass wedding in the first place. He's rich and he's white so let his mama and daddy pay for the whole goddamn thang. I don't like him no-way. And I don't care if you get married in a damn sheet!" Angel was crying so hard she could hardly catch her breath. Like most brides-to-be, her nerves were frazzled. Mildred flopped on the couch and crossed her arms. Angel ran out the door and Freda jumped up.

"Mama, you didn't have to talk to her like that. Damn, it's her wedding. If you didn't have the money and knew you weren't gonna have it, why'd you have to wait until the last minute to tell her?"

"Why don't you just shut up? This ain't none of your damn business, anyway. You been way over there in New York, liv-ing it up, and now you thank you can just come in here and jump in the middle of something and put in your two cents when you don't even know what the hell is going on."

Freda heard Angel's engine start up and told Doll not to let her out of the driveway. Doll ran outside and Little Richard followed her.

"I don't care what's going on. You don't have any business talking to Angel like that."

"I don't, do I? Well let me tell you one thang, sister. I'm about sick of you and everybody else around here asking me to do this and do that, like I'm some kind of goddamn miracle worker. Have any of you bastards ever helped me when I needed some, huh? And now, here you come on our high and mighty horse, with your college-educated ass, like you the Queen of Sheba or something. And I'll tell you another thang while I'm at it. I'm not going to the little whore's wedding since she feel like this. And I mean it! I hope the church fall down and crush every last one of y'all. And I'm not drunk!"

Without realizing what she was doing, Freda walked over and slapped Mildred so hard it hurt her own hand. At first Mildred just looked up at Freda like she was crazy, then she raised her own hand as if she was going to strike back. But she saw that I-dare-you look in Freda's eyes, sank back into the cushions, and started crying.

Freda ran outside to Angel.

"Don't worry, sis, I'll help you. You know Mama didn't mean

what she said. You know how she is. Try not to let it get to you. She's drunk. Now what exactly do you need?"

Angel got out of the car and Freda pulled her sister into her arms. When Angel caught her breath, she told her. "I still need a hundred and twenty dollars to get my dress. I don't have the seventy-five for our best man's tuxedo, and that's about it. I don't want to ask Ethan for any more money, and I already told him Mama was going to help. Freda, why'd she have to say all those terrible things to me? All she had to do was be up front and tell me she didn't have the money in the first place. She had me thinking she wouldn't have a problem. Why?"

"Look, don't worry about Mama. Let her sleep it off. She's just tired and drunk, Angel. And she's broke. And she doesn't have anybody. Besides, you know Mama has always lived over her head. And this is no different. She just couldn't pull this one off and now she's trying to strike out at you and all of us. Try to understand that. You know she wouldn't do anything deliberately to hurt any of us. And don't worry, honey. I've got my Visa and MasterCharge, and I don't care how much all the stuff you need costs. This is gonna be the best damn wedding anybody in this family has had yet."

When Freda walked back into the house, Mildred was sipping on another drink and staring blankly at the wall. She did not move her eyes when Freda poured herself one too and sat directly across from her.

"So, now I guess you feel like a big woman, after damn near breaking your daughter's heart, huh?" Freda said to her.

Mildred took her glass and threw it at Freda, but Freda had foreseen something like this happening and ducked. The glass shattered on the wall behind her head.

"I'll tell you one damn thang," Mildred said, as she got up and walked toward her bedroom. "I won't be going to no wedding, and that ain't no threat, it's a promise." She slammed the door behind her.

Curly Mae arrived the day before the wedding. Like everyone else who had never been to California, she was in awe of everything when she first set foot on the hot LA pavement. And Curly was even more impressed with Mildred's house.

"This house is finer than the ones we got on Strawberry Lane, chile," she said, limping from room to room with her cane.

"I wouldn't say all that, but it's mine, every last drop of it. Come on, girl, let me show you the rest of it. Did you bring your bathing suit like I told you to?"

"Naw, girl. I told you I can't swim with my leg. But I did bring" — Curly scrunched up her shoulders, unable to stop giggling — "some shorts that belong to one of the kids. Cut-offs. I figure at least I can get a little sun on these pale thighs."

Mildred took her through the rest of the house and then outside to show off her pool and flowers. The blossoms looked iridescent to Mildred, maybe because for the first time in months she was sober. But since her favorite sister-in-law and best friend had finally made it to California, today was a good day to celebrate. She went to the kitchen and pulled out a quart of VO, and poured each of them a drink. Mildred had already told Curly that Ethan was white, which didn't faze Curly at all.

"So, how is everythang going?" Curly asked.

"What you mean?" Mildred said, defensively.

"All the wedding plans going on schedule? Is there anythang I can do? That's why I came a day early, so I could help do something."

"I wouldn't know, really. I'm not going."

Curly gulped down her drink. "What you say, girl?"

"You heard me the first time. And don't ask me no more questions about it, Curly." Mildred reached for the bottle awkwardly and poured another glassful.

"Milly, now I know you must have had a falling out with Angel about something, but damn, don't be ridiculous. I came all the way out here to have a good time, see something beautiful — my niece getting married — and I'm not walking into that church without you. You need to swallow some of that Peacock pride and whatever else it is that's bothering you."

"I'm not going, so drop the subject."

"We'll see."

The next morning, the whole house was chaos. Women running around half naked, bumping into each other. Music blasting. Earrings lost. Bras found. Shoes polished. Runs in pantyhose, bath water gone cold. Curly was pulling sponge rollers out of her hair and Freda was in the shower, where two dresses were hanging up so the wrinkles would fall out. Mildred was still hiding in her bedroom with the door closed. Freda had told everybody to ignore her. When she finished drying off, she wrapped Mildred's bathrobe around her and walked directly into Mildred's room without knocking.

"What you want?"

"I came to see how you were feeling."

"I feel just fine and dandy."

"Mama."

"What?"

"Why are you doing this?"

"Doing what?"

"Dammit, Mama. When you gonna learn that being so damn stubborn isn't gonna get you anywhere? All you're doing is hurting yourself and hurting Angel even more. When are you gonna stop feeling so damn sorry for yourself and think about somebody else's feelings for a change? You like hurting people, is that it?"

"No. I don't like hurting people," Mildred said, cutting her eyes up at Freda. "You should know that better than anybody."

"Then think about this. We don't have a father to march any of us down the aisle. But we do have you — our mama — and each other. So how do you think Angel's gonna feel twenty years from now, knowing that on the most important day of her life her mama was sitting at home pouting like some three-year-old?"

Mildred clasped her hands together. "My hair is a mess."

"I'll press it and put some curls in it for you," Freda said, feeling as though she was getting somewhere. She always did have a way with Mildred. Freda was the only one who could raise her voice and Mildred would listen. And now the only one who could smack her and get away with it.

"What I'ma wear?"

"I thought you were gonna wear that dress Doll made for her prom. The peach one that stretches, with the matching jacket."

"I don't know where it is."

"Well, I do. It's steaming in the bathroom with mine."

Mildred looked up at Freda and broke into a smile. "You thank you slick, don't you?"

Freda walked over and kissed her on the head. "Now get your fat ass up and get in the shower. And tie your hair up. We don't have all day."

"You can watch your mouth. You thank you grown, but I'm still the mama in this house. Can I wear them orange earrings?"

"Yes, you can wear 'em, you can have 'em. I don't care. Just step on it."

"Yeah, yeah, yeah. I'm stepping on it. Hollering at me like I'm some child," Mildred mumbled as she walked toward the bathroom.

The wedding was fabulous, of course, and everything went just the way it was supposed to. When Angel saw Mildred sitting at the end of the front row, she stuck her hand out and squeezed Mildred's shoulder as she passed her. Mildred winked at her, glassy-eyed and head all clogged up, and the look on Angel's face said that no apologies were necessary. Freda sat next to Mildred. She was even more choked up than Mildred was, and when Angel said "I do," for the first time in her life Freda wished it was her.

# Eighteen

WHEN CANDY TOLD MONEY she was pregnant, it made him happy. So happy that he married her. So happy that he put in applications at every car company in Detroit, at every construction site he passed, and at every gas station in town. Every day he searched the two-column want ads. ARC Welders (Experienced). Automatic Screw Operators (Experienced). Janitor, $155 a week. Radio Drill Operators (Experienced). All the application forms asked the same questions. Do you have a high school diploma? Have you ever been to jail? Convicted of a felony? Money was too scared to lie.

He did not get a job. He got promises and maybe-soon-but-we-don't-know-right-nows. Come back in two weeks. Try us again next month. Wait till the weather breaks. By the time the snow was a foot deep, Money's patience was as thin as the soles of his shoes. He thought of going back to school, but then the baby would be here soon. And the only thing Candy knew how to do was waitress. Now she couldn't even do that because her feet and ankles had swollen up so bad.

"We need help, Money," she said to him right before Christmas.

"You don't have to tell me what we need," he said, turning his head away. "I'm doing the best I can, and you know it."

"Well, I'm going down to the welfare office today, whether you like it or not. We can't eat no promises."

Money just looked at her and lit a cigarette.

He'd been trying to stay away from the dope man's house and had managed to do a good job of it for a while. But when Candy's water broke and BooBoo came to get him from the Shingle, he found Money sitting on the toilet seat in the men's room, crouched against the metal divider. He was so high that he didn't bother to wipe the saliva dripping out of the corner of his mouth. BooBoo grabbed him by the hair and jerked his face up.

"Money!"

Money opened his eyes and smiled.

"You all right, man?"

"Hey, cuz, what's happening?" he mumbled.

"Candy's in the hospital, that's what. Now come on, let's get out of here." BooBoo pulled Money to his feet and pushed him out the door. His body swayed backward like a brick wall was leaning on him.

"Come on, man, get yourself together," BooBoo said.

"I am together," Money said, closing his eyes again. I'm gon' be a father, he thought. Me, a man with a bright future.

Money had a son.

A month passed. He filled out more applications, but nothing happened. Another month went by. Life was easier behind bars. Predictable. The welfare checks helped, but to Money it was like masturbating. The only reason it felt good was because he couldn't get the real thing.

He'd managed to stay straight for a while, but one night he started getting restless. There was nothing on TV, and there was nothing else to do. Candy was in the kitchen, pressing a girlfriend's hair. He couldn't stand the smell of burning hair. When he was younger, he'd smelled that smell just about every Saturday morning. He sat in the chair in front of the window and puffed on a cigarette, tapping his foot against the tiled floor. Tomorrow he would go to another construction site and ask if there were any openings. But right now Money didn't feel like entertaining thoughts of work. He smashed out his cigarette.

He had to get out of this house. Do something. Get some air. He decided to walk out to Bootsey's. He hadn't seen her in so long.

It was cold as hell, but Money didn't care. He wore two turtlenecks and a pea jacket. He pulled his knitted cap down over his thick Afro so it covered his ears. He didn't have gloves, so he dug his hands into his pants pockets until his thighs warmed his fingertips. He would have called to let Bootsey know he was coming, but he and Candy didn't have a phone, and Money wasn't about to spend ten of the last ninety cents he had.

Dove Road was long and dark. An occasional streetlight lit up the lower part of the sky like a small blue moon. His boots made a clomping sound each time they hit the cold pavement. When he reached the third light, he turned onto Fortieth Street. It was pitch black and looked as if it led only to a vaster darkness. He could feel pebbles pushing against his soles. Why did they call this road a street? He kept walking. The cold dampness filled his nostrils and made the hairs stick together. He held his breath to stop from sneezing.

Finally, he turned in to Bootsey's circular driveway, climbed the steps to the front porch, and knocked on the door. He always thought doorbells were meant for strangers.

"Money!" Bootsey answered the door in her bathrobe. "Come on in. You walked all the way out here in this cold?"

"How you doing? I needed a walk." He came in and stomped the snow off his feet. It smelled good in here, like a real home.

"You want something to drink?" Bootsey asked.

"Sure, why not. Where's Dave and the kids?"

"They went bowling, thank God. I finally get a minute to myself. What you drinking?"

"Anything."

Money looked around while Bootsey went out to the kitchen. She had fixed this house up like some kind of decorator. Pastel blue chairs, thick carpet, French provincial couch. Everything he and Candy owned would fit in this one room alone.

Bootsey came back, handed Money a drink, and turned off the TV. She sat at the opposite end of the couch.

"You hungry?"

"Nope," he said.

"I made some chili and rice and homemade biscuits."

"Thanks anyway."

"How's Candy and the baby?"

"They fine."

They were both silent a few minutes, listening to the wind outside the window and the fire crackling in the fireplace.

"Money, you remember Juanita Witherspoon's son, Danny? They lived across the track?"

"Why?" He turned to look at Bootsey. Somehow Money already knew what she was going to say. He'd just seen Danny yesterday going into Tate's. Everybody knew Tate was passing bad dope. Money hadn't scored in over three weeks. He took a gulp of his drink and sat it down on the carpet. It almost tipped over so he picked it up and held it with both hands.

"You ain't heard? They found him slumped over the steering wheel of his car last night, out on the Interstate, right outside Detroit."

Money turned back to look at the flames. "And?" he said loudly.

"He's dead, that's what. And if you don't check yourself, you gon' end up just like him."

Money's eyes burned. A whole lot of people he knew had died because of heroin. He had damn sure had his share of close calls. And where had it gotten him? Closer and closer to nothing. He sat his glass down. All of a sudden, Money felt lucky.

"We getting out of here," he said to Candy a few weeks later. She was feeding the baby.

"And go where with what?"

"California."

"I thought you didn't like it out there."

"That was then, and this is now."

"If you can't find no job here what makes you thank you gon' find one out there?"

" 'Cause it's different out there. It's worth a try, damn. Give me some credit for trying, Candy. Besides, ain't shit happening for me in this dead-ass town. If I don't get away from here, I'm gon' go crazy. Keep on getting high when I get depressed, which is damn near always. I'm tired, can't you understand that? Sometimes a person just gets tired."

"Whatever you wanna do is fine with me, Money, but you better call your mama." She wiped the milk away from the baby's mouth with the sleeve of her housecoat.

When Candy had fallen asleep, Money collected all the change he could scrounge up and went down to the drug store to use the phone. Mildred answered right away.

"How you doing, Ma?"

"Money?"

"Yeah, it's me."

"I'm fine. I can't believe you ain't calling me collect. How you doing?"

"Not so hot."

"You ain't back in jail, are you?"

"Nope. Ain't going back, either."

"Yeah, well I'm glad to hear it. What about my grandbaby, how he doing? Big and fat, I betcha."

"He fine. Everybody's fine, Mama. I've been thinking."

"That's a good sign."

"Since Candy had the baby, I can't find no work here, at least nothing that pays much more than what we're getting on welfare. And I was wondering . . . if —"

"Yeah, y'all can come out here and stay with me."

"But, . . ."

"Wasn't that what you was gon' ask me?"

"Yeah."

"Then come on. It's about the most intelligent idea you've had in years, boy."

"Hold it a minute, Mama. We don't have no money."

"Sell your furniture."

"What furniture?"

"Well, sell somethang and brang that boy and Candy on out here as fast as you can."

Mildred was already excited. Now she would have some

company, some activity in the house. Doll was so busy sneaking around behind Tony's back that she didn't come to see Mildred that much. And the only time Angel came by was when she and Ethan weren't speaking.

"But I'ma tell you something, boy," she went on. "Don't come out here with no losing-ass attitude, 'cause I couldn't stand it. I get depressed enough as it is."

"Don't worry, I'm coming with the right attitude, believe me."

Nobody wanted to buy anything Money had to sell, and to his surprise, Bootsey offered to give him the money for the trip.

A month later, Money and his family caught a bus to Los Angeles. Mildred and Doll met them at the station. On the way home they made small talk. Mildred smothered the baby with hugs and kisses, but as soon as they got inside the house, her mood changed. She looked Money straight in the eye while he sat on the couch.

"I'ma tell you two thangs right off the bat so ain't gon' be no misunderstandings. Number one. If you look like you going into a nod or I find anythang around here that look like dope, you out of here. Two. You got exactly one month from today to find a job and a place for your family to live. I ain't running no hotel and I don't want no sad-ass sob stories when your time run out. Do I make myself clear?"

"Yeah," he said, lighting a cigarette. "But Mama, what if I don't find no job in a month? What you gon' do, put us out in the street?"

"You already starting out on the wrong foot. You asking the wrong damn questions. Instead of thanking you ain't gon' find no job you need to be thanking about what kind of job you gon' get. Shit. I don't know who you got your brains from. It had to be Crook's side of the family, 'cause ain't nary a member of mine this damn dense except for —" Mildred started laughing. She was glad to have her only son here. "You too tired to take a look at my washing machine? It won't spin." She peered at Money with one eye closed.

He grinned at her and got up from the couch.

Money knew he couldn't afford not to get a job, so this time he lied on all his applications. Yes, he had a high school diploma. A few college credits. No, he had never been to jail, let alone been convicted of a felony. He scored so high on the aptitude test that an aeronautics company hired him as a mechanic on the spot. A month later, they asked him if he wanted to go to school. Money said yes.

# Nineteen

"**W**OULD YOU PLEASE stop at that liquor store over there for a minute?" It was late, and Freda was taking a cab home after working all day at one law firm and four hours at another. She got out of the cab and went into the store. It was crowded. She bought a pint of gold tequila and got back in the cab. Then she slid down in the seat and twisted the cap off the bottle. The first gulp burned as it went down. The second one loosened the ring around her head. By the third one, she knew she didn't want to go back to that miserable room.

She told the driver to drop her off at Ninetieth and Columbus.

"You sure now, lady?"

"Positive." She took another sip and slid the bottle into her purse.

Beaucoup's was her favorite bar. The bartender made the best margaritas she'd ever had. Tonight there were the typical late-night diners seated near the foggy glass windows. Big leafy plants hung from the ceiling. A candle burned on each table, making everybody's face glow. She sat her bag down on the floor, unbuttoned her coat, and hopped up on a stool.

"My favorite person," the bartender said. He was from Antigua, extraordinarily handsome, and gay. "The regular, sweetheart?"

"Yep. It's been a long day."

"What's the scoop?"

"Here I am, supposed to be a writer, but no one wants to hire me as one. Today I had an interview for a job in the newsroom at NBC, and this woman wanted me to take a typing test! 'Do you know how many of our female executives started out in the typing pool?' she asked me."

The bartender liked Freda's spunk and smiled at her.

"I don't care how Barbara Walters got where she is. Experience, she said. How are you supposed to get it if no one will give you a job?" She took a sip from her drink. "Chucky's in Love" was on the juke box. Freda loved that song.

Someone tapped her arm. "Excuse me, is anyone sitting here?"

Freda turned to see the most handsome face she'd seen close up in a long, long time.

"No. No one's sitting here."

"Do you mind if I do?"

"Not at all." She was already nervous and sipped the fizz off her drink.

He ordered a Jack Daniel's and sat down on the stool next to hers. He was having a rough time positioning his long legs, and Freda had a chance to look him over quickly. His lips looked succulent, and his mustache was thick and shiny. His eyebrows were black and bushy and his golden cheeks high. She tried to sip her drink slower than usual.

He finally got comfortable and looked at her.

"What's your name, if you don't mind my asking?"

"Freda. And yours?"

"James. You live in this neighborhood?"

"Sort of." She didn't want to answer too many questions. This guy could be a rapist, a murderer, anything. This was New York. But then there was something about him that made Freda feel at ease. "What about you? I've never seen you in here before."

"I live in Brooklyn. A friend of mine lives upstairs in this building, and I was supposed to meet him at eleven, but he's always late."

"Oh." Freda didn't know what else to say. She already had a nice buzz and was grateful for it. This past week had been one big letdown after another. So now she figured she'd better find out if this guy was for real.

"You work in the city?" she asked.

"No, Brooklyn. I'm a fireman."

"Really? That's dangerous, isn't it?"

"Sometimes. It's hard work, but it makes me feel like I'm doing something constructive."

Freda liked him already. She could talk to this guy. By two o'clock she had told him her life story. James was impressed.

"So, you're a writer."

"Yeah, I'm a writer."

"A woman who thinks. I love it."

He had bought her five drinks and Freda was drunk. He got up to go the bathroom and when he got back he surprised Freda by offering to give her a ride home. "You shouldn't be out by yourself in this condition."

Freda nodded. By now, all she wanted him to do was pick her up off the stool and carry her away somewhere warm. She eased off the stool as carefully as she could. She did not stumble.

As soon as they got into his beat-up car, James took out a small vial with a little silver teaspoon dangling from it.

"Do you blow?"

"Sometimes." As heavy as her head felt, she thought a one-on-one would give her just the pickup she needed.

Freda unscrewed the cap and took two hits. Her head already felt lighter.

"Would you like some company tonight?" he asked her.

"I'm not allowed to have men where I live. But I'll go to Brooklyn if you promise to bring me back."

"Tonight?"

"Whenever." The fact that she had to be at work at eight-thirty the next morning did not enter her mind.

Freda opened her eyes. Sunlight streamed through a window she had never seen. A white paper lamp hung above her head. She felt the warmth of someone's body touching her skin. Her head throbbed. The body next to her stirred. She turned to see who it was. She recognized his face but could not remember his name. Her skirt and sweater were strewn over a chair, her cowboy boots five feet apart, and her bra and panties on the wooden floor. A silver badge sat on the low cocktail table. That's right, he was a fireman.

She wiped the sleep out of her eyes and got up to go to the bathroom. It wasn't hard to find because it was the only other room in this apartment besides the tiny kitchen. She washed her face in cold water and dried it on a used towel. When she turned around, his long, firm body was in the doorway.

"Good morning," he said.

"Good morning."

"You're incredible and beautiful and marvelous. You know that?" He walked over and put his arms around her. Freda rested her head on his chest and wanted to hide there, wanted to stay there for the rest of her life. It felt so safe.

"Do you have any coffee?" she asked.

"No, but I can go get you some. Anything you want. Anything. You name it."

"Just a cup of coffee would be nice."

"If you knew what you did to me last night. There ought to be a law against making a man feel this good."

"You made me feel pretty good too," she said, but Freda didn't remember him so much as kissing her, let alone taking off her clothes. "What time is it?"

"Twenty to ten."

"Oh no! I'm supposed to be at work!"

"Please don't go yet. Today's my day off. Do you have to?"

"Well, I don't get paid when I don't work, and I'm trying to save for an apartment. I hate being late. Can I use your phone?"

"It's on the wall next to the refrigerator."

When she'd finished making her call to the agency, James came out of the bathroom. He was still naked. He guided her to the makeshift bed that was on the floor and laid her down. She was tense. He touched her shoulder, then caressed her body until it had a will of its own. Freda closed her eyes.

She did not go to work for three days.

While James put out fires, Freda played house. She washed his clothes, cleaned out his cabinets, refrigerator, and that grimy oven. She vacuumed and put fresh linen on the bed and clean towels in the bathroom. She watered the plants, James hardly recognized the place.

"You know, baby. I wish you would move in here with me. The thought of not seeing you for twenty-four hours . . . I want you near me all the time."

"But this place is too small for two people. I need somewhere to write."

"We can move. Get a bigger place. Save our money and get a two-bedroom. How does that sound?"

"But we just met, James."

"You know how long I've waited to meet somebody like you? I'm not some bebopper. I'm a grown man, baby, and I know when I've found what I'm looking for."

What did she have to lose? Freda got up from the chair and sat on his lap. She had to stop herself from kissing him.

"Then let's celebrate. You got fifty on you till I get paid?" he asked her.

"All I've got is forty."

"That's good enough. I've got twenty."

James bought a fifth of vodka and a half a gram of cocaine.

They stayed up all night.

The next night, he bought another half a gram, and they finished the rest of the vodka.

By the end of the month, Freda knew why he drove such a raggedy car.

After two months, Freda got up enough courage to call Mildred and tell her about her new boyfriend.

"You love him?" Mildred asked her.

"I think so."

"A fireman, huh? Thank God he's got a good job."

"I'm living with him, Mama."

"You doing that mess again? Girl, why don't you go ahead and marry the man? All you gon' do is find out he ain't perfect and then leave him, like you been doing. When you gon' get tired of this shit?"

"Mama, look. You know how many times I probably would've been divorced by now?"

"What difference do that make? Marrying a man is a way of letting him know you want to be with him forever. It don't make no difference if it don't last but two weeks."

"Mama, I said we're thinking about getting married, didn't I?"

"No, you didn't."

"How are things out there?"

"So-so."

"How's Money and his family? Did he ever find a job?"

"Yeah, believe it or not. A good one too, at a place where they build airplanes. He on time and ain't missed a day. They sending him to electronics school and paying him to go, can you believe it?"

"That's great. I knew he'd pull himself together one day."

"Yeah, I just hope it last. He seem determined, almost like he doing it to prove to me that he ain't a fuck-up. Like he gon' make a lie out of everybody."

"What about Candy?"

"She's a real dingbat if I ever saw one, bless her sweet heart. She believe anythang Money tell her. It surprises me how some women can raise their kids to be so stupid."

"But she is nice, isn't she, Mama?"

"Yeah, and I was glad to get 'em out of here, let me tell you. They stayed here damn near three months and liked to ate me out of house and home. Hand marks all on my damn walls. They killed my fish from overfeeding it, and one of my birds flew out the patio window."

"What about Angel?"

"She fine. Teaching school, you know. English. I can't hardly stand her no more. Ethan done bought her a Mercedes and she only shop in Beverly Hills. She sickening. We don't even see her that much. She pregnant, you know."

"No, nobody tells me anything any more. How many months?"

"I don't know. Three or four. Something like that. She ain't the only one."

"Not Bootsey again, Mama, she just had little Ivory."

"Doll."

"Doll!"

"Yep, this time it's Richard's baby for real. Her and Angel due on the same day. She finally left Tony for good."

"She and Richard getting married?"

"Who knows. One minute he say yeah, the next minute he can't decide. She moved all her stuff into his mama's house. You know his mama gave him that house. I don't thank he gon' make a move until that baby get here. He don't trust Doll two minutes when his back is turned."

"What about you, Mama?"

"I'm gon' do what I told you I was gon' do."

"You're really going back to live in Point Haven?"

"Yeah, why not. I'm sick of California, to tell you the truth. It's boring as hell out here. I don't care what nobody say. Besides, I want to be close to my daddy before he die, and he ain't got nobody to take care of him the way I can."

"You're gonna go crazy back there, Mama, and you know it."

"Chile, if I ain't crazy by now, ain't nothing gon' do it to me. Enough of me. So you feeling pretty good, huh? You cut down on all that dranking, I hope."

"Yep, a whole lot. As a matter of fact, all I drink now is wine. No more hard stuff for me. What about you?"

"Let me thank. I ain't had a drank in four or five days now. I don't need it half as much as I used to."

But they were both lying because Freda was sipping vodka and Mildred was pouring her third glass of VO.


"How much money have you saved?" Freda finally asked James one night.

"Don't worry, baby, by next month, I'll have it together."

"Next month? James, I can't spend another month in this room. I haven't written a word since I've been here."

"Look, don't blame that on me, Freda. You don't have any discipline. I told you, I had a few outstanding debts I had to take care of first. We'll be out of here by next month. I promise. Why don't you go ahead and start looking? You've got a few dollars in the bank, don't you?"

"That's beside the point. We're supposed to go in fifty-fifty."

"We will, but if you find a place, put the deposit on it. I'll come up with the rest, don't worry, baby." He got up from the couch and pulled her into his arms. They did not eat dinner that night.

Freda was still determined to find a new place and the next day she looked through the paper. There were a few places being renovated in Brooklyn that had reasonable rents.

She took the train out to the address in the newspaper ad. It was a brownstone on a clean, tree-lined street. The outside of the building didn't look renovated. The iron gate was open so she walked up the stairs. There was dusty wood and Sheetrock leaning against the stairwell. She heard drilling. The first-floor apartment door was open. Freda peeked in. It had high ceilings and tall windows. The walls were white and the floor was still wooden planks. She walked through it. Brand new bathroom. Two bright bedrooms. One could be her study. Sunlight streamed through the windows and a deck led down into the back yard. They could have barbecues.

She found the owner on the second floor and gave him a month's rent as a deposit.

Freda was making lasagna when James got home.

"I found a place!"

"How much is it?"

"Five seventy-five."

"Are you crazy? I'm not paying that kind of money for an apartment, Freda. Not in Brooklyn."

"You haven't even seen it, James. You wanna go see it? It's beautiful. They're still working on it."

"Why should I waste my time? I'm not spending that kind of money. I know we can find something under four hundred."

"Like this dump you've got now."

"Oh, so now this place ain't good enough for you?"

"I didn't say that. I already gave them a deposit."

"Then get it back. Stop payment on the check."

"I don't want to get it back. It's a nice apartment and between the two of us that's not even three hundred apiece. I could afford it alone."

"You must not have heard me. I told you, I'm not spending that kind of money, and I meant it."

"If you'd stop putting half your paycheck up your nose, maybe you'd be able to afford it."

"Yeah, and if you didn't get so drunk, maybe I wouldn't get so high."

"I'm taking the apartment, with or without you." Freda didn't even realize she'd said it until after she'd said it.

James looked at her as though he hated her.

"Then you can move tomorrow, Miss Hot Shit." He got up, put on his jacket, and walked to the door. "I knew you thought you were too good for me. Be gone when I get back." He slammed the door in her face.

# Twenty

*T*HERE WAS A KNOCK at Mildred's front door. She set the potholder on the stove, turned the fire down on the pinto beans, and went to see who it was. Two policemen stared at her through the screen door.

"Mildred Peacock?"

"Yes?"

"We have a warrant for your arrest."

"Shit." Mildred knew it was those damn checks. She'd written over eight hundred dollars' worth to pay two house notes and stop the phone from getting cut off. How she thought she was going to get away with it had spun past her.

"Can I wash my face and put on something decent?" She had on a pair of blue jeans and a white sweatshirt.

"That won't be necessary, ma'am. If you can get someone to post your bail, you'll be home in an hour. You're going to have to go to court, you know."

Mildred grabbed her purse and locked the front door.

When she got to the precinct, they asked her if there was anyone in particular she wanted to call. She called Doll.

"I need two hundred dollars, and quick."

"Two hundred dollars? For what, Mama?"

"To get me out of jail, that's what."

"Jail? Are you serious?"

"Look, do you have it or don't you? I ain't got all day."

"All I've got on me is about sixty-five, and Richard won't be home until late this evening. Mama, what you doing in jail? You been writing bad checks again, ain't you?"

"What difference do it make why I'm here? Just get me the hell out of here. Call Angel."

"Where are you?"

"Panorama City."

"Angel's on her way over here now. We were supposed to go shopping for baby things. We'll be there as soon as we can."

Mildred sat down on one of the wooden benches. "My daughters are on their way. Are you gon' lock me up till they get here?"

"No, ma'am. You can sit right there. We know you're not a criminal, but you can't go around writing checks when you don't have the funds to cover them."

Mildred just looked at him.

A half hour passed.

"You got a cigarette?" She had left hers on the kitchen table. "Aw, shit! I left a pot of beans cooking on the stove. I gotta call my daughter and tell her to stop by my house first. Can I?"

"It's against procedures, but under the circumstances . . ."

She dialed Doll's number but did not get an answer. Money was at work, and too damn far away. Jimmy, across the street, was at work too. Shit. She lit the wrong end of the cigarette. Shit. What was taking them so long?

"Can you get somebody to go by my house? It could be up in flames right now and I'm sitting here in jail over some damn checks."

"Ma'am, I'm sure if your house was on fire, a neighbor would see the smoke. The worst that could happen is that your dinner will be ruined. Take it easy. You'll be home before you know it."

When Doll and Angel walked in the door, both of their bellies protruding like mixing bowls, Mildred jumped up.

"What took y'all so damn long?"

"Mama, we got here as fast as we could. Traffic is backed up on the freeway this time of day and you know it," Doll said, pushing her sunglasses on top of her head.

Angel paid the clerk in cash.

"I left my beans on the stove, and I know they done burnt up. My house could be on fire."

They all got into Angel's peach Mercedes. Mildred's heart beat like a loud clock. "You think I should'a called the fire department, just in case?"

"No, mother. The beans will probably just be scorched," Angel said.

"What did you call me?"

"Oh, I've gotten into the habit of calling Ethan's mom that. Does it bother you?"

"You ain't been calling me no damn mother, and don't start now. And besides, if you look over here at me, you'll notice that I ain't white."

"Mama, no one's thinking anything like that."

"You know, I been meaning to tell you a few things. Since you married that white boy, you done changed. Now I ain't never had no problems with him. I like him. But I swear, if I didn't know you was my daughter, I'd swear you was a little white girl. You don't talk the same. You don't act the same. You don't even come by and see me no more —"

"Mama, please, give her a break, would you?" Doll said.

Mildred turned to look at her in the back seat. "You know, you can just shut up. At least she *got* a mother-in-law."

"What's that supposed to mean?"

"It means that you a damn fool to give up your apartment and go live with a man you getting ready to have another baby by even if the first one ain't his, and he still ain't put no ring on your finger."

"We're planning on getting married, Mama."

"You know how many times I done heard that shit before?"

Doll didn't even bother answering Mildred. It was senseless to argue with her.

When Angel turned onto Mildred's street, there were three firetrucks at the curb in front of her house.

Angel pulled up behind the red truck and Mildred dashed out

the car and into the side door, which had been pulled off its hinges. The kitchen walls were gray from the smoke. The curtains were singed. Water was everywhere. All the dishes were broken, and the silver pot was on the floor. The beans were black.

"You're pretty lucky," a fireman said to her. "This could've been a whole lot worse if a neighbor hadn't called us in time."

Mildred walked into the living room. Smoke stains covered the white walls. The patio glass had been smashed. All the windows had been broken. She sat down on the wet couch and burst into tears.

"Mama, are you okay?" Doll asked.

"My house. Everything I own is in here. Look at this place."

"Insurance will cover it, don't worry."

"Who gives a fuck about insurance? What about me? I can't live in here now."

"You can come and stay with me and Richard until they fix it back up."

"Or you can come and stay with me and Ethan, Mama." Angel stood in the middle of the room because there was no place dry to sit.

"I don't want to live with neither one of y'all. This is my house!"

The phone rang.

"Answer that, would you, Angel? Whoever it is, tell 'em I ain't home."

Angel tiptoed to the kitchen. "Mama, it's Aunt Georgia."

"What she want?"

"It's Granddaddy, Mama."

Mildred leaped up from the couch. The glass on the carpet cracked under her weight as she stormed into the kitchen and snatched the phone from Angel's hand.

"What's wrong with Daddy, Georgia?"

"He had a heart attack."

"A heart attack? Nooooo . . ."

"He's in Mercy Hospital, Mildred. They don't know if he gon' make it or not. But the Lord is watching over him."

The inside of Mildred's mouth tasted like chalk and smoke. Her lungs would not let in any air. Her hands trembled and she couldn't stop them. It felt like her heart was beating in the center of her head. She couldn't stand all this noise. She wiped her runny nose on the back of her hand and tried to pull herself together.

"I'll be on the next plane out of here. My daddy need me more than he need the Lord."

# Twenty-one

$F$REDA DIDN'T KNOW what time it was when she stumbled in her door. She dropped her keys on the floor and didn't bother to pick them up. Turned on the track lights and dimmed them. Then she took off her jacket and flopped in the middle of her brand new couch. It was white with big flowers all over it. She looked at her typewriter. There was a blank page in it, and stacks of paper scattered around it. It was stupid to have bought a glass desk with no drawers, but it was pretty and sophisticated and she had wanted something to make her feel elegant, something besides a negligee. She walked over to the refrigerator and poured herself a cold glass of wine. Freda had given up hard liquor ever since she and James had split up. Besides, she could drink more wine. She picked her purse up off the floor and opened her wallet to get the white triangle that said "snow" on it. Tomorrow was her thirtieth birthday and she had bought this to celebrate. But what the hell, tonight was tonight, tomorrow was tomorrow.

The phone rang once. Her answering service was still on. Freda set the package on the kitchen counter and uncoded the phone. She got a steak knife and chopped up some of the cocaine. She did a few lines and sat back down. She didn't feel like calling to see who had phoned. Didn't feel like talking to anybody.

She lit a cigarette and kicked off her purple pumps. So, tomorrow was her big day. Freda took a long sip of her wine and emptied the glass. Thirty years old and here I am in New York. Alone. No husband, no man, no prospects, call myself a writer and been working on the same damn article for over a year now. Can't get to sleep without a drink. She got up to pour herself another. She did not want to think about this. When the phone rang again she jumped. Shit.

"It's about time you got home." It was Bootsey. "You didn't get my messages? I left three of 'em. What's the point of having a damn answering service if you don't never call it?"

"Take it easy, girl. I was about to call it now. I just got home a few minutes ago. Damn. Give me a break. Is something wrong? It's not Granddaddy again, is it?"

"Naw, Granddaddy got home last week, and Mama been over there helping him get back on his feet. He's doing much better. You know she's selling her house in California, don't you?"

"No, I didn't."

"Yeah. She got Doll handling all the paperwork. She gon' get some insurance money from that fire, too."

"And where is she gonna live? With you? She can't stand Aunt Georgia."

"No, honey. You know me and Mama don't get along. She's too bossy. She fell in love with this brick house up on Oak Street and she say as soon as Doll send her the money from the house in the Valley she gon' buy it. But that ain't the reason I been calling you."

"Well, my birthday isn't until tomorrow, so what's going on?" Freda reached for her glass.

"I'm leaving Dave."

"You're what?"

"You heard me. Next week. Me and the kids is moving back into our old house. I'm serious. I can't stand another minute of him."

"Wait a minute, Bootsey. I thought you guys were so happy."

"You getting me mixed up with Angel."

"You're serious, aren't you?"

"Did you know I was bald-headed?"

"What do you mean, bald-headed?"

"Just what I said. My nerves have been so bad that all my hair fell out. I been wearing wigs for the past six months. I didn't want to tell nobody. Mama know it now. Anyway, I'm leaving him 'cause he ain't gon' never change."

"Why should he change?"

"You remember a few years ago when I told you how I wanted to go back to school and open up my own bridal shop?"

"Yeah." Freda pulled the phone around the refrigerator and did a few lines.

"Well, every time it comes time to register, he comes up with some excuse why it ain't a good time for me to go. We got money in the bank, but he don't want to take a chance on starting no business with no guarantee it's gon' make it. I'm tired of working at Ford's. And he's so damn lazy it's a shame. I do everythang around here. Cook. Clean. Chastise these kids. And all he want to do is watch TV and fuck."

"But Bootsey, can't you guys talk this thing out?"

"He don't like to talk about nothing. What he says goes, but that's bullshit. I've had it, Freda. I mean, I've really had it."

"What about the house?"

"Fuck this house. It'll be here long after I'm in the nuthouse. And if it weren't for me, do you think this house would'a ever got built? Hell no. I'm the one who worked all the overtime. He was always too tired. And girl, I can't even tell you the last time we went out. If I take another nerve pill, I'm gon' explode."

"You taking those things?"

"I gotta take something. But I don't want to end up like Mama did. All strung out."

Freda looked at the pile of cocaine and the glass in her hand. She was the one who was strung out, she thought, but didn't dare say it. She didn't want her sister to think she was a failure. Didn't want anybody to think that about her. She tried to listen carefully to every word Bootsey said, tried to sound compassionate, but she was too preoccupied with her own sense of loss. She had lost her enthusiasm, had lost her idealism and self-assurance. And now at thirty, she had somehow lost her will.

When daylight filtered through the living room window, Freda woke up and poured the last drop of wine into her glass. The cocaine was gone. Her fingers were stiff, and she could barely stand up. It was her thirtieth birthday, and she was drunk. Something terrible happened last night. What was it? She pounded her fist against her head, trying to make herself remember. Bootsey. Something happened to Bootsey. Freda started crying because she couldn't remember. She ran into the bathroom and washed her face in cold water. It was nine o'clock. Too early to call Michigan. But she had to call somebody. She had gone too far. The telephone book lay on the floor under her desk. Freda leaned over and picked it up. It was so heavy. She turned to the A's. It was her thirtieth birthday and she was drunk. She put the phone book under the phone and dialed the number as best she could.

"Good morning, this is AA," the voice at the other end of the phone said. "My name is Michael, and I'm an alcoholic. Can I help you?"

Freda tried to say something, but her throat closed up. *I'm an alcoholic.* But nothing came out of her mouth. She moved the phone away from her ear. *I'm an alcoholic.* The words scratched her eardrums. She stared at the phone until she didn't have any strength left to hold it. When it fell on the floor, she picked it up and put it back in the cradle.

# Twenty-two

MILDRED SAT in an ugly brown chair in the living room of her new brick house. It was an old vinyl chair with brass tacks in the seams and a back so high it looked like a bass fiddle from behind. It was the only furniture she had here, but she didn't care. She was just grateful that Buster had lent her the money for the down payment and got her away from her sanctified sister. But not long after she'd left, Buster started drinking whiskey and sneaking young girls upstairs to his bedroom through the side door. Georgia was furious, and Buster sent her back down to her own tiny little house so she could share her disgust with God.

Mildred was anxious for Doll to sell the house in California so she could pay Buster back. Seemed like it was taking forever, though. A few weeks ago, Doll had said some Mexicans were interested, but that fell through.

Mildred crossed her legs and took a sip of VO from the tall green glass. She'd bought eight of them from St. Vincent de Paul's for a nickel apiece. She never could pass up a bargain. As a matter of fact, she'd bought an old-fashioned lawn mower for four dollars, which cut the grass down low and smooth in the back and front yards. Mildred wondered how people survived without back yards. She'd also bought fifteen men's shirts for a quarter apiece. Stripes, solids, pastels, and one navy blue with a white collar. A pink angora sweater with white pearl buttons. Somebody would want this stuff, she just knew it.

She took another sip. Since she'd moved in here, seemed like all she'd had for breakfast was rye and ice. Sometimes it burned the lining of her stomach, but by the second or third swallow, all she felt was its warmth. She arched her toes and raked them through the royal-blue carpet. This was about the ugliest carpet she'd ever seen in her life, except for that olive-green stuff Freda used to have when she lived in LA. When the money came from the other house, she was going to pull it up, strip and sand the hardwood underneath, and buy one of those oriental rugs, if she could find one at a decent price. Mildred felt like she always had to plan her life for tomorrow.

She leaned forward when she spotted a streak that looked like smeared smoke on the picture window. Mildred hated dirty windows. Liked everything clean. She had disinfected the whole house with ammonia and Lysol. Even the basement. Mildred got up from the chair and went to the kitchen to get a pail of vinegar and water, then she went back to the living room, and tore off a piece of old newspaper and crumbled it up. Just as she was starting to wipe off the window, the mailman came up the sidewalk and dropped a handful of envelopes in the door slot. One of them would be her welfare check. Then she'd be able to go back and get that forest-green silk blouse and matching slacks she'd seen on the sale rack at Arden's yesterday. Hell, she was going to be forty-eight years old tomorrow. She deserved something new, even if she couldn't afford it.

She sat the pail back down and picked up the brown and white envelopes and flipped through them. A letter from the IRS. Hadn't filed in so long, they'd probably caught up with her. Be just her luck. The trash and light bills. They'd have to wait. Some pamphlet about voting for a city councilman. But she wasn't registered to vote in Michigan. And that notice she knew was coming, telling her the real estate taxes were being reassessed. Her house note was going to be either higher or lower. Right now, Mildred didn't want to know. Last were her food stamp voucher and welfare check. She threw them all on the hall table and picked up her glass. They must thank I'm some kind of money tree, she thought. She took another long swallow. Thank God for liquor.

It was only eight-thirty and the bank wouldn't open until ten, so she decided to take a long bath. Her new bathroom was small and cozy, even if she wasn't crazy about the orange tiled floor. She poured almost a whole cup of yellow bubble bath into the water, untied her bathrobe, closed the door out of habit, and stood naked in front of the floor-length mirror. Her body looked like an old potato. An inch of gray had grown out of her cluster of otherwise red hair. The whites of her eyes looked like the faded pages of an old book.

A sharp pain darted across the lower part of Mildred's stomach. She arched forward to support herself against the mirror. She knew she should've eaten something this morning before she started drinking, but she hadn't been hungry. When the pain had passed, she opened the door and went to get her glass. She closed the door again, turned off the water, and sat the glass on the edge of the tub. The water was too hot, but she gritted her teeth and got in anyway. She sloshed her legs up and down to get used to it and then let her head fall back against the tiles. It was too damn quiet in here. Should've turned on the radio. She wondered what her kids were going to send her for her birthday. Bootsey had given her that microwave. Freda would send money. Mildred didn't know what Angel and Doll were thinking about. And Money, he always forgot. She soaked for at least ten minutes, then reached for the bar of soap, but decided against it. Mildred closed her eyes. What am I gon' do for my birthday? Didn't have any plans. Hadn't thought about who she'd spend it with. Damn sure didn't want to be alone. Last week she'd seen Spooky at the Shingle, but he looked so shriveled up and pale that the thought of him touching her made her nauseated. And Percy might get the wrong idea.

She took another sip and the doorbell rang. Now who in the hell could that be this time of morning? Mildred stepped onto the rug and grabbed the pink towel, then wrapped it around her and went to the front door. Curly stood there grinning. She had something in her hand, but Mildred couldn't see what it was.

"Open this door up, old nappy-headed woman. These mosquitoes is eating me up alive out here."

Mildred hid behind the door as she opened it. "Girl, what you doing out this time of morning?"

"I needed the exercise, and since you ain't invited nobody up here, I thought I'd come and see for myself." Curly lifted her cane up and limped past her as Mildred closed the door behind them. Curly's arm was still bent like it was in an invisible sling. She sat the brown bag on the floor.

"Come on back here, girl, I was in the tub." Mildred dragged the brown chair and pushed it against the wall outside the bathroom. Curly sat down and Mildred got back in the tub. "You want a drank?"

"Girl, I don't touch that stuff no more."

"Since when?"

"Since I joined the church."

"What's joining the church got to do with dranking?"

"I don't need it no more. And what you doing sipping this time of day?"

"You know what tomorrow is?"

"Of course I do. It's your forty-eighth birthday, Milly. I ain't forgot. After all these years I done known you, you thank I forgot? I got something for you in that bag. It ain't much, but I was thanking about you."

"You didn't have to do that, girl."

"I know I didn't *have* to."

"What is it?"

"I ain't telling you. Wait and see."

"Well, I'm going downtown when I get out of this tub. I'm gon' cash my check and pick up some thangs; pay some damn bills."

"This house sure is nice, Milly," Curly said, looking around at the neatness of everything. The gleam on the kitchen appliances, the tiles all intact in the kitchen, the blue carpet, and that fireplace! "The Lord sho' looks out for you, chile."

"If Doll don't hurry up and sell that damn house, he gon' have to."

"You'll never guess in a million years who I seen in church last Sunday, girl."

"Who?"

"Ernestine. She done sobered up, lost some weight, and finally got some teeth in her mouth after all these years. Her hair was fixed so nice."

"No shit. Faye Love told me she was messing around with one of your brothers."

"Which one?" Curly peeked her head through the crack of the door. Mildred's body was covered with lather.

"Zeke," she said, squeezing the washcloth over her to wash away the soap.

"Milly, you can't believe half the stuff you hear in this town. You know that. It's the devil that spreads evil words. Ernestine just seen the light like a lot of us. Everybody 'cept you."

"Look, Curly, don't come in here preaching just 'cause you done turned your soul over to God. I already done had enough of Georgia these past few months. Don't you come in here talking the same mess, please. It's too damn early."

"Milly, I'm not trying to preach to you. But look at what you doing. Dranking VO and it ain't even nine o'clock in the morning. If your soul is troubled, you need to turn it over to God. He'll make you worry-free."

"Aw, Curly, spare me, would you? My nerves is bad and I got so many thangs on my mind I'll do whatever I have to do to ease some of this pressure. I got bills coming out of my ass." Mildred stepped out of the tub, "You know, y'all niggahs kill me. As soon as something terrible happen, the first thang you do is go running to church like God is gon' hop down out the sky and save y'all ass. Well, I don't buy it. Ain't never bought it. It ain't that I don't believe in God, I just don't trust his judgment. If he supposed to be such a savior, why he let you have that damn stroke? Why he take Georgia's titties? Why he let Crook die so young?"

"Mildred, God ain't the one responsible for evil and tragedy. It's the devil. But God is the one that give us the strength to carry on. I can bear witness."

"Can we skip the subject, please, Curly?"

"All it is is the truth, Milly."

Mildred walked out the bathroom with the towel wrapped

around her. "I swear, you so serious. I liked you a lot better before you started going to church."

"I'ma tell you something, girl, and then I'ma shut my mouth. Ever since I had this stroke, I didn't know if I'd ever be able to talk or stand up on my own two feet, and I have thanked God in heaven for every step I take and every word I'm able to speak. The devil sure done his work by me. Shelly most likely gon' spend the rest of her life in and out of prison, Chunky half crazy from them drugs, and last night, chile, some boy beat Big Man in the nose with a poolstick and he up in Mercy Hospital right now."

"Naw, Curly."

"Yeah, it broke and he hemorrhaged some."

"Damn."

"My husband don't even touch me no more, Milly, so you turn to whoever gon' make you feel the most glory and peace. And for me, right this minute, it's God. If it weren't for him, I don't know if I'd even have the strength to get up in the morning and face daylight."

"Well, more power to you, Curly." Mildred was looking through one of her plaid suitcases for some clean panties and a decent bra.

"Why don't you come on and go to church with me on Sunday? Jasper still preaching like ain't no tomorrow. The words be like music filling up your body."

Mildred eased into her underwear, put her robe back on, and went to the kitchen to get her bottle.

"Come on, Milly, do it for your sis'-n-law."

"I'll thank about it. Last time I went to church I got depressed."

"That's 'cause you didn't give yourself a chance to let God in. Once you let him in, it feel so good, Milly, you won't want to turn back."

"Look, chile, I'd love to sit here and chitchat with you all day, but I got thangs to do."

"Well, I just stopped by to drop your present off and to catch my breath. My pressure been going up like crazy. I'm trying everythang I can to relax. Oh well, it's in God's hands. Thank about Sunday now," Curly said as she walked to the door. "I'll thank about it."

"Oh," Curly said, turning to peck Mildred on the cheek, "if I don't see you tomorrow, happy birthday, sis'-n-law."

"Thank you, Curly, and let me know how Big Man is doing, okay?"

Curly lifted her cane up in the air to say okay.

Mildred closed the door, in spite of the rising heat. She reached down and picked up the brown paper bag Curly had left and opened it. It was a photograph inside a wooden frame. Mildred couldn't believe her eyes when she saw the faded picture of her, Curly, and Crook, standing outside the Red Shingle. Hell, that was . . . at least . . . thirty years ago. She was pregnant with Freda, she remembered, because the three of them had gone to the Shingle to celebrate. It was some band playing from out of town, imitating the Platters, and she and Crook had slow-danced in a blue corner. Damn, Mildred thought. Curly sure has a strained grin on her face, maybe because that ugly bandanna on her head was tied so tight under her chin she was probably choking. And Crook, with that devious smirk on his face. Like he knew he was gon' be handsome forever. And me, not a blemish on my face. And happy and everythang. Damn, how time fly. She pressed the picture to her chest and in her reflection from the mantelpiece mirror she saw there was writing on the back. She turned it over. "We always was family. Remember us that way. Love, your sis'-in-law, Curly."

Mildred's tears came quickly as she walked up the carpeted stairs to her attic bedroom. She turned back to go get the bottle of VO and another pain shot through her stomach. She stood still until it passed, then grabbed the bottle and went back up the stairs. When she got to the top, she flopped down on her bed and wiped her eyes dry on the sheets. She unscrewed the top of the bottle and drank from it, then pulled the covers over her because her teeth were chattering. She drank some more. A lot happens in thirty years, she thought. Too much. She took another swig and rolled over on her back. And not enough. The beige ceiling sloped. Mildred took another sip from the bottle and the whiskey ran down the side of her mouth. What the hell, she thought, and rolled back over on her stomach to set it down, but it fell from her hands. What happened to all my strength? She closed her eyes as if she'd been hypnotized. Mildred slept hard, without stirring. When she woke up, Mildred was forty-eight years old and soaking wet from the waist down.

## Twenty-three

*O*N NEW YEARS DAY, Buster died in his sleep. Mildred went numb. She sat in front of her picture window watching snowflakes all day long. She drank something, but didn't know if it was VO or part of that Scotch Curly'd given her for Christmas. Whatever it was, was going right through her. She got up from the brown chair and ran to the bathroom. The Christmas tree fell when her shoulder brushed against it. Mildred didn't turn to see it knock over her good gold lamp, and didn't hear the bulbs crack when they hit the brick on the fireplace. She sat down on the toilet as her bowels ran. She had prayed that Buster would live a lot longer. He wasn't that damn old. She got up to wash her face in cold water, and the phone rang. Mildred picked up the receiver like a zombie.

"Yeah," she said in a tired voice.

"Aunt Mildred," BooBoo said.

"Who is this?"

"BooBoo."

"I thought you was in jail."

"I got out right before Christmas. I hope you sitting down."

"It can't be nothing that bad."

"Mama had another stroke this morning. Her pressure been going up. They say there was a weak spot in her brain in the walls of her arteries and it swelled up like a bubble and busted. We had to rush her to the hospital."

"You say Curly had a bubble bust? She in the hospital?" The words were like a faint echo coming from the back of her throat.

"Aunt Mildred, I can't hear you."

"I didn't say nothing." Mildred said each word slowly, then louder and deliberately. "What hospital she in?"

"Mercy."

"That's what she gon' need." She spotted the toppled Christmas tree, and suddenly it seemed important that she tend to it. "Hold on a minute, would you?" Mildred dropped the phone and walked over to the spruce. Silver tinsel hung from drooping branches and some of it was spread over the royal-blue carpet like silver worms. She grabbed the tip of the tree and dragged it through the living room through the kitchen and out the side door. She kicked the red stand off the side porch, and the tree fell on its side in a snowdrift. Mildred pulled the aluminum door shut and wiped her hands. She went back to the phone but BooBoo had hung up.

She considered going to the hospital, but she felt so tired she sat back down in the chair by the window. Hours passed. She felt like she was suspended, floating. As though no blood was getting to her brain. She had felt like this before. Was it before or after Crook died? All Mildred knew was she hadn't had a drop of strength left in her. Had given up and given in. It had been easy to do. Hell, the kids had gotten on her nerves so bad she had snapped like a rubber band. Just like that. She couldn't remember much else. Except she felt nothing then and felt nothing now.

Finally, she got up in slow motion and walked to the closet. She pulled a coat out and put it on. The gloves Freda had given her were in the pockets. She opened the front door. It was dark outside. Funny, seemed like she'd just woke up a few minutes ago. The temperature had dropped to zero but Mildred couldn't feel it. She walked across the hard snow and it crunched under her house shoes. Bootsey had let her use the Ford for the holidays. Mildred remembered that much. She opened the door, got in, and turned the key in the ignition. The engine growled, then whimpered. She turned the key to off then on again and pumped the accelerator viciously until the engine grumbled and spurted.

She backed out of the driveway and shifted to drive. Three or four cars were coming straight at her, honking their horns. Mildred did not realize she was going the wrong way on the one-way street. She did not turn around. The other cars moved out of her way.

She drove, not knowing where she was going, and ended up on Dove Road. When she got to Fortieth Street, Mildred automatically made a left. It was pitch black. She gripped the steering wheel so hard it hurt her hands. She pressed down hard on the accelerator and the car jutted forward so fast that Mildred was thrown back in her seat. There was a loud pop and the car spun into a snowbank piled in front of a herd of naked trees. Her head snapped forward and bammed against the windshield. It didn't break and she wasn't bleeding. She grabbed the dashboard and fell back against the cold vinyl seat. When Mildred realized she wasn't dead, her body went limp and her hands fell in her lap. She sat there motionless for a few minutes and listened to the wind. To her left it was dark. To her right even darker. The skeletons of the trees in front looked like they were moving toward the car. Mildred still did not move.

Finally, she looked up toward the sky and there was one star in the middle of all that black. One star. Cold tears fell out the corners of her eyes and down onto her coat collar.

Then Mildred got mad.

"All right, you motherfucker. If you up there, I hope the hell you can hear me. I wanna know what the hell you trying to prove? First you take my husband, then my kids, and now my daddy and Curly. Why not me? Curly ain't never done nothing to nobody. I'm the one who wrote all them goddamn checks and lied to the IRS and the welfare people and told my daughter to lie about her baby's daddy. Why not me?"

Mildred waited for the silence to answer.

"Curly been praying for your help for years, and what the fuck did you do to her? Make her have a goddamn stroke and paralyzed her. Why? Why can't you do something right for a change? I thought you was supposed to be so big and bad, could do anything anytime anywhere. Are you there or am I just wasting my damn time?"

She looked around but saw nothing except snow.

"Look, it's a lot of thangs I could've done differently, I know that. And I ain't never asked you for much. And I don't know if this whole thang about life is supposed to be some kind of damn test to see how much I can take, how much any of us can take, but I've had it. This shit ain't funny no more."

Mildred let out a long sigh.

"I betcha this is some kind of game, ain't it? But I'm gon' tell you something, buddy. I'm gon' make it past the finish line."

She opened the car door and got out. It was cold as hell out here all of a sudden. She looked down at the right rear tire and it was flat. Damn. She didn't know how to fix a flat tire. Mildred turned three hundred and sixty degrees and saw nothing. Why had she come all the way out here in the first place? Damn. Why hadn't she put her snow boots on when she left? Jasper's house was damn near a half mile down the road. Mildred knew she'd catch pneumonia if she tried to walk down there in these house shoes.

She looked at the tire and trudged around to the back of the car to the trunk. There was a jack, one of those cross-shaped metal things, and a tire. She pulled them out and dragged them around to the side of the car. Mildred tried to remember all the times she'd seen somebody change a flat tire. She slid the jack under the rim of the bumper until she felt the inside of it click. She pumped the handle up and down and the car rose up out of the snow.

Mildred began to smile.

Next she took the cross and tried to fit it on one of those little screws on the tire, but she couldn't see. She fumbled for a few minutes until she found the right-size hole, pushed it down hard on the nut, and turned the cross until the nut popped off. It landed on top of a crust of snow. Hell, this wasn't as hard as she thought it was. She removed three more nuts, pulled the tire off, and slid the other one on. Then she did everything in reverse. By the time she put the worn tire and tools back into the trunk, Mildred felt like she could probably fly if she flapped her arms fast enough.

She turned the key and the engine purred as if it had just been waiting for her to start it up. She pressed down on the accelerator but the front of the car was still stuck in the snow-bank. Mildred got out and saw that the bumper had snow packed under it. She tried to push the car, but it wouldn't budge.

"All right, if you up there, I'm gon' ask you to help me one last time, and I swear I'll do everythang else myself."

She took her gloves out of her pockets and put them on. Then she took a deep breath and dug her heels into the snow. She lost her balance but instead of falling backward, Mildred fell against the hood of the car. It carried her with it as it rolled out of the snowbank.

# Twenty-four

FREDA THOUGHT she heard the doorbell but wasn't sure. She forced herself up from the wet couch. Her jeans were soaked. The room was a mess. A cart full of dirty laundry sat in the middle of the room. Somebody had died. Granddaddy Buster. Now the doorbell rang continuously. She got up and opened the door. Her head was killing her. Somehow, Freda found herself at the bottom of the stairwell and opened the gate. The mailman handed her an envelope too large to fit into the mailbox. She opened it. One of her articles had been accepted.

She must have floated back upstairs because she had no idea how she was now standing in front of the bathroom mirror, staring at some old woman who looked like she hadn't combed her hair or bathed for months. She was so tired, she had to support herself on the sink.

Okay, Freda. This is it, she said to herself. You've been drunk for three or four days now — shit, you've been drunk for a year. Missed your own granddaddy's funeral. You're gonna have to make up your mind what you're gonna do. You call yourself a writer, but what you really are is a fucking ugly drunk. You better start making some decisions, and fast.

Her hands trembled. Her teeth chattered. She hugged herself

and stared at her reflection. It was Mildred's face looking out from the mirror.

"What I need to do is stop feeling so damn sorry for myself," she said out loud. She started to run some bath water when she noticed the cut on her hand. She forced herself to remember. Yesterday. The last of her depression-glass goblets had slid from her hand into the sink and she had tried to catch it. The cut ran from the M in her palm like a long piece of brown thread. Isn't that something, she thought, how fast the body heals itself.

By the time she got out of the bathtub, Freda felt refreshed. Clear-headed. She was the one who had complicated everything, she thought. For some reason, now, everything seemed so damn simple. It dawned on her that she had a whole lot of things to be grateful for. She had just sold an article to a magazine. Had a file cabinet full of ideas for more. Her family was crazy, but she loved them. And she had Freda. She bent down to dry her feet and stood up to wrap the towel around her. She looked into the mirror and smiled.

She turned off the bathroom light, walked into the living room, picked up the telephone book, and flipped to the A's. She dialed the number of Alcoholics Anonymous, and this time she didn't hang up.

# Twenty-five

"**H**I, SWEETHEART," Mildred said in a singsong voice when she answered the phone. She felt light inside, and for the first time in a long time, she could think straight. She didn't care why or what for or how come. She only knew that for the past ten years she'd felt like she'd been buried alive and had finally dug her way back up to the surface — to topsoil — and right this minute if you had given her a shove, Mildred knew she could dig her way out of any hole, no matter how deep it was.

"Mama, you sure sound good," Freda said.

"You do too. What's up?"

"Nothing, what you doing?"

"Cooking some pinto beans. Where the hell are you? Is those cars I hear in the background?"

"Yep, I'm in a phone booth."

"Well, speak up, I can't hardly hear you."

"Let me walk up the street to a quieter one, and I'll call you back in a few minutes."

Mildred hung up. Why was Freda calling from a phone booth, anyway? she wondered. She had to step over several boxes to get to the kitchen. She was just about finished with her packing. All she had left were dishes and her garden tools in the basement. She was pouring yellow corn bread batter into a baking pan when the doorbell rang. She slid the pan in the oven, wiped her hands on a dishtowel, and went to see who it was.

Mildred's heart stopped when she saw her daughter.

"Freda?"

"It's me, Mama. Open this door. It's cold as hell out here."

Mildred's mouth was wide open and her eyes were dilated.

"I know I must be dreaming, ain't I? You can't be standing here in front of me, now can you?" Mildred pinched herself, then Freda.

"Ouch! I wanted to surprise you."

"Well, this is a helluva surprise, all right. You gon' give me a damn heart attack is what you gon' do."

"What's with all these boxes?"

"I'm moving." There wasn't a trace of remorse in Mildred's voice.

"Moving? When? Where? Back to California? Why didn't you tell somebody?"

"Yeah, moving. Hell no, I ain't going back to no dead-ass California. I'm moving into one of them townhouses in two weeks. You know my daddy always looked after me. He left me enough change to get me back on my feet."

"When did you decide all this, Mama?"

"When they foreclosed on this house, that's when."

"Well, you don't sound too depressed about it."

"I ain't depressed. Ain't gon' get depressed, neither. All it is is a damn house. Brick and wood and plaster. You know how many years I done spent worrying about some damn houses that ain't never gave a damn about me? Anyway, take off your coat. What you dranking?"

"I stopped drinking."

Mildred turned her head to stare into her daughter's eyes to see if she was lying, but Freda's eyes were clear with the truth.

"Did I just hear you say you stopped drinking?"

"You heard me right. And I feel good, too."

"I wish I had your strength, girl. I've been thanking I should stop too."

"You don't have to say that just 'cause I did, Mama."

"I ain't lying."

"What made *you* want to stop?"

"Well, it's a whole lot of thangs. Nothing I feel like going into right now. What you doing here?"

"I got a surprise for you."

"Open your coat. You pregnant, ain't you?"

"No, Mama. I'm not pregnant."

"Then, what, what, what?"

She grabbed Freda's left hand. There was no ring on it. Mildred looked both disappointed and relieved. "You better not go and get married without my knowing about it. I wanna be in the front row. What is it, then?"

"Here," Freda said, handing her an envelope.

Mildred opened it up and counted five hundred-dollar bills. Then she gave the envelope back to Freda.

"What's wrong, Mama?"

"What's this for?"

"Remember when I told you I had applied to all these different places for grants so I could take some time off to write more?"

"Yeah," Mildred said, still pushing the envelope toward Freda, who in turn kept stepping back.

"Well, I got one, for two thousand bucks!"

"But why you giving *me* all this money?"

"Mama, a long time ago I made you a promise. Remember? I promised to send you on a trip and buy you a house one day. Don't you remember?"

"I thank so. Girl, you done done so many thangs for me already. You need to start trying to please yourself instead of me and everybody else."

"Mama, obviously I can't buy you a house, but take it, please, this means a lot to me. Use it for a vacation."

"I told you a million times I don't need to see no tropical islands. All I want to do is get to the Ebony Fashion Fair if it ain't already sold out."

"I've got two tickets for you."

Mildred's eyes lit up.

"Two tickets! You do? Oh, thank you, thank you, thank you! How? And when?"

"I called up and charged them a long time ago. It's all you've been talking about for the longest. You're almost in the front row."

"Get out of here, Freda!"

"You and a guest."

"Don't tell me you don't want to go with me? How long you staying? I know you wanna go, don't you?"

"I don't go for that kind of thing, Mama. Take somebody else."

"Then, here, take this back. I'm gon' be fine, chile."

"Look, Mama. Can I make you one more promise? For some reason, since I stopped drinking, when I say I'm gon' do something, I like to do it. Take this money and I promise not to make any more promises like this ever again, deal?"

Mildred blushed. She looked over at her couch. "I could stand to get that thang reupholstered. And I need to get this partial plate repaired. It cracked." She sat the envelope down on an end table.

"You know something, Freda? Seem to me like all these years I been telling y'all kids what's the right thang to do and how y'all can get over in this world, and I swear, y'all done it all by yourselves. Shit. My period done dried up, did I tell you that? For the longest I worried about going through the change of life. Then I realized I already been through it! I said, good god-damn riddens when it didn't come. I done bled enough to start a blood river, and now, honey, I feel so free. But I'm still y'all mama, and y'all still my kids."

"So, Mama, you sure you don't feel bad about losing the house?"

"Freda, don't ask me no more stupid-ass questions, please. Do I look depressed?"

"No."

"You want to hear some of my good news?"

"What?"

"I'm going back to school."

"School? For real?"

"Yep, Community college. They got this new program for middle-aged folks to get them working again. I'm gon' open up my own day-care center. You know how many women have to work these days? Somebody with some sense need to watch those kids. Why not me? I know I gotta get my license, but that ain't gon' be no problem. All I gotta do is take one step at a time."

"I hear you, Mama."

"You got plans for tonight?"

"Yeah, I got a hot date with the TV."

"Let's get all dolled up and go out."

"To the Shingle?"

"I'll treat you to a nice dinner downtown first and then we can make our entrance at the Shingle. What you say to that?"

"I say let's party!"

They went upstairs to change. They had to use Mildred's room because the other bedrooms were full of boxes. Mildred stood in front of the mirror, naked from the waist up. Her breasts hung down like two small water balloons.

"You didn't happen to bring an extra old bra with you, did you? One that'a look good under that blouse? You know, something with a little lace on it?"

"Mama, you kill me sometimes, you know that?" Freda went to get the bra and Mildred put it on.

"How about them gold earrings you hiding in the top part of your suitcase. Can I wear 'em?"

"I do not believe you, you know that?" Freda brought the earrings back and slid them into Mildred's ears for her.

"Anything else, Your Majesty?"

"Yeah, one more thang. Would you mind plucking your mama's eyebrows before we leave? You know I always loved the way you plucked 'em."

"Yes, I will pluck your eyebrows."

"Have I ever told you how much I loved you."

Freda looked at Mildred, at her mama, as if she weren't hearing her, as if the words weren't coming from Mildred's lips.

"I don't know, probably."

"Well if I didn't, I'm gon' tell you now. I love you, Freda."

They stood there as if they didn't know what to do next.

Then Mildred reached for her daughter as if she were a gift she had always wanted and had finally gotten.

Freda pressed her head into Mildred's bare shoulder. A piece of red hair curled like a C within eye level. Mildred's breasts felt full against her own, and Freda couldn't tell whose were whose. They held each other up. They patted each other's back as if each had fallen and scraped a knee and had no one else to turn to for comfort. It seemed as if they hugged each other for the past and for the future.

Finally, Mildred stepped back. She tripped over an empty box.

"Shit, I'm gon' run my makeup. You know how long it took me to put this mess on?"

"I can imagine — you've got on enough of it."

"Don't give me none of your lip, girl, just make me look like a movie star."

"All right already, sit down."

Mildred sat down in an armless chair. Freda went into the bathroom to get the tweezers and Vaseline.

"Now, rub that Vaseline on 'em till they get good and tender and promise me you won't try to pull my brains loose and make my head hurt and don't yank so damn hard that my eyes start watering like some baby and run the rest of my eyeshadow."

Freda shifted her weight from one foot to the other and put her hands on her hips. Mildred eased her head back in the chair and closed her eyes.

"Mama," Freda said.

"What?" she asked, without opening her eyes. Mildred clasped her hands and wove her fingers together as if she were saying a silent prayer.

Freda looked down at Mildred's face. "Nothin'," she said. Freda was grinning so hard her cheeks hurt.